Weirdbook

VOL. 2, NO. 14   ISSUE 44

Features

Short Stories

Poetry

Artwork

FROM THE EDITOR'S TOWER

This is our 14th regular issue of *Weirdbook*, and things are going strong. The next 7 issues and our 2021 Annual are filled, contracted, and paid for. So our existence is guaranteed for at least 2 more years. We've also successfully (re)launched a sister magazine *Startling Stories*. So these are exciting and optimistic times for all of us involved in *Weirdbook* and *Startling*.

This issue features stories by *Weirdbook* Alumni Franklyn Searight, Sharon Cullars, Adrian Cole, and John Fultz along with poetry by Darrell Schweitzer, Ann K. Schwader, and Lucy Snyder.

I'm also proud that we have new stories from Bram Stoker Award nominee Kyla Lee Ward, Sword & Sorcery legend John Hocking, and Horror Maestro Tim Curran.

I can promise that there is something for everyone in this issue with thrills and chills for all!

Now for some very sad news.

Franklyn Searight passed away in December 2020. Readers will recognize his name from the wealth of fiction he provided for this magazine. He had stories in 7 previous issues, the premier issue of *Startling Stories*, and all 3 themed annuals. He also has a story in our upcoming Zombies-themed annual and lined up for the next 7 issues.

Frank was very much part of what *Weirdbook* stood for: a magazine in the *Weird Tales* tradition. Frank even appeared in *Weirdbook*'s original incarnation back in 1973.

I loved his style of old-school horror and dark fantasy. His stories always managed to evoke an older style of weird fiction while still maintaining a 21st-century sensibility. And this was no small feat considering that Frank sent us these stories while in his late 70s to mid-80s.

This issue is dedicated to his memory.

—Doug Draa, *Editor*

Staff

PUBLISHER & EXECUTIVE EDITOR

John Gregory Betancourt

EDITOR

Doug Draa

CONSULTING EDITOR

W. Paul Ganley

WILDSIDE PRESS SUBSCRIPTION SERVICES

Sam Hogan

PRODUCTION TEAM

*Sam Hogan
Karl Würf*

LET ME BE YOUR SWAMP SNAKE

Adrian Cole

From the files of Nick Nightmare

"Frogs," the old hobo growled at me from the cloying darkness of the street. He was lurching along, barely able to put one foot in front of the other, one step forward, two back, metaphorically speaking. Well, mostly. In fact he added a couple of choice adjectives to the word, indicating he was not enamored of the amphibian tribe. "World's full of unprintable frogs. New York won't hold out much longer."

I left him to his hallucinogenic haze and moved along the narrow alley, which debouched on to the towpath of an old canal. This was a run down part of the city, not a place I'd normally stretch my legs, but I knew a good bar down here with a special brand of malt whiskey they brought in from—well, who knew? I figured it was worth elbowing my way through a few batrachian beasties to wet my whistle with a shot or two.

On reflection now, I may have got that wrong.

As I headed along the canal side, hemmed in by shadows and leaning brick walls, barely lit by a vampire moon leached of all its color, I heard something out on the coal-black surface of the canal. Very little river traffic passed up or down those waters these days. This craft had no motor. Its long, thin shape glided alongside me and its lone occupant, leaning on a pole like the pilot of a gondola, called a surprisingly cheerful greeting. I gritted my teeth and waved back. It was Fred the Ferryman, and he was not famous for bringing good news.

"Fred," I said, standing over him as his craft eased to a halt alongside. As always it was draped in tendrils of fog.

"At your service, Nick," he said, bowing. He was little more than a thick bundle of rags, his beaming, round face swathed in a gray scarf and topped with a flattish cap. His eyes sparkled vividly. "Why walk when you could embark and be transported?"

"Probably because you'd slip me into some other place where the nights are darker, the skies are definitely cloudy all day and most of the words heard thereabouts are discouraging."

"Getting a tad poetic, aren't we?" His grin widened.

I stood very still, picturing again the old tramp I'd seen a few moments back. "My guess is, this has got to do with frogs, right?"

Fred bowed again. "Bravo, maestro! Step aboard."

I did so, steadying myself, and sat on the single seat. Fred poled us off. "A friend asked me to fetch you," he said. "He's very unhappy. It's the frogs. And what he fears could be a sort of apocalypse. I'd like to think he's exaggerating, but, well, you know."

"Which friend would this be?"

"The Mire-Beast. It's quite a journey and we'll have to cross over at some point. Why don't you just relax. Have a doze. I'll wake you when we arrive."

I showed him my teeth, though not in a smile, and sat back, ruminating. The Mire-Beast, once of the NYPD, a man then known as David Goroth. He'd been seriously damaged under a crushing fall of masonry and rebuilt after a fashion by some pretty twisted scientists. Things had gotten worse for Goroth. They'd given him a new body, the huge, misshapen hulk that was the creature we knew as the Mire-Beast, ejecting its former persona, Alexander Cradoc, who'd returned to his native England.

Goroth, in his new form, had been involved in a huge dust-up between me, a few of my pals and members of something we knew as the Dark Army, a powerful collaboration of very unpleasant specimens hell-bent on overrunning as many worlds as they could. We'd held them up, not obliterated them. So if Goroth was feeling glum right now, it likely meant the Dark Army was flexing its muscles again.

Fred poled us out of the canal and along the Hudson, and the fog banks moved in predictably, smothering the view, not that it had been salubrious. It was impossible to say how far we traveled, or at what point we slipped over into some other place, possibly the Pulpworld. If there was a city on the invisible banks, it wasn't the New York I knew as home. Things had gotten very quiet. I did hear an occasional *splosh* in the water, and twice something very large slid along under us, nudging us gently but otherwise mercifully not interested. Fred lit a lantern that hung on another pole at the rear of his craft. It gave out a bright yellow light but did little to penetrate our surroundings. Probably not a bad thing.

Eventually I knew we'd left the main body of the river and were moving up a wide creek, its waters sluggish and oily. They had a rich, pungent smell, a combination of rank weed and decay. Hell, we were entering swamp territory. Home was indeed a long way behind us. But it would have suited the Mire-Beast, a creature that thrived on this kind of location, as far from humanity as it could get. Alexander Cradoc had suffered for a long time in his imprisoning body, and now the wretched David Goroth would be enduring the same misery, doubtless yearning for release.

Fresh sounds emanated from the vapors on either side of us. Mainly a chorus of deep croaks that could only have been burped by any number of our amphibious friends.

"This is frog heaven, right?" I said to the Ferryman.

"They do seem to like it here," he agreed. Very little ever fazed him, but I did notice he put some extra muscle into his poling. We bumped up against a landing that loomed out of the fog ominously. I clambered up onto to its weed-encrusted boards. Fred saluted me, telling me I'd be met and that he'd be on hand again when I needed him. He then dissolved into the murk. I was used to that, but even so, this was the last place anyone wanted to be stranded. And definitely no rare malt whiskey on the end of my little jaunt.

There was light of a kind: greenish and sickly, the product of certain organic growths you would not find in hometown New York. What passed here for fireflies, hornet-sized monsters that zipped around like bullets, also glowed. I went slowly down the landing, careful not to slip on the weathered boards. I did not want to end up in the surrounding swamp, which could have been dumped here straight out of equatorial Africa. As far as I could tell there was nothing on either side of me apart from that bubbling ooze and the tangled banks of low trees that drooped possessively over it.

Ahead of me the landing curved around a wide area from which gray swathes of gaseous cloud billowed upwards. Something else emerged from the muck, bulky and broad, its bizarre features highlighted by the glow. This was the stuff of nightmares, except that I recognized the creature as it dragged its way through the swamp to the landing and hauled itself up to join me. It looked like it had been formed out of the swamp, a mix of mud, stone and root. Its wide blob of a face turned to look down at me—well, it was seven feet high—the red eyes regarding me, somehow imbued with pain.

The Mire-Beast.

"You wanted to see me?" I grunted.

The huge head nodded and the long gash of a mouth opened. There were no visible teeth, but something wriggled about in there. I tried not to shudder. "Nick Nightmare." The voice rumbled up from that vast chest. "You know about the frogs?"

I glanced around me. The croaks among the reeds and mud banks had intensified. My guess was, the place was seething. "I gather they're planning a little *coup d'etat*."

"It's no joke. If someone doesn't do something about it, Nick, about a billion frogs are going to swim down the Hudson and fetch up in New

York—in our world, not this one. They already own this one."

"And is there a reason they'd leave such an ideal environment as this?"

"Food. They'll eat everyone."

"I'm not a qualified zoologist, pal, but don't frogs eat flies and insects and grubs and such like? Frogs don't eat people."

"These do."

That's all I needed. Carnivorous frogs. "And someone has to do something? That someone being me? A two-bit private dick against a billion meat-eating frogs. What's wrong with that sentence?"

"I'll help. And the Bog Witch holds the key."

"Ah, there's a Bog Witch. That changes everything. Should buy us another ten minutes."

The Mire-Beast, the wretched David Goroth trapped in that grotesque parody of a human body, was not inclined to conversation. He turned away and indicated a gap in the dense vegetation beyond the landing stage. I found a path there, a series of matted hummocks, compressed reeds, that shook as I stepped on them, moving deeper into the shadows. The light decreased, but there was enough to see by. Around me the quasi-daylight barely penetrated the vegetable walls and from them came an incessant chorus of insect and amphibian sound, not least the croaking of a batrachian multitude. I tried not to imagine my flesh being stripped from my bones by countless fleshy mouths.

We reached a larger mound, where a few stunted trees poked up from the black loam, drier land bound together by weeds and roots to form a sort of haven, although I use the word loosely. Beneath one of the trees, sitting cross-legged on a large black stone was the oldest woman in the universe. I'm not being ageist. She really was very old, practically mummified. Hairless, her skin parched, her arms and legs almost devoid of flesh, she regarded me from eyes that had long since clouded over. Blind eyes, I would have supposed, but she had far greater powers. Her presence hummed like a generator. She held a crooked staff, its point dug into the ground and my guess was she drew up all the energy she needed from it.

"Nick Nightmare," she said in a voice like an amplified whisper, if that doesn't sound too Irish. "A little island of sanity in a universe gone mad."

"Shucks, ma'am, no one's ever been that nice to me," I said, trying not to smile.

She did and her toothless mouth widened as the smile became a cackle of soft laughter, if that doesn't sound too Irish.

"I take it you're the Bog Witch," I said, bowing slightly.

"Indeed I am. I have watched over these glades for many generations. But at last, ultimate evil has entered them. Terrible powers, intent on unleashing mayhem in your world. You have tasted their deviltry ere now."

"The Dark Army."

"It never rests. Always looking for a foothold and worlds to conquer. Always recruiting demons, demi-gods and the vile outcasts of the dimensions. Here, in this forgotten realm, its members have imbued the Frog God with power, and with it a lust for omnipotence. They have promised it much, bound over in blood, in exchange for its service."

"They want to consume New York. My home town."

"They do. And pave the way for things beyond your imagination."

"Oh, my imagination is pretty colorful, ma'am. So—I take it you want me to put a stop to this hanky-panky. Even though I am a mere mortal, with a few trinkets to ward off an evil eye."

"Give a man the means to an end, and he'll deliver," she said. "What you need is Sebok's Staff. That and its bone headpiece."

"That figures. And you just happen to have this item to hand?"

"No pain, no gain, Nick Nightmare. You should know that."

I should have that tattooed on my chest. I managed a non-committal grunt.

"Sebok was an ancient Egyptian God, warden of the crocodiles, among other things," she said. "He served the pharaohs of the two lands and slew their enemies through control of the great river's water creatures. Much of his power was invested in his staff. The headpiece is carved from the skull of the lord of the crocodiles, a great beast who, it is said, lived for a thousand years."

I cut to the chase. "Where is it now?"

"Here, in this backwater, hidden from man for centuries. Its power has never diminished."

"That's hunky-dory, ma'am, but how does a crocodile totem counteract this *Frog* God and his minions? Frogs are amphibians, right? Crocs are reptiles."

"These are no ordinary frogs. Mutants."

"Figures—they're reptile frogs?"

"In a manner of speaking. Sebok's Staff has control over crocodiles, alligators, reptiles, and other things. In your hands, Nick, it would give the Frog God pause for thought."

"Okay, give me the tool and I'll finish the job." I held out my hand, more in hope than expectation.

"She doesn't have it," said the Mire-Beast. "We have to fetch it."

"That'll be the pain bit."

"Deep in the swamp there is an altar," said the Bog Witch. "Sebok's Staff is secured there. The altar is on a small islet, surrounded by the Frog God's host. You must pass through it to get to the altar. The two of you have powers of your own. Strengthen your resolve and the staff will be yours."

I turned to the Mire-Beast. "Your loins girded up?"

The vast hulk was incapable of smiling, but it growled and I took it as assent.

"You have your guns?" the Bog Witch asked me. So she knew about my twin Berettas.

I patted my coat. "Don't go many places without them, ma'am."

"One more thing," she said, her blind eyes fixing me. "There is a guardian."

"Naturally. There always is."

"She will not part with Sebok's Staff willingly."

"Who is she?"

"The Sleeping Sister. Sissyllys. You will know her when you see her."

The interview appeared to be over, and I'd landed the job. My huge companion trudged across the back of the mound and we were off, pushing through the cramped vegetation, trying to blot out the ceaseless noise of the swamp. I drew my guns. My guess was, our progress would not be smooth.

The Mire-Beast was far more efficient than any machete would have been in my hands, creating a passage for me. The worst I had to deal with was the threat of an attack, and innumerable insects, which I laboriously swatted as we worked our way deeper and deeper into what seemed to be an endless green hell. In the muck around our path, things slithered and hopped in the pools, or slid through low branches, coiling and uncoiling, hissing, but somehow not inclined to strike. Probably the Mire-Beast exuded a psychic will, radiating a warning to all but the most powerful of the swamp denizens to back off. I did loose off a couple of shots when things got too suggestive of pending aggression, and it did the trick. My guess was, it wouldn't last.

I got that right.

The squat trees parted to reveal a wide expanse of thick, muddy swamp, its surface glazed with green scum, flat and featureless, its edges cloaked in vapors that rose up from it in billowing yellowish clouds. It was an enclosed world, near-silent and stinking of rot. The path I was on dropped out of sight below that festering mire, so there was no way I could progress. And I sure as hell had no intention of letting the Mire-Beast carry me across. He didn't offer.

Instead he lowered himself into the gunk like it was a health spa. I watched as his great bulk was immersed up to his shoulders and he waded out from the shore, looking for something. Around me in the gloom I heard the gathering of flapping, winged things, probably looking for lunch. Right then I was on the menu. Hell, I *was* the menu.

"Some kind of raft would be useful at this point," I called.

The Mire-Beast ducked under the surface, bubbles breaking it to mark his path along the bottom of the swamp. He burst up from below, muck and slime slithering off him, and pointed along the bank. "Stone pathway," he said.

I moved around the swamp on unstable chunks of the bank until I reached the indicated place. There were big stones there, an inch or two below the surface, leading outwards. "Seriously?" I said to my companion.

Just to demonstrate how tickety-boo it all was, he jumped up on to the first of the submerged stones and crossed from one to the next without sinking. I held both my guns and made my move, balancing myself carefully. Okay, I could do this. I was trying to remind myself what the blue blazes I was doing here, but no sane reasons popped into my head. I just kept moving, further and further out across the swamp. I wasn't wearing my best shoes—that was my other pair—but these were going to be ruined.

Now the swamp was coming alive. Things stirred in its glutinous expanse. Croaks increased in volume and shadows moved like serpents through the vapors. I appeared to be standing in the middle of an open area, a long way from shore. Vulnerable. Something broke surface ahead and I almost fired off a couple of rounds at it, I was that nervous.

"The causeway," said the Mire-Beast. To underline his point, he swam forward and hauled himself up on to the flat, wooden area. I moved over the last of the submerged rocks and likewise climbed up. A low, wooden jetty, the thing wound onward into more mist, but it was above swamp level and at that point in my journey, most welcome. Something snapped at the place I had just vacated. I swung round, about to fire, but whatever it had been had gone back under.

We got moving along the causeway. It was slippery, many of its boards rotten, and I was almost pitched over the side as sections of it lurched, unstable and potentially collapsing. We were definitely no longer alone. Out in the mire, many things were following us, their bulging eyes popping up and observing us. The Bog Witch had warned me that we'd have to pass through the ranks of the frogs to get to the island. They didn't disappoint. On the plus side, they were only small critters. It was just the number of them. That number had a lot of naughts on the end.

As they swam in droves alongside the causeway, it became clear that some of them weren't that small after all. I commented on this to the Mire-Beast.

"Those are the toads," he said.

"Anything else out there I should know about?"

He chose not to respond. Instead we moved on, more speedily. Behind me I heard the wet slap of something on the boards. I turned and saw a shape, large and bulbous, gleaming with swamp muck. It opened its mouth and I could see deep into its maw. It was toothless but as welcoming as a man-trap. I fired at it and the creature croaked indignantly and hopped back into the swamp.

The Mire-Beast had pulled up, flexing his huge clawed hands. Beyond him I could see the causeway was blocked. At first it looked like a fallen tree but then the whole thing wriggled and split up into about a thousand small, hopping shapes. A wall of frogs, reinforced with a score or more of the bigger toads. All those boggling eyes, fixed on us, was a disconcerting sight. The amphibian army did not want us to pass. Behind us more of the things were hopping up onto the causeway. I felt it shift under me, like it was about to turn belly up. Right then I did not want to plop into the mire.

Instead I rushed forward, both Berettas blazing away. The result was instantaneous. Numerous creatures burst under the blizzard of lead, their pulped flesh scattering over the swamp, while others hopped aside. Those that played it all heroic and came at us, including some toads as fat as pigs, ran into the maelstrom that was the Mire-Beast. In a blur, he swung this way and that, sweeping the croaking monsters hither and yon, in most cases ripping them into chunks of meat. Some reached him and tried to fasten those slimy, fish-wet mouths on his torso, but they had no effect. They tried it on me, too, but I had enough time to blast them into a drizzle of blood and gore. Sure, it was messy. But we got through and out the other side.

The swamp on both sides of the causeway was heaving as if we were somewhere out on a heavy sea swell, bracing against a storm. My guess was, bigger things were going to emerge from the swirling chaos and make a play for us. I was about to ask the Mire-Beast how much further to the island, but I saw it ahead. It was a big hump, maybe a couple of hundred meters across. A few trees poked up from its curve, but it looked solid enough. Behind us the frogs and their bloated chums were gathering and preparing for a second concerted attack, but we hightailed it across the last of the causeway and on to the island. We turned and what I saw almost stopped my heart.

The swamp surface was no longer visible. It had been replaced by the amphibian host. I mean, those things were packed so close to each other— big ones, small ones, monsters—all you saw was frog flesh. Or toad flesh. Or—well, whatever the hell the rest of them were. All set on cuddling up to me and my companion, and not in the nicest possible way. I thought maybe I'd slightly underestimated the task set for me here. I'd reloaded my guns and prepared to let fly once more, but the Mire-Beast called me to him.

"They can't get on to the island," he said. "It's protected. They'll completely surround it, but that's all."

"That's *all*?" I echoed. "Is that supposed to reassure me?"

"Sebok's Staff repulses them."

He ignored my little rant and shambled on across the island, pushing through thick leaves and creepers until we came to the central glade. It was some fifty meters across and had been paved some time in its past, the big slabs of its floor cracking and pushed up in places by the rampant vegetation. A few pillars poked up from the thick grasses round its edge, broken and looking as if they been gnawed on by something with very large teeth. Across from us, looming over the whole place was a spectacular statue, carved either in bronze or some other tough metal. My blood felt suddenly cold as I looked up at the thing. Statue it may be, but it was terrifying.

It was the raised head of a serpent, three times my height, its mouth open, its fangs gleaming in the light from overhead. Something dripped ominously from them. The eyes were two immense jewels, probably rubies given their deep red color, and they were wide open. I was damn sure if I moved from side to side they'd follow me.

"Don't worry about the teeth," said the Mire-Beast. "That s not poison. This thing is a constrictor."

I saw now the body of the creature, curving down from the enormous head and wrapping itself around the rim of the clearing. It was big enough to have taken on a couple of freight trains, with room for most of the trucks. But it wasn't poisonous and better still, it was a statue. In front of it there was a big flat stone resting on two short, squat ones, something from the Stone Age maybe. Resting on the stone's surface, which was strangely free of any kind of growth, was a long staff, topped with a weird shaped head cut from something off-white. Bone.

"The Staff of Sebok," said the Mire-Beast.

"Help yourself," I said. "Let's use it to clear a path back to the sane world."

Before my companion could comply, there was movement to one side of the clearing and we were joined by the weirdest guy I'd ever clapped eyes on. Seriously, I have seen some freaky people, but this guy scooped the award for Mr Impossibly Ugly. Essentially he was a human frog. Ridiculously wide, with batrachian skin, blotched and slimy, an inflated gut and huge thighs, he hopped forward and kind of crouched close to the flat stone. His head was enormous, with no neck or visible ears, but the eyes and nose were not far off being human. I wasn't sure the mouth was, although this amphibian amalgam spoke, albeit in a *basso profundo*.

"*Lovely* to meet you at last, Mr Stone. I won't call you Mr Nightmare. The only nightmares here are the ones you're likely to have." The bloated body shook and it took me a minute to get it. The thing was laughing.

"So how are things at Toad Hall?" I quipped.

Again it shuddered. "A jest! How *delicious*! Wrong character, I'm afraid, though. I'm—well, I do have a name among my minions, but you'd need an entirely different set of vocal chords to pronounce it. I'm the Frog God. It's a little truncated, but it'll do. Not that it matters. You won't be with us for very long."

I lifted my twin Berettas. He was a soft target.

"Oh, please, do put those ridiculous things away. I may not be a full blown deity, but I can assure you, I do have powers. You could blaze away all day, Mr Stone, but you'd be wasting bullets." The bulging eyes swiveled round and regarded the Mire-Beast, which hadn't moved. "David Goroth. An absolute *pleasure* to meet you. My colleagues did a real job housing your wreck of a body in that positively *awesome* alter ego."

Goroth said nothing.

"You've come for Sebok's Staff," said the Frog God. "I've got a much better idea." A long, forked tongue slipped out of the wide mouth and licked at the chin beneath it in a particularly repulsive movement. "You had a tough time back in good old New York."

Goroth remained motionless. I'd heard about his life as a cop. His nasty accident and his crippled body. He'd been promised something better. They made him into the Mire-Beast.

"Why fight us, David? Why stay locked up in that *hideous* guise, when you could be back at home, enjoying life as never before?"

Goroth stiffened.

"Oh, yes. My colleagues have the technology to rebuild you. Send you back. As you once were, before your accident. All the hopes and aspirations you had, your family, everything you struggled for, all restored. How refreshing. How *revitalizing*! You know we can do it. After all, we did it for your predecessor."

I knew he was right. The original Mire-Beast, Alexander Cradoc, had been restored and sent back to his life in England with his wife, no longer part of the team that bonded together to combat the Dark Army. This was a big, big incentive Goroth was being offered. If he took it, not only was my goose cooked, but the rest of my team would be hamstrung.

There was a long silence. Even the frog chorus had zipped it. All eyes were on the Mire-Beast. I tensed. I knew that if Goroth took the carrot, my guns would be no use against him. I thought about making a grab for the staff, but knew I had no chance of getting it before those huge, shovel-like hands got hold of me. As it was, the creature turned slowly and regarded me with its crimson eyes. It was impossible to read anything in them, or the mind behind them.

Usually the Mire-Beast moved ponderously, but there were times when it could defy the eye with a burst of speed. Like now. It swung round and snatched up Sebok's Staff and tossed it to me. I caught it and stood like a kid caught with his fingers in the candy jar.

The Frog God sat bolt upright. "That was an *incredibly* stupid thing to do," he said.

"I like being the Mire-Beast," said Goroth. "Nobody kicks me around and I get to use muscles I never even heard of. And best of all, I get to kick the butt of big slobs like you."

The Frog God was on his feet, squatting like a sumo wrestler, his body slick with secretions, his tendons and muscles rippling obscenely. "You want a fight, David, you've got one. A duel! Yes. You have Mr Stone as your second, while I have—her!" He pointed to the serpent sculpture. Which moved. That wide open mouth flexed and the eyes were even more alive.

I backed up a little, holding up the staff. It felt like a piece of wood and bone, no more than that. The serpent dipped its head but as I pointed the staff at it, it drew back, hissing like a steam engine. If it had swooped it could have taken me in one gulp. It would have had more of a problem with Goroth, but for the moment it hung back, swaying this way and that as if looking for an opening. The staff seemed to be exuding power of some kind.

Meanwhile the Mire-Beast and the Frog God went for each other in a full-on clash. Apart from the slap of flesh on flesh and the thump of fists, the contest was fought in silence punctuated with deep croaks and grunts. They grabbed each other, rolling and tumbling, shaking the ground, their mouths clamping down on each other's soft spots, assuming they had any. Fluids were spilled and bones may have been broken in what was obviously a very even battle. I watched the giant serpent. Its eyes were curiously riveted on Sebok's Staff, so I waved it about like I knew what I was doing. Anyway, it did keep the monster at bay. I could see its coils beyond the circle of stone: the whole thing was alive. I would have made a break for it if it hadn't been for those coils. Staff or no staff, I wasn't going near them. It looked like we had an impasse.

For a while I thought the Mire-Beast had met his match. The Frog God was evidently imbued with colossal power, squeezing and trying to crush his opponent, but the Mire-Beast was a curious construction, its body changing shape, squeezed like mud, contorted like earth, always breaking the Frog God's hold. Eventually the Mire-Beast lifted his huge head and gave vent to a sort of shout, a uniquely horrible sound, like something a demon might release when enraged. He followed this with redoubled efforts and I saw through the confusion of twisted limbs the head of the Frog God. Goroth had a grip on it, lifted it and brought it down on the stone slabs. There was a sound like the explosion of a fat sack of gelatinous ooze. The Frog God's feet twitched. Goroth stood up, kicking what was now the carcass of his opponent to one side. It slid across the slabs, leaving a wide, wet smear, as well as the head. Former head. It now resembled a mound of steaming, molten wax.

The Mire-Beast took a deep breath. "One to me, I think." He stepped back slowly and stood beside me. We watched the huge serpent together, sure it would bear down on us, intent on vengeance.

I could hear something. I thought it came from far away, but it was inside my head. Sibilant sounds. Slithering, sensuous, serpentine. Hell, was this thing trying to communicate? I glanced at the Mire-Beast and could tell he was also hearing the seductive voice.

Hunger. That was the key. This monster had been dormant in its sculpted form for a long time. Now, awake, it felt starved, on a scale that defied reason. That desire for food washed over us in waves, knocking us backwards like a physical tide. Those eyes blazed, turning for a moment to the mangled corpse below it.

"You want to take a bite out of that sucker, be my guest," I said.

Amazingly the serpent dipped down and did just that. A wriggling tongue, criss-crossed with scarlet veins, shot out and curled around the fallen Frog God, quickly dragging it into the mouth, which closed, the serpent shuddering ecstatically. We saw the shape of the victim slide down the mottled throat and beyond. Gone in a few seconds. Still hungry. The huge snake dipped its head and licked up the remains of the head. I felt the creature's satisfaction, its pure enjoyment of its revolting meal. Just as I felt the return of its hunger. The *hors d'oeuvres* were fine, but it really wanted the full meal. That would be me and my triumphant sidekick.

Unless -

Sebok's Staff would control the frogs, toads, crocodiles and what have you, the Bog Witch had said. I stepped backwards, still holding the staff aloft. The Mire-Beast and I backed away from the serpent, but it followed us, the waves of hunger pulsing ever more strongly. The Mire-Beast was one tough hombre, but could he match this absolute monster? I didn't ask.

Food! The word rolled around inside my head like telepathic thunder. It battered us both back towards the edge of the island and the causeway, which was now almost totally covered in amphibious life. Frogs and related horrors were piled head-high in an effort to get at us. It looked as if we were going to be the meat in a very nasty sandwich. I swung round and made passes with Sebok's Staff, hoping for a result. I got something—the frog masses held back, the mountainous mass shedding scores of hopping, leaping creatures that fell back into the swamp.

Something loomed over me and I ducked down, dropping to my knees. The serpent had dipped that awesome head, its mouth wide, but it wasn't me it intended to snap up. It went for the frogs. It dipped again and the

Mire-Beast and I had to slide to one side of the causeway as the serpent tore into the heaving mountain, swallowing countless dozens of the creatures wholesale.

Food! It came again, that joyous mental boom. And I shared some of that joy—the food was not me or Goroth. It was a banquet, a glutton's dream, the gorging of a gourmand beyond imagining. Chaos had broken out on the causeway as the countless creatures there fought each other to get back into the swamp. The serpent's head swung this way and that like something from the age of dinosaurs, its mouth crammed with wriggling, croaking amphibians. I used the staff to ward off any of the other creatures and started back along the causeway, the Mire-Beast right behind me. The artifact proved its worth as the frogs were just as afraid of its exudations as they were of the serpent. While the endless feeding went on behind us, we made it as fast as we could to the end of the causeway.

This time I didn't hesitate to get back on to the underwater stones and hop my way back where we'd come from. I couldn't quite shake myself free of the idea that the serpent would want us for the last course. Everything around us became more and more subdued until we were immersed in complete silence. The swamp was listening to us as we moved away from the scene of carnage. Nothing moved, above the mire or below it. Even the buckled trees seemed to have stultified, as if we were moving through a painting.

I was mighty relieved to get back to the place where the Bog Witch had her encampment. She was again sitting cross-legged on a large rock, her milky eyes fixed on some inner vision.

"Ah," she said, her ancient face breaking out in one of those crooked smiles. "I see you have the staff."

I'd been gripping it tight and right now I didn't have much intention of letting it go. "It passed the test run," I said. "No need to wrap it, I'll take it with me."

I expected her to argue, but she shook with soft, phlegmy laughter. "You'll be needing it, Nick Nightmare. The Frog God may be gone, but that won't stop the Dark Army from re-convening."

"You know what happened back there?"

"From the moment you woke Sissyllys. My sister. You did well. She likes you, Nick Nightmare."

"Your sister is a snake?"

"Not always. Like your friend here, she was transformed. Once she was a beautiful woman, like me."

I wasn't about to argue.

"The Frog God snared her and used Sebok's Staff to turn her into that creature you saw. Now—listen! Take Sebok's Staff back to your own world and guard it carefully, as you have done with other such items of power. Before you go, I will teach you how to use it, what convocations, curses and conflagrations of energy you can use."

I didn't relish the thought of that, but needs must when the Devil drives, or in this case, tries to kick your butt.

Thus I spent some time with the Bog Witch and her bizarre entourage, learning some new tricks. The Mire-Beast withdrew. I got the distinct feeling Goroth had enjoyed himself for once. I suppose in a warped way, he was back into law enforcement, more effectively than in his previous existence.

"Good luck," said the Bog Witch to me as I prepared for a fresh rendezvous with Fred the Ferryman. Out in the tangled trees I sensed something listening in, something very large and—*coiled.*

"She likes you, Nick Nightmare."

"Well, that's good to know."

"Remember, if you use the staff to summon the Silent Sister, there'll be a high price. She won't eat you, but she was always very possessive."

"Yes, I'll pass on that, no offense intended."

WARNING

Darrell Schweitzer

(after M.R. James)

The curious gent, I'm afraid,
went digging at night with a spade,
and, seeking a treasure,
succumbed without measure
to the thing from the trench he had made.

A WHISPER IN THE DEATH PIT
Kyla Lee Ward

Dr Jessamine Wiung was lead archaeologist on the expedition con-
ducted earlier this year, by the Department of Oriental Studies, to the site
of Kayalyk in south-eastern Khazakstan. The following email was received
by the head of department on August 16th. It was the final communication
from the expedition camp before the assault by as yet unidentified persons,
which claimed the lives of two of our colleagues.

The university, in consultation with the families of the deceased and
the missing, has decided to release the full text, together with a draft trans-
lation of an important inscription from the site. Please bear in mind that
the latter has not yet been officially published and contains clear errors,
as well as a degree of fancy. But her reflections on Kayalyk may well con-
stitute Dr Wiung's last written work. It is hoped that the free circulation
of this material, as well as honouring the members of the expedition, will
stop the spread of rumours that, as well as ludicrous, are disrespectful to
their memory.

* * * *

To the world at large, those first images of the Death Pit will forever
represent Kayalyk. But I retain a different picture. Situated between the
mountains and the river, the site is indeed remote, yet also spectacularly
beautiful. This morning, I saw wild ibex grazing not twenty metres away
from our encampment. As I write, the last light of the sun is still visible
behind the peaks and the excavated courtyard of the monastery is a pool of
shadow. Soon, there will be nothing to see but the unbelievable plenitude
of stars. The lights of Koilyk village do not reach us here.

I first saw the city ruins as a graduate student in 1998, when I assisted
Dr Aliyu Aliyev in the first of a series of beneficial exchanges between the
university and the Institute of Archaeology RK. We were studying regional
dialects and collecting folktales—she always said the two were inextrica-
ble. It was in these circumstances that I heard the legend of the monastery
of Ak Araw, the name translating roughly as "pale tree". I ask that you permit me to reiterate the relevant details, so you will understand the precise
nature of this latest emergency.

From the eighth century onwards, Kayalyk was a major hub of the

Silk Road. Parties from China, having survived the Taklmakan desert and the Tien Shan mountains, would frequently take the opportunity to on-sell their goods to Middle Eastern and even venturesome European traders, and pass the winter here before daring the return journey. This collision of cultures, doctrines and technologies made, as in Taraz, for a unique and dynamic milieu, persisting until the city was abandoned towards the end of the thirteenth century.

Koilyk #34 (Aliyev, 2000) recounts that, in the years before the coming of Genghis Khan, a "jade demoness" came out of the desert and corrupted the abbot of one of Kayalyk's Buddhist monasteries with promises of immortality. Soon, the entire community, including a formerly segregated order of nuns, had abandoned all regulation in favour of orgies alternating with torturous rites of abnegation and the brewing of strange potions. Caravans were plundered to provide ingredients and children disappeared at night. Corruption entered the river and the crops failed. In desperation, the citizens appealed to the Khan, offering the unconditional surrender of the city if he would but rid them of this terror. A contingent of Mongols marched upon Ak Araw, only to find it an empty shell. Its occupants had become immortal and flown to the western paradise.

I first noted the correspondences between the folk tale and the Chinese alchemical parable in my paper "The Jade Demoness: a journey of motifs" (*JoOS*, 2001). The thirteenth century Héxī'āshū lù ("Dew Writings"—see Van Galen, 1972) preserves the tale of Yù Sōngshù, a princess of the Jin Dynasty, who shunned marriage and the court to became a Daoist practitioner and disciple of the Sage Pang Liu. "Jade Pine" (the name collates two traditional symbols of longevity) had long been thought to represent the elixir of immortality, arising from the death of her master (the proper combination of the elements) at the successful conclusion of the Work—in this, Chinese alchemy is indeed similar to its western counterpart. In this paper I proposed that, setting aside the typical folkloric flourishes, it was not hard to picture a disciple or group of disciples who fled beyond the northern border during the purges conducted by the Jin, settling in Kayalyk and pursuing immortality through the accepted means of meditation and alchemy. The destruction of the monastery by Genghis Khan was at least theoretically possible, placing the conclusion of the story around 1220 C.E.

But the Death Pit presents a grimmer ending. Confronted by an army known for its atrocities, the inhabitants of the monastery entered the subterranean meditation chamber and collapsed the passage behind them. In classic Daoism, ascension as a true immortal traditionally involved immurement in a cave for a period that might last centuries. This may have been a final attempt to grasp the crown of their practice, or it may have been the mass suicide which was certainly the result.

There were many reasons to conduct a fresh investigation of Kayalyk, not the least being the site's elevation to World Heritage status in 2014. This expedition was always cast as an adjunct to the excellent and ongoing work being conducted by the Institute of Archaeology RK and initially, I welcomed the participation of my old mentor, Dr Aliyev, with great enthusiasm.

It was her translation of the stela we found in the courtyard that confirmed the identity of our discovery—Ak Araw was myth no more! This, too, has largely been submerged in the spectacular footage of the naturally mummified bodies and the chamber, with its stellar patterns upon the roof and brilliantly coloured floor mosaics featuring plants and animals of the region. But the stela's importance cannot be overestimated, in terms of cultural history and the context it provides to the larger find.

Not a classic sutra, it nonetheless must have been important to the practice of the monastery. I reproduce here the full translation:

> *What, then, is the day?*
> *Eternity is the day.*
> *What, then, is the night?*
> *Everlastingness is the night.*
> *What, then, is the roof above?*
> *The never-ending sky.*
> *What, then, is the floor below?*
> *The boundless realm of earth.*
> *What, then, of the pillars?*
> *The mountains ever-rising.*
> *What, then, is thy meat?*
> *The presence of my sister.*
> *What, then, is thy drink?*
> *The presence of my brother.*
> *How good, how pleasant to join thee in the garden!*
> *How fine, how fragrant, the thousand-petalled rose!*
> *How fine, how pleasant, to feel the coiling dragon!*
> *How good, what sweetness, to hear the phoenix sing!*
> *What, then, is thy breath?*
> *Knowledge of the truth.*
> *What, then, is thy blood?*
> *Perfection of understanding.*
> *What, then, is thy life?*
> *To speak the sacred words.*

One morning in early July, a student volunteer from the Institute insisted to me that one of the bodies sighed when she touched it. Several of her fellows claimed to have heard whispering while in the Pit, that could not be traced to any person present. These rumours spread and were augmented to such effect that some of our personnel refused to return to the Pit or handle the remains, placing the burden of logging and conservation on our contingent. This loss was in no way remedied by the increasing presence of the curious and pecuniary, to be sure, but also by belligerent groups from Koilyk village, the subject of previous reports, who drove around the outskirts of the site by night, shouting threats, and whom I suspected in the subsequent rash of thefts and sabotage of our equipment.

Initially, Dr Aliyev found it fascinating to observe how the discovery of the Death Pit was being incorporated into *Koilyk #34* and she attempted to engage the volunteers in the process of study, as a means of exorcising their own fears. The locals used the old tale to forecast the consequences of our disturbance of the bodies, but for the main seemed gripped by a non-specific dread.

There are forty bodies in all, in varying states of preservation. Many remain in an upright, meditative posture. Both male and female, the sexes alternate although male/male and female/female have been confirmed. All subjects wear robes of coarse, grey silk and the heads are shaven. Although all may be assumed as residents of the monastery and the majority are surely from the Kayalyk area, the variety of ethnicities is apparent to even the most casual eye. There is no trace of coercion, in the array or such bodies as have been properly examined. Their tissues contain a substantial presence of alkaloids and metals—standard ingredients of the elixir! Which may have contributed to the exceptional preservation of some of the mummies. We have not yet touched the central pair, who kneel opposite each other as if this were a marriage ceremony rather than a funeral. Those two are in truly incredible condition. I make no rash claims, but the woman displays an ethnicity consistent with Northern China: her companion is a Khazak with possible western traits.

Daoism today is a lively religious expression for millions of people across the world. It approaches contemporary life with both continuity and a wonderful flexibility of tradition that has always focused on development of both the community and the individual. We have received expressions of interest and support for our work from many Daoist communities, even though the practice of the monastery appears to have been truly unique. In any case, religious scruples are unlikely to have contributed to the unrest amongst our volunteers or in Koilyk, where the majority of the inhabitants are Sunni Muslims. No, I fear it is the example of Hollywood that sparked this surge of "mummy madness", with a more worrying possibility that I will come to soon.

You may well believe we have all been under a great deal of stress and the physical labour is taking its toll. But I had believed the professional archaeologists were coping. This was an error of judgement for which I take full responsibility: as the expedition leader, I should have been more aware. But despite being in her sixties, Dr Aliyev was shaming the rest of us "youngsters" with her energy and commitment. She had been spending a considerable amount of time down in the Pit, recording and identifying the various symbols incorporated into the mosaic. When she confronted me during today's lunch break, I was truly surprised. She said that it had never before struck her that these people had believed, had been utterly certain of their ascent to paradise. Should we not recognise this? Could we find some way to conduct our work while respecting their decision? Although she said this all in a reasonable tone, her hands were shaking.

At this, I abandoned my retort about thirteenth century Kool Aid and told her much the same things I had the Khazak media: that we were treating the mummies with the utmost respect and bringing them to "life" in a world they could never have imagined. In turn, we were learning invaluable things from them. At this, she sighed and said in her opinion we should remove no further material, bodies or otherwise, from the Pit. The reason she gave was the encroachment of Autumn and the attendant risk of storms, but as she said this, her hands shook even harder and she gripped the notebook she carried strongly enough to tear it.

I thought she might have been threatened. There is no question but antiquity thieves are circling and in this part of the world such operators are both organised and armed. Indeed, I now suspect their hand in the demonstrations of the villagers. My subsequent enquiries amongst the local personnel turned up nothing in this regard, but a student did let slip that after speaking to me, Dr Aliyev had returned immediately to the Pit.

This struck me as contrary, given her outburst, and I was thunderstruck to discover that she had gone down alone, in contravention of nearly every regulation we have. The rest of our people were in the conservation tent, dealing with the morning's extractions. As I approached, I saw the lamps we have installed in the Pit were still off, and she had not signed into the Pit log book. I must admit, I stormed down the passage with every intention of demanding an explanation for her behaviour, when I was relying on her to bring her fellow Khazaks to their senses! But whether you are superstitious or not, it is hard to shout in the Death Pit and perfectly impossible to stamp. The delicacy of the find aside, there is a sense of solemnity, of stillness, that defeats even the most righteous anger or fear for a friend. And I confess, when I heard that whisper trailing through the darkness, my heart nearly jumped out of my chest.

It was her, of course. My Khazak is good and I retain my familiarity with the local dialect, but this appeared to be an archaic form. I could make out maybe one word in four but that was enough to identify the verse from the stela. At this point I turned the lamps back on: the stars on the roof flashed, the brilliant depictions of fruit and flower leapt into life around symbols suggesting everything from hieroglyphs to Manichaeism, and Aliyu rose with an expression of absolute terror on her face. We have removed 12 mummies thus far, clearing a wedge from the outermost circle towards the innermost pair, and it was here she had been kneeling, much like a mummy herself. She waved at me, notebook in hand, as if the light had robbed her of the power of speech. As said, it is hard to shout in the Death Pit, so I merely waited as she came towards me, still not speaking but gesturing me away, back into the passage, as she again turned off the lamps. I obeyed, but even once we were within the reach of daylight, she wouldn't tell me what was wrong. In frustration, I seized her notebook. She raised her hand, then seemed to think the better of the action, and let me read it.

This is what I read, in her hasty scrawl, complicated by questions, references and the multiple revisions that accompany translation:

> *What, then, is thy meat?*
> *The presence of my sister.*
> *What, then, is thy drink?*
> *The presence of my brother.* Brother, do you hear me?
> Sister, I hear you. But this means you are separate from us and this should not be.
> Something has changed. Listen!
> Our voice is…less.
> We were many, now we are few.
> What has befallen those whose voices are still? Have they ascended?
> I think something comes among us, bringing destruction.
> *What, then, is thy life?*
> In danger, brother, danger.

I asked Aliyu what this meant. She said that the only way for me to understand was if I returned to the Pit with her in darkness. I would have to be absolutely silent, unless I could memorise the chant in an approximation of medieval Khazak, which was as close as she had been able to get and which seemed to working. I must not, under any circumstances, disrupt her again: it was imperative she go back down there right now and *guide them back into their meditation.*

I spoke gently of the conditions under which she had been working and how we were all extremely tired. I agreed that resealing the Pit might be the only way to preserve the find during Winter, but in the meantime we should continue with our duty to conserve the mummies and send them on to the Institute.

She looked at me and in that moment, I was once again a 26 year old doctoral candidate, being farewelled by my mentor at the airport in Astana. Only this time, instead of seeing pride in her eyes, I saw a deep disappointment. She said. "Do you remember Pang of Datong?"

Of course I did, from my own, old paper. I found the reference in Chiang's 2003 work on the splintering of Dao sects during the fall of the Northern Song. Pang of Datong was reportedly arrested by the first Jin Emperor and divided into "the four parts of a human being and the fifth exclusive to man, and each separately boiled" for being unmasked, as I now recalled, as a ghost immortal.

A ghost immortal is a Daoist bogey, someone without the patience or discipline necessary to become a true immortal. Instead, they settle for a lesser form of existence that needs to absorb life energy to survive: a popular pastime of mummies the world over. These are moral tales, illustrating the evils of pride and materialism, or of clinging to worldly attachments. Dr Aliyev, I'm sure, knew them all.

She had forborne till now, she said, out of respect and a wish not to cause panic. But if I did not agree to close the Pit *immediately*, then she would deploy all her influence not to calm the volunteers and the villagers, but to whip them into a frenzy. She would tell them that my equation of Pang of Datong with the sage Pang Liu (which I made speculatively, merely to suggest historical context) proved I was aware of the *real* danger and was ignoring it. She would incite them to close the passage and abandon the dig, and see to it that I bore the blame. This was Khazakstan after all, and the Institute was her domain.

How much of this was bluster, I cannot say. But finally, I understood that *she* believed.

So now you see my situation. Although I do not believe she could lead the mutiny she proposes, she could cause disruption, which could compromise the security of the site in the face of genuine danger. I ask only that the university back me in the action I propose to take. I have rallied the others and if you will assure me of your support, we will remove Dr Aliyev expediently from the dig. I believe she has gone back into the Pit, which will allow this to be done out of view of the students. Kris has agreed to drive her to Almaty along with the next load of artefacts, the duration of which journey should allow negotiation with the Institute. Share with them any of this material you think necessary. I ask you to please see that Dr Aliyev is treated well. I am deeply saddened by this turn of events but this is the only way I can see to proceed.

* * * *

After discussion with the Dean, our head of department responded in the affirmative. We can only assume, from where the bodies were found, that Dr Wiung did indeed confront Dr Aliyev in the Pit and was in the processing of escorting her back to the surface when the attack occurred. Although the police investigation is ongoing, we find no reason to doubt Dr Wiung's suspicion of antiquity thieves, taking the disruption as an opportunity to raid the site. Finding our colleagues and Dr Aliyev in the Pit, they killed the two men and abducted Drs Wiung and Aliyev. Perhaps they forced them to identify the most valuable of the remaining artefacts, resulting in them taking the central pair of mummies and some of the smaller vessels and burners.

At the time of writing, both women are still missing. No ransom demands have been received and it is considered likely they too are dead. Although Dr Wiung's story ends here, some further entries were found in Dr Aliyev's notebook. Thanks to the Institute of Archaeology RK, who share our grief, we reproduce these here in recognition of Dr Aliyev's sense of the sanctity of Kayalyk. If the conflict between this and Dr Wiung's sense of responsibility towards the expedition contributed in any way to the tragedy, it can only be considered a terrible coincidence.

* * * *

What, then, of the new voice? It speaks the words.

Corrupted, my brother. It speaks strangely, with no true understanding.

Your people have lost their way, as did mine.

What, then, of our fate?

Shall we abandon your people when their need is so great? It is as my master said, before he was twice-killed. Beyond the rules, beyond even our own ascension, our great duty is to preserve the lore.

Shall we be monsters, then?

We shall be teachers, of the kind this barbarous, new world demands. Brother, it is fate that has awakened us.

With grief, I see that it is so. Embrace me, sister, in our garden this last time.

Speak to me, brother, the sweetest of all words.

What, then, is thy meat?

Oh brother, I hunger!

What, then, is thy drink?

Brother, I thirst!

Such agony! To come aware once more! To know of the space between us, the boundaries of flesh! Such agony, as the heart twitches, as withered lungs begin to fill!

What, then, is thy breath?

Scents of sweat, my brother, of perfume, oil and blood.

What, then, is thy blood?

Foul, my brother, thick and cold, yet thanks to the elixir, it flows.

What, then, is thy life?

It lies in *them*.

✗

ABSENT A PASSION PLAY

Allan Rozinski

In the windows of the stores,
in magazines, on billboards and screens,
manikins are dressed to kill,
or to simply advertise their wares;
and then there are the
marionettes, automated,
in constant motion,
window shopping
with imagined needs to fulfill,
while elsewhere
pliable puppets submit themselves
to be molded, bent or broken
to fit the roles they've chosen, or
to play the parts they'd auditioned for.
Hordes of extras join the cast
without consideration or protest
in exchange for payment
or for the hopeful comfort
of some semblance of applause,
and, at each level above,
in turn, it builds, stage upon stage,
an endless spectacle at large,
a free-form bunraku theater
inspired by the Grand Guignol,
absent a passion play.

✗

DEADEST MAN IN TOWN
Franklyn Searight

Watching the man in green as he moved about was as entertaining as a dog fight, as long as it was not your pooch involved in the melee. He moved with a decided swagger and fluid movement requiring fewer muscles and bones than the average person.

"Well, well, well," he said, pulling a chair away from the table and sitting down. "Haven't seen yer in quite a spell, Arnie."

The man addressed did a double take, and then another, spilling some of the coffee he was raising to his mouth. Catching Arnold Monroe by surprise and rendering him speechless for more than a minute was unheard of—but it happened this time. He did his best to repress any further emotion, but his eyebrows rose in astonishment. His insides felt as though they had been turned upside down and inside out, and mixed together in a vegetable blender. He was a smallish man with a protruding belly who had hoisted too many cans of beer over the years. In addition, he was an auto mechanic, now retired, one of the best, and currently the president of the South Fork town council.

"Been a long time, Vince," he finally said, scratching the unshaven, bristles on his face, acknowledging the man in green.

Vincent Fletch, tall and slender as a flag pole, agreed. "Fer sure. Yer looking well."

"Can't complain—can't complain. My rheumatism flares up a bit now and then, though. Try not to pay much heed to it."

The visitor nodded sympathetically. "Feel for yer. Have my own tribulations, deed I do!"

Vincent wore a mint green suitcoat over a grassy colored vest partially covering an emerald green shirt; his feet were shod with dark, iridescent socks and shoes seen below his verdant-hued slacks. Arnold thought he appeared something like a leprechaun.

My gawd, he wondered. *Where in tarnation did his old buddy ever find such a getup?*

"How's the wife?" Vince asked, crossing his lanky legs and leaning back.

"Middling, I'd say. She's gone to fat, though—put on forty pounds since you last seen her."

"Mite too pudgy. Rheumatism will be eating away at Mildred soon, lessen she loses a bit of poundage."

"You can tell it to me," said Arnold, "but you can't tell it to her. Can't tell the woman a dern thing, you can't!"

"Knows it all, huh?"

"Knows *everything*! Walking 'cyclopedia, she is! The one thing she don't know is just how stupid she is sometimes!"

The man in green chuckled and ran his fingers through dark, curly hair that needed a good combing.

"Typical woman, huh?"

"S'pose so, but not all of 'em be as dumb as Mildred."

"Guess yer right, but I always thought she be pretty—a shapely specimen of the feminine persuasion. College graduate, too, ain't she?"

"Yup, she be that. And something else you cain't forget—she won't let you! You'd never know it though, to hear her speak. Maybe she's smart when it comes to book larnin', but it's 'bout it. She'll tell you too—over and over again if you'd sit there and listen to her. I walk away once she gets started."

The two old friends stopped talking for a spell, wondering what to say next, but both of them comfortable in the silence. Vince glanced around the pine-clad wall of the *Cozy Spoon*, the town grill he hadn't seen in quite some time. His eyes focused on the old, moldy-looking moose head above the door leading to the rest rooms. It had been fairly new when he had last been in the place, but now looked ragged and worn, as though it had been infested by fleas or other mangy varmints.

"Where's the waiter, anyway?" the man in green finally asked. "He looked over here a minute ago; thought he'd be right over to take my order. Least he could do is bring me a cup of java."

"Prob'ly didn't notice you," Arnold suggested.

"Think so? Maybe 'cause I don't want him to. People don't see me if'n I don't want them to."

"But I can see you. See you fine."

"Cause I want yer to."

"Oh," said Arnie, as though it explained everything.

"I can do 'bout whatever I wants to—within certain limits, of course."

"Oh. Of course."

"Who is he anyway?"

"Be Lennie Wilkes. Works part time here at the *Cozy Spoon*. Little soft up here," Arnold said, tapping his head with a slightly bent finger. "Least, it's what people say. Left school in the fourth grade an's been bumming around the town ever since. Musta had a million jobs, but cain't seem to hold on to one more'n a month or two. People feel sorry for him."

"Oh, yeah?"

Arnold waved at the waiter to come over.

"Bring a mug of coffee for my friend," Arnold instructed him.

The youth's long and pointed, acne-splotched nose sort of wriggled as he stared at Arnold in wonder. The white shirt he wore was rolled up beyond his elbows, revealing a tattoo resembling a turtle sticking its head out of its shell.

"You heard me! Coffee for my friend!"

"What friend?" Lennie asked, weakly, glancing around the room.

"Just get another coffee, Lennie," Arnold said, with a knowing smile on his face.

Lennie left to fill the order, looking around three times before he reached the counter, then went behind it and reached for the coffee pot.

"He's a nice enough fellow, though," said Arnold, watching the youngster pour the brew into a clean cup. "Means well, but just plain stupid—like Mildred."

The man in green chortled again. "Prob'ly not good in the sack, either."

"How would I know?"

"I mean Mildred."

"Well, yeah. Mildred's not so good anymore. Hot flashes, she gets. Change of life comin' on, she says. Drinks now, you know?"

"Didn't know. She's nearly forty-five now, right?"

"Yup. Two years younger'n me. I ain't slowed down a bit, though—see the Wider Parton couple times a week—lives down by the creek. Don't need Mildred."

"Too bad I'll never see fifty, myself—never know what it'd be like to be fifty."

"Prob'ly much like the day before when you would have been forty-nine. The years pass by, one after 'nother. How old were you when you died, now?"

"Must be seventeen years ago, I 'spect," the man in green said thoughtfully.

"Yup. be 'bout right. Still remember the summer evening; hot and sweaty; no way to cool off or take in a lungful of cool air. I had turned on the radio to listen to the ball game when the announcer man come on with a special report."

"That the night, huh? Hot? Don't recollect much 'bout it myself."

"Yup, that the night. Broadcaster told the listeners 'bout how Old Seventy-Six came roaring through the intersection, not knowing the gate weren't down, plowed right into your car, and sent it flying like it were a stack of Tiddlywinks. Smashed it to smithereens. Weren't Bernie's fault though; no one could have stopped the train in time."

"Maybe if he be agoing slower?"

"Nope. Train still would've rammed into you and drug you fifty yards down the tracks afore braking to a stop—made the goddamdest noise and mess you've ever seen.

"Folks didn't know who the driver were, at the time…not until the next morning."

"Oh, yeah? My face that bad? Weren't my driver's license in my wallet?"

"Maybe it twas. Never found it till a few days later, out in the field, all ripped and shredded. Easy to identify you though, once they found your head."

"My head? Where was my head?"

"Hacked off from the rest of you. Little Sally Pulaski found it in the field next to the tracks next mornin', 'bout fifty feet from the rest of you."

"My, my. Musta given her quite a turn."

"Yup. Town folk didn't think she'd ever be the same again. Mildred had a fit, of course."

"Did she, now?"

"Yup. This was afore we were married, of course. You were dating her then, and she had a mite fearsome crush on you, you know?"

"Did she, now?"

"Yup. A mighty fearsome crush. After, she turned to me for cons'lation. I was there, and I was available. Seven months later we be married."

"Should have been me," the man in green reminisced, feeling a tad sorry for himself.

"Yup, if'n you say so."

"She should have been with me in the car."

"Didn't know that."

"Had a date that night. Matter of fact, I was on my way over to her place to pick her up, when WHAM!"

"Wham, is right! Hurt much?"

"Didn't hurt a bit. Don't remember much, either. I was *dead*, man! Dead as a mosquito smacked with a mallet. Killed right off. No chance to say goodbye to anyone er recite my prayers."

"Sorry, I misspoke. Remember when they found your head in the field—fifty feet from the track."

"I believe yer. Think if Barney had been going a bit slower…"

"Still would have happened, Vince. It were your own fault. Gaud only knows what you were doing on the track with the train coming at you."

"Don't know. Cain't remember much of anything 'bout that night."

"As I recall, you were all busted into pieces. Tad Perkins, down at the funeral parlor, stitched you back together again as best he could, I s'pose."

"Why'd he bother tryin'?"

"Mildred. She batted her big blues and begged him to put you back together."

"Stupid, but it sounds like something she'd do."

"Yes, it does. Said she couldn't stand the thought of you being flung into the bone yard in a dozen pieces."

"Stupid."

More silence followed as the two men gathered their thoughts. Vince reached for the coffee Leonard had set down, and his hand passed through the cup.

"Dang! Keep forgetting. Cain't grab anything; not anymore."

Arnold shook his head, slightly amused, and asked, "So what brings you into town now?"

"Getting restless, I was. Been under the sod for a long time; missed the good old days with yer and Larry, huntin' in the winter, fishin' in the summer, bowlin' at Midge's, drinkin' at the Four Aces—yer know."

"Yeah, the Four Aces."

"Saloon still around?"

"'Tis."

"Bernie still there pouring drinks? Cheating the customers when they ain't watching careful like?"

"Naw. Bernie's been gone seven years now. Never met him on the other side, huh?"

"Nope. Not many come through I knew in life. 'Course, both of yer parents, and yer niece Agnes. Couple chaps I knew at grammar school. Heard 'bout others who passed, but never came across'em. Don't know why. Bernie never showed up. Yer sure he's gone?"

Arnold grinned his infectious grin, and patted down his white, thinning hair. "Course, I'm sure. Maybe he went the wrong way: down instead of up."

"Yup, could have happened, all right."

"So, tell me: How was it you were able to claw your way out of the box, and then dig yourself up six feet to the surface?"

"Nary a s'picion, Arnie; nary a one. Fact is, my *body's* still in the hole, rotting away, feeding the rats and the vermin."

"So, just who or what is it I'm looking at right now?"

"Yer be looking at a manifestation," he answered, pronouncing the word slowly and carefully. "There're things yer don't know 'bout—things yer don't *want* to know 'bout, Arnie."

"Still, doesn't s'plain why you're here, Vince."

"There's a coven of witches here in South Fork. A clutter of twelve of 'em. Been drifting in over the years, one by one, taking up residences, making themselves welcome in the community—being outstanding citizens so's to cause no s'picion."

"You're not serious, Vince. Are you?"

"I am. I heard tell of the visits they make up Cemetery Road to the top of the hill. Stealthy like, silently, in the evening and the darkest of the night, stealin' certain mushrooms and herbs for casting secret spells, opening graves and taking out body parts to use in their conjurations."

Arnold drew in his breath slowly, afraid to believe or not to believe, unsure of what to say or do.

"You just trying to scare me, aren't you, Vince?" he finally said.

The dead man looked at him with a crooked grin. "Am I? That what yer think?"

Just for the tiniest of a second, Arnold thought he saw a white, curly worm of some kind moving between the man's teeth, then dart under his tongue and out of sight. A nauseous quiver of revulsion tingled along his spine.

"They're having a special meeting tonight at Crooked Lake—all twelve of 'em. Down at the picnic grounds near the beach."

"Who tell you?" questioned Arnold.

"Don't have to be told—just knows. Knows lots of things, Arnie. Fact is, the Big One told me. Gives me an assignment, he did. Told me to sneak up to the meeting tonight, and spy on 'em. I want yer to go with me, Arnie!"

"Huh? You been in the ground too long, Vince. You're plumb out of your friggin' mind!"

Vince reached for the coffee cup once more, and again his hand passed through it unobstructed. "Damn!" he exclaimed. "Keep forgetting I'm not all here."

"Not quite," Arnold opined.

"Sure would like a taste of black potion, though."

"But 'bout tonight…the special meeting of the coven…we'll be *joining* 'em, Arnie."

"Oh, yeah? Long stay in the pine box ain't improved your reasoning any, has it? I can see how it would concern Pastor Michael and his congregation, and maybe John Toller at the funeral parlor, but why are you interested in the activities of a coven?"

"Ain't 'specially interested in them sinful folk, but the Big Boss is. It was He who tells me to dispatch them unsavory occultists—soon as possible."

"Big Boss? Who that be?"

"Mr. Biggie…the Guy in Charge…the Chap who set the planets and such in their orbits, and sort of keeps an eye on things down here…sep'rates the wheat from the chaff, so to speak."

"You mean God?"

"Course, I does. God…our Creator; Commander of the Force. Call Him or Her what yer will, it's the One in Charge. The Big Boss!"

Arnold nodded his head sagely. "Gotcha, Vince. Don't go to church anymore, 'cepting' when Mildred gets a bug up her butt, thinking we're living like the heathen, and drags me along with her."

"Prob'ly not often, though, huh?"

"Once or twice a year. More 'n that'd be overdoing it. Overkill. Don't quarrel with her, just go along with it. Easier to follow her like a puppy dog than it 'tis to argue with her.

"But what does this Mr. Biggie intend to do 'bout the coven?"

"Bust it up! Get rid of it! Big Guy puts me in charge of doing it."

"You been appointed to destroy the coven?"

"Yup, and He says it gots to be done soon!"

"Why doesn't He do it Hisself?"

"Well, rather than wave a magic wand, Big Guy sometimes gets Hisself some help. Yer must know God often gets things done by relying 'pon the hands of those He's created to do His will."

"What if there be no hands to use, Vince?

"Why, then, he prob'ly just launch a thunder bolt or somethin' at the coven and eradicate it away—all at once. Problem is, He might miscalculate and take out the whole of South Fork!"

"Wouldn't want that to happen."

"No. Course not. So, I've been given the assignment."

"Big job, Vince."

"Yer bet it is. But there cain't be much of a penalty for failure. What's he gonna do? Banish me to the nether regions?"

"He able to?"

"The Man can do anything he want."

"All powerful, huh?"

"He be that. Puts the color in the roses—makes 'em bloom. Turns ittybitty minnows into enormous basses and pikes. Oh, I could spend days telling yer 'bout all the nifty things He can do."

"I'll bet you could, Vince. I'll bet you could. But just how do you intend to chase them sinners out of our community?"

"I has a plan."

"Oh, ho!"

"But to carry it out, I needs an assistant, and that where yer come in, Arnie."

"Don't look at me like that, Vince. I don't like the shifty gleam in your eyes."

"Too bad, Arnie. Yer been chosen to be second in command."

"You being the first, of course. No thankie, Vince. I decline the honor."

"Tain't an honor, and yer cain't decline. Yer haven't been chosen by me—although I do think yer be an excellent choice—Big Guy in the Sky selected yer hisself."

"Whoa, Vince. Why me? He don't know me from Adam."

"That s'posed to be a joke, Arnie?"

"No, not an intentional one. Sounds funny, though."

"I'm not laughing, Arnie. Neither is God. In much the same way as He needs hands to get His work done, I needs to have a helper to accomplish my assignment.

"Yer to be my helper, Arnie."

"What if I wants to decline, Vince?"

"Tell it to God, Arnie, not to me."

"I understand why God needs a helping hand now and then, but why do *you*?

"In the same way God relies upon me is why I have to count upon yer to get things done. See the coffee there? I'd love to have a swaller but cain't. Look!"

The man in green extended his right hand, his fingers curling around to grasp the handle of the cup. His hand passed completely through it.

"See, Arnie? I has no substance. No actual reality, so's to speak. As I said afore, I'm a manifestation. The real me is still six foot under the grass. If I wants something done, I have to have someone do it fer me."

"You want me to hold the cup up to your mouth and pour the coffee down your throat?"

"Course not! I'd only go right through me and leave a big puddle on the table for Lenny to clean up."

"Just what does He…or you…'spect me to do?"

"Not quite certain yet. Still working on the plan. But I'll pick yer up at eight o'clock tonight, and we'll head fer the coven meeting down at the lake. I 'spect there'll be plenty fer yer to do, meaning whatever I cain't do fer myself, which I s'pose'll be just 'bout everything, 'cept for the thinking part."

"So, I'm just an obliging pair of hands to do your will. That it?"

"That be 'bout it, Arnie, but it won't be *my* work yer'll be doing, exactly, but the good Lord's."

"Sort of like Pastor Michael having ushers pass the plate during the service, or getting someone to rake leaves off the church lawn in the autumn, as a volunteer."

"Yeah, 'bout like that."

"So, let me sum this up," said Arnold. "The Lord knows of this coven and has appointed you, as his emissary, to destroy it, to do what He'd rather not do His self. You accepted the appointment and has chosen me as your envoy to do those things, using my hands, which you cain't do."

"Exactly," agreed Vince. "Took a while, but yer've caught on, right good. What kind of vehicle yer got?"

"Got me an 88 Ford pickup truck."

"Runs okay?"

"The way I pampers it? Course it do. Runs better'n okay. Runs good!"

"That be fine, Arnie. And...bring yer gun. Knows yer used to have one."

"Still do. Ol' Smokey—haven't shot it in a coon's age, though. Bought a second one a few years ago—lighter caliber—to shoot snakes with while I'm ahuntin'. I'll bring it along for you, Vince."

"Don't bother bringing one for me. I couldn't hang on to it, let alone pull the trigger."

"Hard to understand why the Lord would want a gun to be used. This His idea?"

"It is, but don't try to understand it, Arnie. The Lord works in 'scrutable ways. See yer tonight 'round eight o'clock."

Vince extended his hand and then withdrew it quickly, knowing Arnold would curse him a blue streak if he reached to grab it, and it was not there to shake.

Vince stood up. "Gotta go."

"Okay," said Arnold, and he reached over to retrieve his coffee cup. When he looked back, the man in green had disappeared. He shook his head as though what was left of his hair had been mussed up by a sudden breeze. He rubbed his eyes, wondering if this last hour had been a dream or a figment of reality. He had always known the truth when he heard it, he thought, but he could not make up his mind about this particular episode. Tonight, unless he had been mysteriously transported to the Land of Oz, he would be working in the service of the All-Mighty!

It was a time of the month when the moon appeared in all its glory, shedding an unusual amount of light on the landscape below. Arnold Moore always enjoyed watching the awesomeness of a new moon begin its progress across the sky. With a degree of giddiness, he would speculate nature must have somehow inserted a new, more powerful battery into it, increasing its illumination multifold.

He had been in the living room watching the Yankees on TV getting the bejesus booted out of them. When the wall clock indicated the time was ten minutes to eight, he stood up, sighed, and moved the revolver he had been cleaning from the coffee table to his hip pocket where it snugly fit. He hitched his pants up a trifle higher, and moved outside onto the front porch.

With one hand he patted the hidden weapon, and with the other he carried a half-consumed can on Colt 45. Mildred was already in the bedroom, sacked out, soused as usual, and sleeping it off. He didn't want to tell her anything of what was going on, anyway. She would leer at him, hiccup, and make some nasty observation.

He sat on the swing, lifted his legs to rest his feet on the top railing, and took a healthy swig of the cooling drink. He released a healthy "aah", burped loudly, and set the can down on the boards beside him.

Would Vince actually come here tonight, he wondered? Hell, he still didn't know if he had experienced a curious dream this morning, or not. If it *had* been mere hallucination, there would be no extraordinary appearance of his old friend this night—or any other. If what had seemed to happen actually *did*, well, he was ready to do the Lord's bidding, as Vince had explained it. Becoming involved with a coven was not his resolve at all, so it must be of God.

A tiny, barely auditable buzzing caught his attention, growing louder every moment, and seconds later he swatted at the audacious mosquito settling on his arm, fearless as could be. He missed—as usual. The airborne bully must have an inborn sixth sense allowing it to know the precise moment a crushing palm would squish it and, with but a micro instant to spare, it would be off and circling about, biding its time, ready to risk disaster when the moment came for one more chance at a fresh supply of blood. Quite like many vampires Arnold had read about.

Idly, Arnold gazed out over the landscape in front of him before taking another swig of beer. Shadows were abundant and crowding closer as darkness rapidly approached; the moon was poised as though he might snatch it with his hand, and the forested terrain laying across the road was deep in the shadows of semi-darkness, revealing a belt of trees blending together as one long line of darkness across the horizon.

Bisecting the woods was Cemetery Road, little more than a dirt trail beginning at the highway across from where Arnold and Mildred lived and then crawled up the hill to where the burial ground was located, beyond his vision. This particular cemetery was where Vincent Moore had been planted some seventeen years ago, he reflected.

The burial service had occurred on a dismal, overcast day, he recalled, with a light drizzle which seemed determined to last for eternity. There was mud all around, which didn't improve the onlooker's disposition in any way, and the light drops continued long after the box was lowered into the ground. Pastor Reynolds, the precursor to the current Pastor Wilcox, had tossed some dirt into the hole and said a few solemn words of comfort. He did not go on and on, as he was frequently wont to do, realizing the people wanted the ceremony to be over with as quickly as possible so they could leave and seek shelter from the elements. There really was not a lot for him to say, anyway, although he did have the remarkable ability of rambling on and on, stringing his words together during a half hour's passage of time. Vince was, well, Vince. He was a common man, neither awfully bad nor exceptionally good, known by everyone, if only to be greeted in passing, or sitting next to in the movie house, or chugging beer at the bowling alley. Pastor had quickly finished his piece and thanked the folks for coming out.

Arnold glanced at his watch—two minutes to eight. He lifted his head and could see movement of some kind at the far end of the narrow road. Just a blot of shadow at first, moving through the growing twilight, becoming larger as the seconds ticked away. The blur expanded into a shape and was just nearing the highway when it resolved itself into a long, narrow, upright figure. It continued across the road, and by the time it was half way across, a head could be seen resting upon a neck attached to a torso and long legs.

It was Vince, all right. Arnold could tell by the time the figure had crossed the road. He sighed. Some sort of action *was* going to take place this night, one not to look forward to, but also one he would not attempt to evade. If it was, indeed, God's will, then he would do his best. It was all there was to it, being the sort of guy he was.

He grabbed the can of beer from the floor, raising it to his lips as Vince reached the sidewalk leading up to his house, and drained the contents. He might as well. By the time they got back tonight—if they ever did—it would be warm and stale, anyway.

"Evenin'," said a voice from the shadows, coming from the man in green, reaching the end of the walk and climbing the porch steps.

The globe on top of the shoulders resolved itself into the grinning face of Vincent Fletch.

"Evenin', Vince," returned Arnold. "Weren't sure whether you be turning up tonight, or not."

"Wouldn't miss it for the world," said Vince, reaching the top of the steps. "Going to offer me one of those?" he asked, pointing to the can in Arnold's hand.

"Can't fool me again; wouldn't do you a speck of good, would it?"

"Nary a speck, but the kindly gesture would surely be appreciated. God knows, I'd love to have a cold one right now. Haven't had a drink—or anything else, fer that matter—in seventeen years, and boy, I sure do miss the brew!

"Where's Mildred, my old girlfriend?"

"In the back room—sleeping it off. No point in bringing her out here to see you. Drunk as a skunk, anyway. She'd 'spect you to climb atop one of them purple elephants she sees when she gets this away."

"Darn! Hoping to see Milly again after all these years. Pretty bad, huh?"

"Couldn't be worse, Vince. She'd cheer you up a bit though; make you glad you didn't have to put up with her these past years."

"She know what yer be up to tonight?"

"Naw. Wouldn't interest her a tall, anyways. She'd be interested in seeing you, though. That'd snap her out of her stupor, right quick. More 'en likely, she'd faint dead away and, ifn she woke up and found you still here, she'd run screaming back into the house, screeching 'bout haunts and heebie-jeebies."

"How come yer don't do it, Arnie?" the man in green asked, poking a little fun at his old acquaintance.

"Too blamed stupid, I 'spect. This prob'ly be a dream, anyway, and I'd want to see what happens next."

"Won't have to wait much longer. Yer truck in the driveway?"

"Yup. All gassed up and ready to go."

"Running smooth?"

"Purrs like a bobcat."

"Ha! Ha! Yer were always good at machines, Arnie. Got cher gun?"

"Got my gun—but she don't purr. Goes blam, blam!"

He slapped the bulge in his back pocket.

"Cleaned and oiled," Arnold said. "Did it this afternoon. Ain't much of a shot with it, though, you understand."

"'Spect yer won't need to be."

It was then Arnold remembered he had neglected to do one important thing after cleaning his weapon: replace the cartridges he had removed.

"Dang," he said, "my mind has been napping. 'Spect I should put in some bullets, huh?"

"Most effective that way, but prob'ly won't matter no how. Just the sight of it should be enough. They don't know yer ain't good with it. I 'member just how bad yer were. The broadside of a barn was always a safe place to stand. Might put a few rounds in yer pocket, though—just in case."

Arnold nodded and went back into the house for a few seconds, and returned jamming something into a front pocket.

"Good to have, but prob'ly won't have no occasion to use it. Folks around here never used to carry firearms, no how."

"Still don't, 'cept for hunting."

"If'n them coven folk want to hurt yer, they'd make a doll resembling yer and jab it full of needles. Make a pin cushion out of it—and yer. Or, if they don't want to go to so much trouble, they might cast a quick spell over yer, mutter a few words of mumble, jumble, and dispatch yer that away."

"Don't scare me no how, Vince."

"Don't know why it would scare anyone. Perhaps, though, if'n a person believe in hooey, it will work. But, me? I don't care one bit. I'm dispatched, anyway!"

"So you are, Vince."

"So let's be on our way. Coven'll meet tonight at nine o'clock whether we be there or not, and I'd prefer we be there, even a bit early, so's to find a grandstand seat to watch 'em from; that'd be to my liking."

Together, the men left the porch and passed over the weed-cluttered lawn to the pickup truck. Arnold opened the door on the passenger side for Vince, he being unable to do so himself, and watched his friend settle onto the seat. He closed the door, walked over to the other side and positioned himself behind the steering wheel.

"And away we go," he said, as the vehicle shot backward, out of the driveway.

"Something like the Lone Ranger and Tonto, huh?!"

* * * *

The silvery sheen of the moon reflected off the particles of fine, ground-up quartz covering the top of the bluff upon which they lay. The beach, down below and in front of them, was vacated by the typical rowdies making their usual appearance during the daylight hours. It was not difficult to tell where the coastline ended and the water began despite the darkness and shadows accompanying the night. They could see Crooked Lake sparkling in the silvery rays all the way out to where a thin line separated the water from the opposite side. In closer, calmer water made its way landward, washing its way onto the beach, suds crawling up the spectral sands as far as it could reach before backing up and returning to the frigid waters.

"Nice up here," said Vincent.

"Very nice," agreed Arnold.

"Sure would make for an agreeable picture," Vincent ventured. "The trees, the moon on the lake, and all. Never had a camera myself. Too much trouble and expense. Store bougt'n ones better than homemade, anyway. Taken by professionals."

"Yup. Got me a drawer full of post cards back home. Never owned a camera either, not till recently. Got me an iPod—a Nokia Android-based smart phone. Works like a camera, too. Won it off a city-slicker salesman out of Chicago in a poker game. Took all his money, and when he wanted to keep playing 'loud him to put his gadget in the pot. Thought he'd cry when he lost it, too."

"Work good?"

"Don't know. Haven't tried it out yet."

"Still no one down there."

"Sure you got the right night? Right place?"

"Course, I do. Big Guy don't make mistakes, does he? He should know. Course, it's the right night and place. Right time, too."

"He should know, all right. Course, He don't know everything, do he?"

"'Spect he don't."

"Damn right, He don't! Years ago, after you met yer Maker, I ask Him 'bout Mildred. Told me she make a wonderful wife, and I should marry her."

"That right?"

"Goes to show you He don't know everything!"

"What time yer 'spect the witch folk be getting here?"

"The mighty told me nine o'clock. Not a minute afore, ner a minute later."

"That's when they be here? Past eight-thirty now, so we don't have us a long spell to wait."

"Fine. We got time to look at the stars, then."

"You an astronomer, Vince?"

"Naw. Can pick out the Dippers, though; Cassiopeia, the North Star, things like them."

"More'n I can do. Such Knowledge worth havin', Vince?"

"Prob'ly not. Not 'lessen yer find yerrself on a quiz show, or somethin'."

"Tain't likely, Vince. If'n you cain't lick it, smell it, wear it, or give it to your girlfriend to look pretty in—tain't no good, atall."

"For that matter, Arnie, what good be *anything* worth knowing? Cain't use none of it while yer laying cramped up in yer box, six feet under."

"Guess not. You mentioned clothes, though. You were buried all in black, as I recollect; but now everything' you wear is *green* Where'd you get them fancy duds?"

"They be on loan—temp'rily like—the good Lord provisions me nicely."

"Treats you good, does He?"

"Always has, both alive and deceased. Course, I'm easy to look after; don't move around much in that pine carton, and all."

"Will he be wantin' them green duds back when this be all over with?"

"Don't know. Hope so. Makes me look like a goblin."

"Be thinking, more like a green lizard, Vince."

"That's as may be. In either case, I'll be glad to shuck 'em, even though my funeral garb's getting pretty ragged and tacky lookin'."

"God's been good to me, also, Vince, 'cepting for Mildred. Wonder if…"

"Shhh. Lookie down there!"

Arnold swiveled his head and looked in the direction at which Vince was pointing with his gnarled finger, topped with a greenish colored nail, and was surprised to see a movement down below. A dark shadow was emerging out of the woods and edging across the sands. It might have been mistaken for a long slab of driftwood if it were not for the slow but steady movement. The fellow—or woman, he wasn't quite sure just which, not from this distance—looked to the right, down the beach, then to the left, and then suddenly raised its arms and waved back towards the woods from where it came. Seconds later, Vincent and Arnold spotted a group of people emerging from the tree line, responding to the motion of their leader.

"Looks like he ain't alone, don't it?" Vincent declared, assuming the advance person to be a male. "Look at all his friends coming out of the woods! One, two, three …whole bunch of 'em!"

One by one the people left their concealment. The moon had earlier emerged from behind a bank of clouds and revealed them to be hooded, creepy looking creatures in the silvery moonlight, glancing from side to side to be certain they were not being observed as they approached their leader who had signaled to them. Next to where he stood was an enormous chunk of driftwood which must have weighed a ton. It had lain there for years, poking out of the sand, a permanent fixture, bleached white as a ghost by the winds and the storms that sometimes howled up and down the coast, pounding the shoreline. The group advanced to one of its ends, then moved on a few more yards and dropped what they had been carrying unto a pile growing higher and higher.

"Looks to be branches or logs," Vince said in a low voice. "They intend on building them a fire, then."

"And they come prepared," Arnold added.

They watched as the mound grew larger and larger, enough to provide for an enormous conflagration when ignited. One of the figures stepped back and, with a long stick, proceeded to draw a wide circle in the sand around the fire pit with a diameter of about fifty feet. The rest of the group left the area, but only for a brief respite, returning to the forest for more armloads of fuel to add to the heap.

"Why don't they just gather driftwood?" Arnold wondered.

"Prob'ly not enough of it lying 'round."

"This going to be a real biggie blaze," predicted Arnold.

"Big fire for big goings-on," Vince anticipated.

"I think we got us a seat too far away," Arnold complained. "Hard to see much of anything, they so far away. Cain't we get some closer?"

"S'pose we could. These sure ain't the best seats in the house, are they? S'pose we stay low and back up a bit without them seeing us. We'll circle down the pathway to the beach below, and get closer to 'em."

"Good thought, but not so near they sees us."

"Course not."

During the next minute they were able to crawl a dozen feet or so away from the brink of their vantage point, stand up, unseen by those below, and then slip and slide down an incline to the edge of the forest. Half way to the bottom, Arnold lost his balance and stumbled and rolled a dozen feet until he caught himself and then proceeded more carefully. Once there, the two bent low and made their way through the dark shadows toward the big lake. Still a hundred feet or so from the crowd, they dropped to their knees and crawled further through the dry, gritty sand.

"This be far enough," decided Vincent in a whisper. "Don't want to get too close and cause 'em to see us."

"What do you s'pose they do if they spot us?" Arnold whispered back.

"Don't rightly know. Big Guy didn't mention the possibility. Yer got yer pistol, though. Yer can defend yerself. Me, I don't need no defending, being already one of the dearly departed."

"Yeah," said Arnold, reaching around to pat his weapon reassuringly. "One of the advantages your kind enjoys.

"Uh, oh," he ceased whispering, unable to feel the bulky projection he expected to find in his back pocket.

"What do yer mean by 'Uh, oh'?"

"I mean the gun is *gone!*" Arnold asserted, his voice beginning to rise. "I know I had it there, and now it's *gone!* I musta lost it in the sand when we was sliding down the hill. I'm going back to find it."

Vince made a grab at his arm to stop him, forgetting he would be unable to touch him, let alone detain him.

"Don't be a ninny, Arnie. Yer'd never be able to find it in all the sand— and at night! Even if yer did, it'd prob'ly be so clogged with grit it wouldn't fire, proper-like. We'll have to get along without it."

"Easy for you to say, Vince. They wouldn't see you even if you were standing next to 'em, tweaking their noses, less'n you wanted them to. You can walk away when e'er you want. What would I do then?"

"I wouldn't desert yer, Arnie, if it's what yer be thinking."

Arnold wasn't quite so certain, but there was nothing to be gained by making an issue out of it. Neither one of them wanted to leave just yet, anyway, so they might as well sit back on their haunches and watch what was going on. As they talked in low voices, they studied the group more closely, walking about within the circle, impatiently waiting for the activity to begin.

"Whooa," said Vincent. "Lookie there, Arnie!"

The taller one, who had arrived on the beach first and appeared to be the leader, bent over, lit a match, and applied it to shavings he had been making. The tinder caught almost immediately, the fire burst forth and began to spread until a flowering flame mounted skyward, providing more light by which to see the eerie scene enacted before them. They were surprised to see, enabled by the additional lighting, the leader was endowed with a set of horns sticking out from his forehead as though they had been snatched from a cow and glued on.

As though an inaudible signal had been given, someone turned on a battery-operated cassette player they had brought with them. One of the fellows pulled at his hoodie until he was able to slip out of it.

"Now what they be doing?" wondered Arnold softly.

One by one, both men and women shed their clothing and lay the items on the ground outside of the circle, in the sand. Their hooded sweatshirts came off first, then shirts and blouses, followed by pants and dresses, and finally their under garments.

"Dern!" exclaimed Arnold. "We be so far away we cain't see much of anythin' might be interestin'."

"Wouldn't interest me, no how, even if I was out there with them, shucking my britches," Vince observed.

"Well, it would me, though," conceded Arnie. "S'pose we get a bit nearer to 'em?"

"Yer cain't fool me, Arnie. Dirty Old Man, yer be! Still, I s'pose it wouldn't hurt to get a mite closer—long as we don't bring attention to ourselves."

"You don't fool me neither, Vince. Must get pretty randy in the long box you calls home."

"Heh, heh, not a bit, Arnie. Not a bit."

"Then again, what if they spot me? How we going to defend ourselves 'gainst that mob?"

"Just be careful yer not seen; be quiet like, and we won't be spotted. I do admit my curiosity is aroused for a closer look."

"Me, too, Vince; I'm just as aroused as you are."

They crawled a dozen feet closer before deciding it was far enough.

"Looky," said Vince, his eyes glued to the participants standing around, nude as jaybirds, unembarrassed by their state of nakedness as revealed by the growing blaze.

"Ain't that just somethin'!" exclaimed Vincent.

"Sure is. Say, lookie at that one!"

"The overly buxom one?"

"Yeah. Could be the Widder Parton? Sure look like her!"

"Don't know her, but fine looking woman, from what I see," said Vincent. "If'n anyone could identify her, yer be the one."

"It *is* her! Sure nuff! Never knowed she were a witch, though—if'n be it's what they calls themselves. The little tramp's been *cheating* on *me*!"

"Lower yer voice a tad, Arnie. Too dark to see much, even though their fire be catchin' right nicely. Bet she looks outstanding in the daylight, or in the bedroom."

"She do, all right. Careful what you say, though. She *my* woman!"

"Is she now? What does Mildred have to say 'bout that?"

"She don't say nothin' 'cause she don't *know* nothin'. And you better not be telling her what she don't know!"

"Careful, Arnie. Yer voice getting louder now. It'll carry to them if'n yer not careful."

"Just what I need alright—being caught out here with the Widder, her not wearing a stitch of clothing."

Arnie toned his voice down to a reasonable volume, but was still able to be heard by his comrade.

They both fell silent, watching as the group begin to dance around the fire toward the heavens in a crackling blaze, brightening the scene before them, casting as much illumination as might a mega-volt spotlight!

"This be cool," said Vincent, hugging the sand, momentarily forgetting the dancers were unable to see him anyway, one of the few advantages of being deceased he could think of.

"Worth the price of admission," Arnold agreed, "whatever they might happen to be doing next."

Bosoms, large and small, stood out in profile, silhouetted by the fire gleaming off their bodies, caught in a sensuous trance of mesmeric move-ment, growing sweatier from the exertion being expended and the heat of the fire. The Widder Parton was prominent with her breasts swaying and swinging to the sound of the recorder booming out its jungle cadence. Their dancing became wilder and they began to chant as they squirmed and writhed furiously within the ring, thrashing convulsively. Lightning zigged and zagged above the firmament, and thunder bombs exploded across the darkened sky as though a devastating war was in progress.

"How many do you 'spose there be?" asked Arnold.

"Don't know for certain. Lordie say there be an even number. I'd guess maybe six witches and six warlocks. But some folk say a coven has thir-teen."

"Warlocks?"

"Warlocks be male witches, Arnie. Don't yer know nothin'?"

"Damn it!" exclaimed Vincent, a minute later. "Their leader, the goof ball wearing the fake horns! I knows the guy! I 'member him from long ago. Take the headpiece off, put some pants and a shirt on him, and yer'd recognize him, too. Be the Chief of Police, Ed Bates!"

"Still is, sure 'nuff. Recognize him now. Never did like the arrogant pup! Give me a ticket five…six…years ago. Ain't likely to forget."

"Nasty guy when I knew him, too."

"And…and…gol dang, if the lady next to him ain't the minister's sister, Maude Wilcox. Man, oh, man, wouldn't Preacher go into a tirade… have a humongous tizzy…if'n he knowed she be here tonight?"

"Unlike the good Lord, man of God don't know everything, do he?"

The music swelled into a thunderous crescendo as the troop of dancers pranced around…and then abruptly stopped, as though someone had flipped a switch demanding motionless silence. The congregation ceased its gyrations and many of the performers fell to the ground in exhaustion, while others stood there, proud and fearless, their arms raised as though they were reaching for the stars. Slowly, the wicked wizards collapsed to the ground, caught their breath and then stood up. The participants fell silent except for the panting of laboring lungs over exerted.

Suddenly the leader stepped back and yelled to the sky: *"Yog-Sothoth!"*

"Yog-Sothoth," responded the brother and sisterhood of the craft, drawing closer.

"Yog-Sothoth, hear our plea!" he exhorted, "in the name of the invincible Old Ones, hear our petition!

"Vent your terrible wrath upon your enemies, Mighty Yog, those who would gainsay your evilness, denounce your wickedness, topple your blood-smeared altars, spit upon your graven image and exterminate your supplicants who stand before you now!"

The petitioner went on and on, spewing vindictive hate and demanding vengeance upon the blasphemous ones who would interfere with their consecrated doings, each word inciting his followers to a frenzied fury. When he finally stopped speaking, it was to allow the participant's time to reaffirm their oath to obey the sacred laws of their secret society and to confirm their promise to continue their worship of the invincible Yog.

At last, exhausted, they became silent again, and what followed next was an awesome sight provoking terror in the most intrepid residents of South Fork if they had been there to witness it. Even Vincent Fletch, who believed himself immune to such frightfulness, felt himself shuddering in spite of himself!

The horned gent in charge continued, asserting his right to defend the Awfulness of the Night they adored, when a voice, eerily hollow, erupted out of the semi-darkness above them.

"Enough, my followers! I heed your petition! Cease your lamentations and recriminations!"

It stopped speaking until the congregation followed its orders.

"Kneel, my devotees, bend your knees to the majesty of Yog-Sothoth!"

The deity, or whatever ranking it held, waited for its disciples to follow its command.

The astonished flock knelt to the ground.

Out of the partial darkness appeared a leering face, one of evil incarnate glancing from the right side and then to the left of the stunned believers, then set its stern gaze directly down upon them.

"I hear your pleas, and will avenge and protect you. Your wickedness finds pleasure in my sight! Continue to obey my will and consecrate my presence, and your enemies—my enemies—shall fall like wheat separated from the chaff before the reaper!"

Following the presence, a body materialized as though squeezing itself through a hole in the ether, a jumbled gathering of iridescent globes moving as though directed by some unknown musical director.

"I go," it uttered, *"but warn you to rid yourself of the two unbelievers among you who have the power and the means to thwart your plans.* "I leave you now. Do my will!"*

The voice was hushed. The visage and torso evaporated like a disappearing cloud formation, the firelight dimmed, and the fanatical mob found itself alone—except for Vincent and Arnold, still nearby, unseen witnesses who rubbed their eyes as though they had witnessed a magician perform the greatest stage illusion of all time.

"Vince," said Arnold. "What do he mean by 'Two unbelievers among you?'"

"It be us, dummy! Who yer s'pose it mean? It either sensed us or saw us and ordered our execution."

"You mean they were instructed to kill us?"

"Not us, Arnie. *Yer!* I'm already dead! *Remember?*"

"What do we do now, Vince? You got me into this predicament!"

"And I'll get yer out of it, too. I won't desert yer now, Ol' Buddy."

Those around the campfire began to stir, as though they had just emerged from a trance. The horned one arose from his kneeling position. It was not difficult to see the leader, Ed Bates, the Chief of Police, trembling, practically traumatized. Had this been the first time the entity they worshipped made an appearance? He acted as though it was. Seconds passed before he regained control of himself and spoke to the assembly again:

"All right," he demanded. "Who among you profane our meeting?"

"Not me!" cringed one of the disciples.

"Not I," trembled another, in a weak, but more grammatical and barely audible voice. One by one they swore they were not the ones Yog had spoken of, each denial turning the leader into a state of perplexed confusion.

"You deny your treachery, do you? Come now: admit to your duplicity.

We will forgive and all will be well with you."

"As though anyone would believe him," whispered Vincent to his nearby cohort. "If he discovers the imposters, they'll wind up on a spit and be roasted over the inferno."

"Come now," the leader exhorted, his voice rising in alarming dissonance. "Step forward and admit your disloyalty and you will be richly rewarded. Golden coins will shower your feet!"

No one responded to his appeal. After a few more attempts he gave up and glared at them.

"So be it, then. I have no recourse but to contact the *Oracle*."

A chorus of "oos" and "awes" responded to this announcement!

"This concludes the official portion of our meeting," the leader intoned. "Disperse now, enjoy yourself as you will, and await communication of our next gathering."

One by one the practitioners paired off, male with female or, as in one instance, male with male, and disappeared from the scene, each making their way into the woods or over to a different but convenient sand dune behind which they could conclude their evening's activities.

Vince and Arnold stood up and approached the vacated fire to look around, confident they would have abundant time to hide themselves again when they heard the return of the horde. The smell of smoke and charring wood was almost overpowering.

"Well, now we've seen a meeting of the coven," was Vincent's comment.

"And we find the membership exceptionally violent. I agree with God it be banished."

"No question 'bout it."

"How you plan to dispose of this heathen cult?"

"No plan, but I do have the glimmering of an idea."

"At least it's a beginning. Give me a hint of what this 'glimmering' be."

"Yer heard Ed tell his group he would consult with the *Oracle* and find out who the miscreants be, the unbelievers in his group."

"I did. But we also know those reprobates be *us*."

"I believe yer stated the situation quite clearly, Arnie."

They poked and prodded, looking about for anything the group might have left, and searched among the various articles of clothing strewn about, left by the membership until their return. Those items, along with the branches, lustily burning themselves out, were all that remained. They walked about the circle, careful to avoid stepping on the hot coals.

Nearly half an hour passed before they heard sounds of the returning membership, and knew the prudent thing for them to do would be to vacate the area as soon as possible, without being seen. They returned to their earlier position where they had hidden themselves to view the proceedings.

As they were leaving, the coven adherents strolled back, laughing and making light of the proceedings, put on their garments, and made their way to the woods and the parking lot where their vehicles had been left. The last to leave were Ed, the horned priest, and the Widow Parton. They said not a word as they put on their clothing and followed their flock away from the scene.

All the way back to the truck, left near the parking area but out of sight, Vince and Arnold talked about the unexpected manifestations of evil they had seen.

"Looked like one of them special affects you see at the picture shows," Arnold commented. "Or an eerie TV program. Oh, I forgot, that probable afore your time, ain't it?"

"Course not. Television started back in the 1940's, right? Long afore I was even born. 'Course I 'member it! Movies even eerier. Programs like *Godzilla* or *The Blob*. Lots of other gory productions popular then, too. They'd chill anyone's blood."

"Guess you're right. You ain't been dead long as I thought, have you?"

"Long enough, Arnie. Long enough! I 'member reading horror books, too, as a youngster. Stuff by a gent named Lovecraft. Good stuff!"

"Yeah. The only thing is, them stories be fiction. What we saw tonight was *real*!"

"Yup. Was real enough, all right."

"If'en I dream tonight, it be filled with horrors like that."

"Something I don't look forward to, Vince. I dreams 'bout *real* horror, like as when Mildred's credit card bill comes due, and I have to pay it."

"Heh, heh," was Vince's response.

Once they were settled in the truck, Arnold said, "Seems to me we accomplished only half of what God recruited us to do. The important part, the hard part, must still be done."

"What that be, Arnie?"

"Why, to dispose of the coven. Smash it to smithereens! Deep-six it! Put it out of business. What we still have to accomplish, ain't it? Don't want them people 'round here doing the evilness they be doing."

"Yer right. Guess I sort of forgot, just for a moment, the part 'bout the Lord God's decree."

"Don't rightly know how you'd forget the most 'portant part, Vince."

"Well, I 'spose I just did."

"So now you 'member it, what's the inkling of a plan you mentioned to me?"

Vince glanced over to the driver who was concentrating on the road and the long patch of twists and turns coming up.

"Hmmm, well, pr'haps I did suggest something like that. What kind of hint did I give yer, Arnie."

"Gol dang it, Vince! You didn't give me no hint! You told me you'd tell me later. Well, now be later."

"Hmmm. Well, come to think on it, maybe I did. Did it have somethin' to do with finding the Oracle, I wonder?"

"Don't know, Vince. It were you, who had the 'sinuation you ne'er give. But, come to think on it, Ed did mention consulting the Oracle, who-ever he be."

"Dang it all—wonder what it was I had in mind. Who do yer s'pose the Oracle chap be, Arnie?"

"No idea," said his companion, holding tightly to the steering wheel as they drove down an especially dark expense of rutted roadway, boarded by bushy trees slightly leaning over the road.

"Come to think on it, maybe I did have a slight twinge of an idea, but cain't 'member now what it was. But since I don't know who the Oracle is, and neither do you, how 'bout you asking someone who does know?"

"I don't know anyone who does, Vince."

"Maybe yer doesn't, and maybe yer does. Yer could ask the Chief of Police, but he don't know neither. Yer might have better luck if'n yer ask someone else, someone be more willing to tell yer."

"And just who might it be?"

"I be thinking of the Widder Parton."

"Hmmm," said Arnold, scratching the stubble of beard irritating his face, "Maybe she do, and maybe she will, but not if I start asking her right off to reveal secrets of the coven to me."

"Then ask her in a way won't trouble her no how. Tell her someone told yer she's a member of a coven, and yer'd like to join one, too. She'd like that just fine."

"Maybe she would, and maybe she wouldn't. The way she was hang-ing on to the horned Chief, though, I thought maybe she be going to dump me for him. They did seem to be pretty chummy together, and all."

"Thought yer two be lovers or somethin'."

"Course we be, but after seeing them together tonight…"

"Think she's going to cuckold yer fer him?"

"Don't know. Been thinking, I wouldn't care if she did, no how. If she be two-timing me, well, maybe I should be doing the same to her! 'Course, Ed just might be the one with the car, and he drive her to the meeting with him. Maybe nothing 'tween them a'tall."

"Cain't see what difference I'd make, anyways. Yer, be deceiving Mil-dred; what be wrong with Parton be fooling yer?"

"It's different. Me and Mildred ain't close no more, nohow.

"What if Widow want me to tell her who told me she be awitchin'? Then what I tell her?"

"Tell her someone named the Oracle told yer, and yer'd like to know more 'bout him afore yer became a member."

"'S'posing the 'him' be a 'her'?"

"The Oracle be a 'her'? Well, could be, I s'pose. Didn't think of that. Yer got me there, Arnie. Maybe yer could ask the question without spec'fying a gender."

"Might be I could. But even if'n she do know, and even if'n she do tell me, how it going to help destroy the sect?"

"Don't know, but if'n it give us one piece of information we don't already have, it may help."

"Useless information what it be."

"We don't know 'til we know what it be."

"How that be possible?"

"Arnie, how do yer ever get yer britches on in the morning, anyhow? Tie yer shoelaces? *We don't know yet!* First we takes one step, and then the next. First order of business is to find the Oracle!"

"'S'posing Nan don't want to tell me?"

"And with yer luck, Arnie, it just might happen. But we won't worry none 'bout it until later."

"You could always ask God who the Oracle be. Bet He'd know."

"'Course he would. But God be a busy God, and don't want to be troubled by such questions. Why He uses mankind to do his bidding. Told me to handle it, and I will."

"You know, Vince, when you said you had the inkling of an idea, I thought it 'twas an impossible inkling to have."

"I 'magine so. And now?"

"And now, I think you might be on the right track."

The two fell silent as the vehicle swung off the dirt road on to the highway. Arnold was able to increase his speed, and within a few minutes they were approaching the sleepy village of South Fork. Only a few scattered lights were on, an indication most of the residents had retired for the evening. He steered his truck onto the driveway of his home and parked it there.

"Tell yer what, Arnie. Yer find out from Widow what yer can, and I'll stop by someday, prob'ly sometime after Mildred goes to sleep, and we'll talk 'bout it then."

"All right, Vince. I'll be seeing Nan tomorrow, Wednesday being our usual meeting day, and see what I can find out 'bout the Oracle for you."

"I'll stop back to see yer sometime after yer do."

The following morning dawned clear and bright with just a touch of haze being blown away by the pleasing breeze. The air was crisp, but warming nicely, promising another agreeable day for those interested in such pleasantries. Arnold did not care. Blistering cold, or hades hot, it was all the same to him. As long as his truck was purring like a contented kitty—and, as a skilled mechanic most of his life, he kept it running smoothly, making him happy as a hound dog treeing a coon—as long as good health allowed him to pursue his varied interests.

Nancy Parton was one of his varied interests and had been for the last several years. He was enamored by her attractive presence, her quick wit, her willingness to please him as a congenial companion should. His intimate interest, in accord with her own for him, would be frowned upon, if they knew of it, by the Reverend Wilcox and his congregation. He was a God-fearing man and wanted to please the Lord, to honor Him and do His will—but it had been Mildred, and not him, who had ended the closeness of a loving relationship. If anyone should bear the trauma of guilt, Mildred should be the one, for forcing him into the arms of another. He did not want to leave her, he was not that kind of man and, besides, the parishioners, all longtime friends, would heap the greatest of the fault and scorn upon himself.

He had also been a lonely man until the Widow had come into his life, making the best of a bad situation. He had met her seven years earlier, long after his marriage to Mildred had nosedived into the outhouse. If anything should happen to his wife at this time, he would not waste a moment in taking Nancy to the altar as his second spouse. But it was in the hands of the Almighty, and he no longer gave it any thought.

It was nearly twelve o'clock noon when he turned off the highway onto the dirt yard of Nancy Parton. He had spooned up two bowls of cereal for breakfast—the crispy kind—but was already hungry again. He could have left a few minutes earlier and stopped at the *Cozy Spoon* for a quick burger, but he knew the widow would have something ready for him to eat when he arrived. Unlike Mildred, Nancy would not allow him to go hungry. The meal she provided might not be fancy, but it would be tasty and wholesome, and he would appreciate every bite he took. He knew she frequently fried up a mass of chicken on Sundays, and it was possible she might have saved a bite of it for him.

Arnold rapped sharply on the door of her humble abode. It was an old edifice— some even termed it ancient, but it was all her late husband could afford at the time of their marriage. She was content with what she had, however, all anyone should expect, unlike Mildred, who was seldom satisfied with anything. Nancy kept the interior of her place neat and clean, with a place for everything and everything in its place, so no clutter was there to offend the eye, like other women he knew.

"Hi, Hon," he said in greeting, as the door swung open. There she stood, a beaming smile upon her face, her heavenly, azure eyes gleaming with the delight she felt as she led him inside. He kissed her gently, hugged her ardently, and softly told her how much he missed her. She reciprocated in kind, leading him into the kitchen where she had a cup of coffee, recently brewed, waiting for him.

"Thankee," he said, reaching for the sugar bowl. He fed two heaping spoons full into the mixture, enough to satisfy his sweet tooth for a while. "How you getting along, Nan?"

"Right nicely. I been slicing and squishing strawberries this morning. Gonna boil 'em down and can 'em later today. Got my Bell jars cleaned and ready to fill."

"Taste right good come winter time, I think," said Arnold. "Add lots of sugar to 'em."

"You know I will."

The two engaged in their normal chit-chat for a while, and then Nancy went to the stove to fry some burgers for their lunch. Arnold was disappointed when he learned there would be no fried chicken for him this day.

"Something to ask you, Nan," he finally began.

She turned to look at him, spatula in hand, and he continued, "Somebody tell me you know something 'bout the coven folks been talking 'bout 'round here."

The Widow Parton had nothing to say for several long seconds. Her eyes squinted, drawing her brows together in a puzzling manner.

"Coven? What you talking 'bout, Arn?"

"Witch work, Nan—been going on 'round here for a long spell. I been thinkin' it sounds like a mite bit of fun and excitement. Thinkin' maybe I'd like to join up with the group, myself."

"Don't know what you talking 'bout, Arn. Why would I know anything 'bout such goings on? You must be outta your mind, saying something like that! Who told you I was a coven member anyway?"

"Cain't say, Nam. But are you?"

"Never, you mind! And if'n I were, I wouldn't want you to join one, no how. Now, who tell you?"

Arnold, in his reluctance to give her a straight answer, was suddenly inspired and said, "No one special. Guy's called the Oracle."

"Now I knows your afibbing' me, Arn! No one named the Oracle told you!"

Now confused and muddled, he retorted, "How does you know, Nan, lessen you a member of the secret clan yourself?"

Nancy Parton put her hands on her hips and continued to stare at him. "I knows because I knows," she maintained.

"I want to know just *how* you knows, Nan."

Nancy began to sputter, almost speechless. She dropped her eyes to the floor and remained silent, her composure staggered.

"I wants to know how *you* know 'bout the Oracle, Nan—now you tell me!"

Nancy sighed deeply, and looked him directly in the eyes, gaining confidence from some unknown source within herself.

"All right, Arn. If'n you must know, I *am* a member of the coven. And not only that, I happens to *be* the Oracle! That's how I knows your afibbing me!"

"What's?" Arnold exclaimed. *"You be the Oracle?* Why din't you never tell me 'bout it afore?"

"You never asked me 'bout it afore, Arn."

"Nan, sit down and tell me all 'bout this. Them burgers can wait. I admit, I already knew you was a cult member, 'cause I was there at the lake last night and saw what you folks were up to."

"You...you were there...a watching us?"

Nancy could not believe what she was hearing. "You couldn't have been. I didn't see you there."

"But I was."

Doubt was in her eyes, but she asked anyway. "Just what did you see, Arn?"

"Saw you and the other witch folk dancing naked around the fire, I did. Saw something awful come out of the air you people worships! Saw your gang split off into couples and going off by yourselves.

"And you...you went with the horny guy! I knows it was Ed Gates, blundering Chief Bates. Like to give him a poke in the eye!"

"My *God*," she exclaimed, coming to grips with the reality of what he was saying. "You *were* there—you *did* see us! You *must* have been one of the two disbelievers Yog tell us 'bout!"

"That's right, Nan."

"Who were the other guy?"

"Cain't tell you Nan. Wouldn't believe me, no how."

"Pro'bly wouldn't. Seems to me you have more to tell *me* than I have to tell *you*."

"Might be so—maybe not."

"So you saw us, did you? Well, I didn't pair off with Ed Bates, not in the way you s'pect, at least. We strolled down the beach and talked 'bout the vision we see in the sky looking down at us, wondering if'n it be mass hypnotism, or we be mes'mrized in some sort of enchantment, or we be under some witching spell creating the illusion for us. That's all we did, I swear."

"Okay, Nan, I believes you."

"'Sides, Ed wanted to ask me what I knew 'bout the nonbelievers Yog mentioned. He'd told the group he would consult the Oracle, which is *me*. Lot of good I could do. I had no idea who the intruders were, and I told Ed. Didn't know t'was you and someone else!"

"That right, Nan. It was us alright. But we had no idea the Oracle be *you*."

"Well, it be. I couldn't give Ed Bates any answer 'cause I didn't know it was you 'twere there. So, now you knows."

"Yes, now I know."

"So, it's what we were talking 'bout. And we weren't out in them woods playing hanky-panky like the others were."

"I believes you, Nan. But why do they call you the Oracle?"

"Oh…err…? Well, now you knows, Arn, there's something I 'spose I should have mentioned to you long afore. Got something for you to see.

"Come along."

Nancy turned off the stove and let the burgers sit there, sputtering in their own oily grease, while she guided him to a door in the back leading into a small shed attached to the property. Arnold had never been in it before and thought it was just a closet he had seen on earlier visits to her home. His interest in the little room perked up considerably as he saw it contained a card-table sitting in the middle of the floor, with three chairs grouped around it.

In the center was a large, glass globe.

"My crystal ball," Nancy informed him. "The other objects sitting around next to it, they's just other objects of my perfession."

She reached over and picked up a deck of what seemed to be playing cards, but were actually a set of seventy-six Tarot cards. Next to it was an Ouija Board.

"What's all this for, Nan?" he asked, failing to understand.

"I'm a *witch*, Arn! Have been for years. Long afore I met you, during my marriage and after. This be how I make my living. Not a great one, but a good one. Don't have no one to take care of me, Arn.

"Must admit I'm not all I seems to be—don't always lead a normal life. I has my secrets. The country folk—them as lives back in the hills and Dunwich—they knows 'bout me—calls me the Oracle. Comes to me during the evening hours, sometimes for advice, mayhap to buy herbs or potions, dried frogs or lizards, gris-gris bags, hexing dolls, or other things like that. Pays me to caste spells on enemies, seek revenge, heal stricken cattle. Things like that. They knows I'm a skilled practitioner of the dark arts, along with the white ones, of course, and other magical things."

"How come you never tell me this, Nan?"

"Feared you would leave me, Arn. Not come to see me no more—avoid me. Men are funny 'bout things like that. Knows your Mildred's man, but you're *my* man, too. At least, part time. Wants to keep it that away. Don't want to lose my man, do I? 'Sides, there's things a woman wants to keep to herself—don't want to tell, 'specially if they be a romantic couple, like us be. Witching is one of 'em. Didn't think you'd be interested in such things, nohow.

"Joined the coven nearly a year 'go, now. 'Twas fun at first…exciting…but now I'm afeared. I'd leave the group if'n I could, but Ed, he don't like quitters. Tells me them trying meets up with sudden accidents.

"Don't want *you* to join the group, either. Don't want something to happen to you, too."

"I don't *really* want to join the cult—just said it to get you to talking 'bout the Oracle. But I don't want you to quit, neither, Nan. Least ways, not yet—not till the coven is busted up, the membership hightailing it out of here, and not inclined to join up again."

"Why you want to, Arn?"

"Got my reasons, Nan. Don't never you mind. Why'd you ever get into witching, anyway?"

"Got bills to pay, Arn; groceries to buy; how'd yer think I gets money to live on? 'Sides, witching comes natural like to me. Always has, even as a little girl. My momma was one, too. Got to make a living, and it's all I knows how to do. Don't know what I do if'n I gives it up. With it, I'm an independent woman—takes care of myself. Without it, I'd be a ward of the state, or somethin'. Cain't do anything else, can I?

"I'll take care of you, Nan."

"You a sweet man, Arn," she said, putting her head on his shoulder and hugging his arm, "but you already has a wife. One's enough for any man to take care of. Don't want you to join the coven either.

"But now I'm scart. I'm in far deeper than I want to be—feared of Yog—thing ain't at all humanlike! Wants to leave the group if'n I can find a way. Will you help me, Arn?"

"Course I will. But tell me a tad 'bout Chief Bates. How come he be the leader, wearing them phony horns and the like?"

"Oh, Ed be just a big bogus, Arn. Say he be the son of Margaret Alice Murray who he claim knows all 'bout witchcraft. Died in '63, I think he said. Because of her, he say he be the leader, the High Priest. While back he make me the High Priestess. Don't care what he calls hisself; he just be a big fraud."

When parting the evening of the coven, Vince had requested Arnold to do nothing about the matter until hearing from him again, other than attempt to learn the Oracle's identity. Meanwhile, Vince would chat with the Man Upstairs, reporting to the Big Boss what had occurred—as if He did not already know—and receive further instructions as to what He wanted them to do. He would return and advise Arnold and they would make further plans.

"Damn!" said Arnold to himself. "I've learnt who the Oracle be, and it be weeks now since the dead guy's been here! Wish he'd hurry up and come. I'm tired of waiting."

Almost a month had passed, giving Arnold ample time to reflect upon the situation and consider all the angles and possible solutions to the problem. The latest full moon had nearly reached its ascendency, and was scheduled to appear this night in all its brilliance. Also slated to appear was the coven, as decreed by the High Priest. This had been told to Nancy, who relayed the information to her man.

Arnold appreciated the news, but did not really care a great deal. He was fed up with the entire situation and wanted it to be concluded.

Besides, he had already devised a plan of his own. Although it was not as foolproof as he would like, he believed it had a reasonable chance of success. As the president of the South Fork City Council, he had a certain amount of influence with the other board members, and together they could apply a certain amount of leverage on the police chief's activities. The Horned One was planning to retire in a couple of years, and it was in their power to deny Ed his pension if he was found to be a man of debased character and the leader of a satanic cult engaged in immoral activities. Arnold was certain they would vote to have it forfeited, even though Ed was otherwise entitled to it. He would fume and swear and vow bitter vengeance, but there would be little he could do about it.

Arnold would explain this to the police chief, along with an offer to keep silent about what he had witnessed at the last cult meeting if Ed promised to disband the group and make no attempt to revive it in the future. Oh, yes, Horny Ed would agree to dismantle the cult as long as his pension and the assurance of a secure and lucrative retirement was certain!

After thinking it over and over again, he could see only one possible flaw with this plan. Namely, Ed might decide to just eliminate Arnold before he could reveal his clannish secret. Would the Chief of Police, sworn to uphold the laws of South Fork and protect its citizens from any and all tribulations, take such an action? Arnold was not sure, but he might, and he could think of no reason why he would not. More than likely, though, he would comply. There being no other flaw in his plan nor other approach he believed would result in success, he was resolved to follow through with this strategy despite any action Ed might take.

It was evening, and Arnold was sitting on the porch swing. The full moon was starting its jaunt across the darkening sky, as expansive as ever, beginning to look like a swollen cantaloupe. Arnold had been told two weeks earlier by Nancy the coven would be meeting this night, information given to her by the police chief, but Vince had failed to show up, as promised, and might know nothing of the High Priest's plans. Arnold certainly had no intention of going on his own and watching the coven by himself; if they went at all, it would have to be next month when the yellow globe would be at its full again.

Arnold was mistaken.

He took another swig of the Coors next to him, and was about to go inside for the evening, when he noticed movement on Cemetery Road leading to the highway which his residence faced. Several minutes passed as it drew closer and resolved itself into the figure of a man.

"What in tarnation!" he thought. "What would anyone be doing up there at this time of night? Must be nearly eight o'clock."

It took but a moment for him to realize there was only one person it was likely to be.

As the man approached, a car came down the road, its muffler howling in pain. The Buick was traveling fast, over the speed limit, but not by much. The pedestrian reached the street, paying no attention to it, and started to cross without looking both ways.

"Uh, oh," thought Arnold, witness to the certain tragedy, realizing if one of them did not stop, there would-be a bloody smear on the pavement. The two continued at their present pace, the face behind the wheel glancing down at what might be a cell phone.

A certain accident was imminent.

The two travelers met at the same spot, at the same moment of time, but what one would expect to happen, did not.

The man continued to walk straight ahead, and the car passed right through him, or maybe it was he passing through the car.

There was no accident, as anyone watching would expect. The car continued on its way. The man, tall and slender, and dressed all in green, looked up as he finished crossing the highway and paused at the edge of the road. It was Vincent, of course. Arnold did not have to wait to recognize him. Vince was the only one it *could* be. He looked up as he reached the porch with a look of rapt attention on his stoic face, nodding at his friend.

"Showing off again, as usual!" Arnold observed, acerbically needling the newcomer. Vince had certainly known the automobile was coming, and could have avoided it if he had wished, but he had chosen to demonstrate to any observer one of his truly terrifying attributes.

"Evenin', good buddy," he said in greeting, reaching the porch and climbing the steps.

"Hello, Vince. Weren't sure you'd make it tonight. Gettin' late."

"Had to, Arnie. Big doings goin' on."

"You should be more careful crossing streets. If the driver of the car hadn't been looking down, he would a seen you and, to avoid hitting you would have skidded off the highway. Could have had a bad accident, maybe turned his car over, or perhaps plowed into my house and made me deader than you."

"Cain't be deader than me, Arnie. I's the deadest man in town! Wouldn't have happened, anyway." Vince set himself on the porch swing next to his annoyed friend and looked longingly at the can of beer. "Even if the driver be lookin' right at me, he wouldn't see me. Remember? Only one around here who can see me is *yer*."

"I 'member. Guess there be no harm done. What 'big doing's' you talkin' 'bout?"

"Well, yer know. Widow told yer, didn't she, the coven meet tonight? Same time, same place as 'afore?"

"She did. How you know?"

"Because *He* knows everything. That's how come! Man Upstairs, he tell me everything I need to know. Tell me of yer plan to rid South Fork of them cussed witches be; told me to tell yer it wouldn't work—would backfire, like, on yer."

"Really? And what's so wrong with my plan?"

"Ed's not a fool; he a nasty man. Moment yer threaten to expose him, or soon after, he put a bullet in yer brain, and keep going right on with his sorcerous ways."

"Hmmm—thought it might happen. Hoped it wouldn't."

"Well, it would a happened. The Big Guy, he devise an addition to yer plan. I'm here to tell yer 'bout it and to help yer out."

"Help *me* out? You mean *me* to help *you* out, don't you? This be *your* doings. What's his better idea?"

"Yer have a camera, don't yer?"

"No…well, yes…got me an iPod, a Nokia Android-based smart phone, I do. Won it off a salesman out of Chicago in a poker game. We won all his money, and when he wanted to play more—recoup some of his loses, we let him put his gadget in the pot. I won it with three Jacks!"

"That's fine, whatever an iPod be. We join the forbidden conclave tonight, just like afore, and take pictures of their sordid activities, their dancing and chanting, and so on. Yere give 'em to Bill, the publisher of the *South Fork Weekly*, in a sealed envelope with instructions they be opened and printed in the paper in case anything happens to yer. Oh, and don't tell Ed who has the pictures, just they be published if'n he don't do what yer say. He won't harm yer 'cause he be immediately exposed."

"I see. Once Bill has the photos, then I goes on with my plan just as it was outlined to you—tell Ed he loses his pension less'n he gets rid of the coven?"

"Think of the pictures as a little insurance policy."

"Sounds like a good idea God come up with."

"The Good Lord knows what He be doing, for sure. Get yer iPod, if it's what yer call it, along with yer keys and yer pistol, and we be on our way."

"My gun is back at the lake, buried in the sand, 'member?"

"So it be. Bring the one yer were going to have me carry.

"Plenty of time to get there, conceal our self as afore, and wait for the infernal membership to arrive and the evening's entertainment to begin."

* * * *

During the truck ride to the park they discussed Arnold's sudden surprise when Nancy told him of her dual role in the community: a congenial member of the municipality and a practitioner of the forbidden craft, known by her customers as the Oracle.

"Never would have guessed it of her," her paramour admitted.

"Me, neither," concurred Vince. "Must admit though, she do need to earn a living doing *something*. Might's well be with a job she's well suited to do. Doesn't mean she's a bad person, though."

"You're right there, Vince. Nan's a good woman. She tell me when the cult started getting ugly, doing the mean, nasty and degenerate things, she wanted to get out of it."

The activities of the evening began much as they had the month before, although Vince and Arnold avoided the bluff above the beach this time, and went directly to the area where they expected the coven to meet. The night was as pleasant as before, with a cooling breeze caressing Arnold, tingling his skin as they waited for the nefarious association to arrive.

The mosquitos were few and left Arnold alone, possibly because he was in such close proximity to a dead man. Flies, he reflected, might be a totally different annoyance. Vince, of course, was not bothered at all, likely because he had no blood in his veins or arteries to drain. Twenty minutes after they arrived, the membership began showing up in groups of twos and threes. The widow arrived with a different man this time, and the police chief came by himself.

For a few minutes, after dropping the branches and twigs they had brought to the fire site, the group stood around, idly chatting. Ed Bates adjusted the horns to his forehead and immediately assumed a new persona. His voice vibrated with authority and certainty as he ordered the members to congregate around him. He seemed to be no longer the Chief of Police but the servant and foremost disciple of the unknown forces of the night. He was, without question, the High Priest. When they were all together, he struck a match and ignited the desiccated pieces of wood, and the adherents stood about, watching the fire catch and blossom into a conflagration soon illuminating much of the surrounding area. Almost at once, as though on cue, the calming breeze surged its intensity, as though pulled in by the force of the heat, and the sky grew darker as clusters of cloud cover swept out of nowhere to vanquish the moonlight. The cassette player began to beat out a jungle-drum rendition of forest lunacy, and the membership disrobed, much as they had done a month earlier. Arnold was quick to notice Nancy did not remove everything, but left enough to cover the more enticing curvatures she wanted to conceal.

"Good for her," whispered Arnold in a voice Vince could barely hear.

Arnold took out his iPod and began to film one scene after another until he had a good sampling of the activities, the police chief prominently featured. The two hidden visitors stared and gaped as the members danced and cavorted around the fire, spinning, leaping and gyrating with frenetic abandon, sensuously flinging themselves about and raising their hands high in supplication to the dark forces seeming to gather in the unholy shadows cast by the fire.

Wonton movements and shrieking abjurations fed into the frenzy of the group, and the sound of beating drums blasted forth their song of blasphemy to the moon above, now being uncovered by the cloud banks moving away. Louder and louder sounded the pulsating beats and the chants until the drifting billows had parted to reveal a moon appearing to laugh downward upon them. Suddenly the earth was shadowed by a scudding storm cloud moving into the area, unleashing a torrent of water and drenching the participants and the surrounding countryside. A thunderous roil from the great bowling alley in the sky could be heard as pin after pin was shattered, while loud crashes of thunder clanged about their ears and forks of splintered lightning tore through the firmament.

At last, the primitive music stopped and the participants came to a rest, some of them weary, others totally exhausted. Arnold watched as the minister's sister and a few of the others dropped to the sand and stayed there, silent except for their heavy breathing. Ed, the main warlock, stepped forth.

"*Yog-Sothoth!*" he cried to the heavens, his arms raised high in supplication.

"*Yog-Sothoth!*" screamed the multitude.

"*Hear our pleas!*" bleated the minister's sister, suddenly recovered and standing up to recite her line, sounding like an actress speaking a part she had rehearsed.

"*Hear our pleas,*" chorused the throng in unanimous support.

To Vincent and Arnold, the group sounded like binge drinkers, as most of them actually were, having taken the opportunity to imbibe the fruit of the vine, moonshine, and other popular beverages of assorted alcoholic content, during the hours before they had arrived.

Suddenly, out of dark nothingness, with no fanfare other than another roll of thunder, the extraterrestrial entity arrived as it had before, blasphemous and hideous, all knowing and supremely arrogant. It fastened its gaze upon the assembly.

Arnold was spellbound, but continued to record an assortment of scenes.

"*I see you have not disposed of the nonbelievers! Did my words of warning mean nothing to you?*

Its query was directed at the horned guy who stuttered in an attempt to reply.

"*I warned you to take care of the matter, did I not?*"

"But I did, Great Yog! I *did*! The entire membership has been thoroughly investigated, their lives opened wide to reveal any insidious deceit or treachery we might have overlooked. It is only they who are here tonight! I swear! What more could I have done?"

"*You should have exposed them and destroyed them. You did not. You have failed.*"

"But who *are* they, Great Yog? *Who*?"

"*Those concealed beyond yon sand dune—that's who!*"

The mouth of Yog-Sothoth opened wide and out from it, like the appendage of an anteater, snaked a rope-like filament, many yards in length shooting forward and downward until it reached Chief Bates; there it wrapped itself around his fleshly neck.

"*You have failed, and will have no second chance to repeat your offense!*"

Like a boa constrictor, the tentacle-like tongue squeezed, contracting unremittingly while the horned one screamed in inexplicable agony as his head was severed from the neck, and toppled to the ground.

Arnold stopped taking pictures, beginning to quiver as he realized they were no longer needed.

"*Lordie, Lordie, save my soul!*" he mumbled repeatedly in a hoarse whisper.

"*Amen, and amen,*" Vince responded in a murmured undertone.

The crowd, stunned into absolute silence as they viewed the fountain of blood gushing forth, soaking the sand, finally found their voices and gasped in unison. They inched away and watched, spellbound, as the torso sank to the beach like a puppet with broken strings. The horny head rolled a few feet away and stared up at them. Two of the coven members fainted as the tongue retracted into the semi-deity's maw.

"Disband! Yog-Sothoth wants nothing more to do with you! Find another god to worship, if you must, but go, leave and never return."

That being said, the preternatural entity continued: "For those of you who choose to defy my will, beware; my vengeance is swift and terrible!"

The hovering figure of frightening, cosmic proportions, moved from its position to where Vince and Arnold lay concealed. Its tongue shot out again, wavered, and reached to grip the neck of the green man. Vince remained as motionless as a stone. Curiously, it probed the crevices and recesses of his face. Suddenly, it drew back, as though transfixed by an electrical shock.

"This man is already dead!" Yog disclosed. "And this one is under a protective spell!"

The awful tongue rolled back into the appalling maw.

"No matter. It is time for me to leave."

To the gathered throng, it issued its final declaration: "Disband your membership. Flee to the furthest corners of your world, each of you, and do not reassemble. Never trouble me again, lest you feel my awful wrath!

"I have spoken!"

With that, the ropey tongue peered out from the mouth for a second, threateningly, and then withdrew into the cosmic being. Yog rose high into the sky and then vanished into the darkness of the night.

Arnold slipped the iPod into his pocket without conscious effort. It was time for everyone to leave, and they did so without delay. Never again did the witches walk the streets of South Fork, which quickly returned to the peaceful community it had been.

By the time Vince and Arnold were ready to leave, the coven had already left, with the exception of the Widow Parton. The man she had come with had been so terrified he had been one of the first to bolt away from the fire circle, race to his car, and speed off into the night. Arnold was pleased to take the widow, who had no other means of transportation, back with Vince and him. His strong feelings for her had been rekindled by her comportment that night. Nancy had eyes only for Arnold, as the dead man walked along beside them, unnoticed, having no wish to be seen by her.

During the time spent driving back to South Fork, Arnold asked her what she intended to do, now that the other-worldly entity had ordered the membership to disperse.

"'Tain't for me to argue with it," she decided. "Believes what it said 'bout attendin' to those who disobeys it. Present condition of Ed Bates be proof. Guess I'll yank up stakes and go live with my sister in Schenectady. Last time I heard from her, she mentioned one of her boarders had left and she'd sure like for me to come up and live with her."

"You'd leave me, Nan?" asked Arnold.

"I would, Arn. Not that I'd wants to. Not as though I had much of a choice though, is there?"

"I'll miss you, Nan."

"Miss yer too, Arn."

They dropped the lady off at her little home. Vince moved to the front seat of the vehicle and the two continued on to Arnold's place. The driver shut the motor off, then picked up his iPod to see how his pictures had turned out. He stared at the results and softly swore.

"Gol, dang!" he exclaimed. "Nothing! Must have put the battery in wrong or it's worn out or defective. 'Bout time I learned how use to this thing!"

"Don't bust a gut worryin' 'bout it," said Vincet. "You don't need them pictures of the coven, anyways. Not no more."

"Guess I don't, do I?" Arnold agreed. "Problem's solved." He left the truck and ran around to the other side and opened the door for his companion to exit.

"C'mon in for a spell, Vince. Put your legs up and watch some telly with me. Stick around till Mildred gets up and give her a scare will last the rest of her lifetime."

"No thanks, Arnie. My work here be done, fer now. I needsa long, long rest; regen'rate my strength till the time comes when the Guy Upstairs needs my assistance again."

"I hear you, Buddy."

Vince waved his hand, unable to shake Arnold's, and stepped back a bit to face him. "Yer take good care of yerself. I'll come ter visit yer again one day, or maybe yer be the one who comes to call on me—permanent, like. You be a phantom then, too."

The man in green walked away and kept going, crossed the highway to Graveside Trail and continued upward, his form growing smaller and dimmer until he was out of sight.

Arnie went inside, popped a can of Coors and leaned back in front of the television set to see what was on at this time of night. Mildred would be up in a few hours, sobered, and start in on him again for being such a lazy, good-for-nothing klutz.

✗

PENUMBRA OVER MILLWALL
Jan Edwards

Foul, yellow-tainted smog had settled into the streets like water filling the dents and creases of a boot print. London was renowned for such pea-soupers and Georgi was grimly amused at how some thought it a part of old London's charm. *Perhaps it is*, she thought, *provided a body is not cursed with poor lungs or fragile heart*. She had neither but was gradually becoming convinced frost bite was not out of the question.

She peered at her watch for the umpteenth time and cussed; her words curtailing dully in the heavy mist. She had already cancelled dinner at Claridges to answer a summons from Tamesis to the embankment steps just below Greenwich College. After an hour and a half in biting cold she had come to the conclusion the meeting was not going to happen, which was curious. Whatever the river goddess's peculiarities Tamesis was generally punctual.

Fog siren's hooted and boomed all along the river, but she had neither seen nor heard any boat pass, nor a vehicle on the street, by in all of the time she had been waiting there. The smog had sent every bus and taxi cab in London to ground, meaning she had a long walk in this corrosive atmosphere. That just about put the lid on the entire evening.

She swore again and struck out to the east, toward the Naval College, in order to carry out her second command for the evening; a mercy dash to the Isle of Dogs and the home of Nellie Hall, an old staffer in the Ministry of Arcane Events. Officially Nellie had been a cleaner for the Department. In reality she was a font of London myth and skilled Medium who still received payment for her work long after retirement.

Brady had told her to visit Nellie and collect urgent documents, and perhaps, given the weather, fetch the old girl a meal at the same time. It was hardly a job for an Officer-Agent. Any post-boy could have done it and on such a night she would far rather have stayed at home, but one did not argue with the old man; plus she had a soft spot for the old lady. If Colonel Brady said Nellie had urgent papers then so be it.

Georgi snapped up the last fragrant portion of cod and chips from a frying bar along the way and strode as fast as the gloom allowed. At the domed southern entrance of the Greenwich foot tunnel she hesitated, peering into the stairwell and wrinkling her nose at the rank, fishy stink of the river. Since the submarine debacle she had found confined spaces some-what unnerving. "Just get a grip," she muttered.

She clattered down fifty feet of spiralling stairwell, and started along the four hundred yard run beneath the Thames at a clipped pace. Half way along the arched tunnel she paused and looked back the way she had come. She'd not seen a soul, yet the floor glistened with wet prints that merged into one sodden trail. Her hand had begun to itch and that branded third digit was twitching maniacally. Noden's macabre gift never lied. Some-thing was out there, and they were not human.

She took ran the final hundred yards and took the stairs at a trot, burst-ing out of the roundhouse on the north entrance and distancing herself by a good margin before stopping to draw breath. She coughed, the thick air tearing at her throat and nose, making her gasp all the harder.

She could just make out the glow of the dome's glazed roof. To her left a smaller, diffuse pulse indicated what might be a street lamp. Conditions made it difficult to see anything clearly that more than a hand-span from her face but other than the swirl of moisture clustered around the fog-dimmed lamps she could not detect any movement. It did at least explained why nobody was coming in from the northern end. Even those who knew the place well would have been disorientated. Lack of visions coupled with the eye-stinging, lung scouring, coal-tainted fumes would keep all but the most determined safe at home behind closed doors.

Only the thought of old Nellie, alone and waiting, prevented her tak-ing the saner course and heading for home. A promise is an officer's sacred bond and Captain Georgianna Forsythe would not let an old friend down. She pulled up the collar of the great coat she had worn in favour of her usual flying jacket and struck out across the street until she found the pav-ing edge of Dougs Path's. She deduced, rightly, that she could hardly get lost if she followed the curb to the junction where she turned right. She was gratified to see the twin headlights of a *Number 56* bus at the stop just ahead of her.

Georgi hurried forward to grasp the passenger pole and set foot on the bus's grubby platform. There was no rumble of diesel engines nor grumble of impatient passengers and the bus interior was as mist-raddled as the out-side, but she saw enough to ascertain that it was devoid of people.

She supposed it possible the driver had considered it too dangerous to go further, even with if the conductor walked ahead, carrying flares. If the 56 had been abandoned, however, it did not explain seats strewn with belongings. Handbags, shopping bags, briefcases, hats, coats; all thrown around the space as though some mad wedding guest thought to make con-fetti from whatever came to hand.

Georgi's hand slid through a smear of cold goo bisecting the back of the nearest seat. She peered at the sticky, brownish smear on her fingers and then sniffed at it with a certain caution. The taste test was unneeded. She had seen blood and death too many times in the service of the King for any lingering doubt. The thought of what might have caused the destruction of a whole bus full of people and leave little more than this filled her with an awful foreboding; a feeling backed to the hilt by the nagging ache in that fish-scale ring on the third digit of her left hand.

She moved back to the platform and considered retracing her steps to the south bank. The food package warm against her hip reminded her of her orders to both deliver Nellie's supper and collect that report. Though now more than anything she really, really, wanted to find out what had aroused her arcane early warning system.

The deep, guttural bark seeped through the fog. It sounded familiar, except it was like no dog that she had ever heard, and too deep for the unearthly scream of a fox. Nor was it a distressed horse from some milk float or brewers dray.

Georgi froze, analysing the sensations in her hands and her mind as she had been taught to do. A water-vision dazzled fleetingly in the front of her brain and she smiled grimly. It was not much but it narrowed the field a little. Something from the pantheon spawned of sea and river had raised her inbuilt alarms.

Further cries echoed between Georgi and the river. She still had no idea what could make such a sound, but there were at least two of them and their howls did not sound particularly friendly.

There came a slithering and a slapping as one of the somethings felt its way along the outside of the bus. Her skin crawled in empathy with her pulsing left hand. The smog was the deepest she had ever seen, and somewhere within it beings of some unearthly ilk were calling. Not just two now but a disconcerting many, in a frog's chorus of querulous yip and answering yalp from all points south and east. Two shapes moved in and out of the brownish gloom. Shapes that were both indistinct and alien. She knew now what they were and knew absolutely that she should avoid their attention at all costs. Killing them individually was not the problem but in doing so she risked summoning that which controlled them, which she was more eager to avoid.

She patted the Webberley inside her coat. Its weight was reassuring but not a great deal of help when she had not brought any spare ammunition. Once she emptied the chambers it was no more dead weight, and she needed to be able to see a target for those limited shells to count. Avoiding the need to fire at all was her best option. She drew the weapon in any case, pocketing her torch and readying herself to make a break for open streets.

The bus lurched as something heavy swayed against the side. There was a brief silence and then a strident "YIP". From close by it was answered with a deeper "Yalp", and the vehicle rocked once again.

Another "YIP", another slow moving shape looming from the murk. She launched herself away from the vehicle platform and sprinted blindly toward the opposite side of the street. A chorus of yips and yalps gave way to more feral yowling that was taken up from almost every point around; rising in pitch and volume until there was little else able to percolate her darkening thoughts.

She missed the kerb, despite it being only a few paces away, and found herself running down the centre of a side road. Her pursuers seemed not to have any great turn of speed, or were as dubious of running blind as she was. Whatever the reasons sounds from the creatures gradually receded and her hand ceased to itch. She slowed down, trying to make out where she was. A sign told her she was passing Mudshute, home to the Rope maker's sheds, all of which were unlit. Nobody lived here, and in such weather none worked either.

She had an urge to cough up the fumes that her exertion was drawing into labouring lungs and steeled herself against making noise that might give her position away. She risked slowing to a walk to listen for signs of pursuit. In the dense air sounds were truncated; lacking reverberation. Nothing much to hear but the fog sirens and a lone crane still chattering its chains across toward the docks. It was difficult to pinpoint distance or direction but so far as she was able to work out they were some distance off. yips and answering yalps from the open space to her right told her she could not afford to stop for long however.

Along this stretch, if memory served she was certain she would find a phone box. She thought she could call the Department and warn them. The streets were empty but she was afraid for the safety of anyone unfortunate enough to be abroad, and yes she needed to hear a sane voice to offset the awful distraction offered by those ululating, inhuman, creatures.

The rolling mist cleared a little and in a sudden small window of clarity she saw the unmistakable squareness of a Post Office telephone box glowing through the vapour. Around it lurched a trio of creatures the like of which she had only seen once before and had hoped never to see again.

They were around her own height. Their heads and backs were dark grey and scaly, glistening like wet mackintoshes. Their underbellies were flaccid and pale. A ridge of scales run from their skinny buttocks to domed heads that seemed almost fish-like, with their huge, unblinking eyes set so wide they stretched to the sides where ears should be. Long stringy forearms dangled past bent knees and they stooped as they walked, like oily, hairless baboons. She knew what they were and they filled her with loathing and dread.

Deep Ones.

They moved back and fore, pawing at the glass, apparently unable to determine how to enter the box. They were emitting more croaking yaps; communicating their frustration and abject confusion to each other. As well they might. Her own confusion was barely less. She had never heard of them travelling so far from their native breeding grounds on America's north east shores and seeing them here on the opposite shores of the Atlantic was deeply worrying.

Georgi backed into the mists before any of them turned toward her and fumbled her way along the edge of the kerb. Nellie's terraced house, nestling in the south-eastern edge of Millwall Docks, could not be so very far.

Dim radiance from the next street lamp drew her west. Lamps meant road junctions and hopefully a street name or two. Georgi approached the sphere of light cautiously for fear that the light would attract Deep Ones like a flight of ugly, wingless moths. All seemed quiet. As they appeared to hunt in packs, or perhaps, given their appearance, in shoals, and the yips and yalps were all behind her, she felt confident enough to stand in the light and look up at the wall corners for signage.

Undine Road.

At last. She took out her torch to search for door numberings. She passed 50 and slowed. 54a would be dead ahead.

"Yip?" was followed, from horrifyingly close behind her with a grating, "Yalp."

"Damn and blast," she muttered. "Little bastards have been stalking me." Their ability to reason belied all her assumptions of bestial intellect. Evidently some of these creatures were the equal of humanity or at very least thought themselves thus.

She eased a lungful of air, trying to prevent any noise carrying to the preternatural hearing of her pursuers. She needed to think. A wolf in the forest and shark in the sea will hunt their prey with low cunning, but they should not outwit an officer of his Majesty's secret service. She did not think she could outrun them, nor could she hope to perform acrobatics that could lift her above their heads.

One of the creatures was close enough to touch, the other still a dim shape some four paces beyond. Georgi raised the Webberly and popped of two rounds; and was satisfied to see both attackers tumble into the gutter. Raising her left hand she urged blue fire after gunfire. The bodies bucked and twitched under her onslaught uttering piercing, almost plaintive, whistles and yelps as they died.

She leapt away into the mist before anything could home in on her position as fast as poor visibility would permit, keeping close to the walls so as not to veer from her target; after six strides she dared turn on her torch.

Fifty-four was painted neatly on the planking beside her. Nellie's home was in the alleyway just at the side of this. She dodged into the gaping darkness, sprinted the few short spaces to the step and rapped on the door. A shuffling noise from inside and then nothing. Whoever, whatever, was on the other side was listening as ardently as Georgi did them. For one grim moment she feared she was too late, that the beasts had already forced an entry. She bent to the letter-flap and opened it.

"Nellie." She hoped her stage whisper was not enough to carry beyond the two feet needed to reach the inside. "Nellie. Are you there?"

"Captain Forsythe?"

"Yes." Relief at hearing Nellie's rasping demand was immense, tempered only by the chorus of yips thrumming in the street beyond the alley mouth. "Let me in," Georgi hissed.

The sound of something dragged aside and of bolts being shot and then the door opened. Not waiting for invitation Georgi slipped inside, shutting and bolting the door behind her and, without need for asking, manoeuvred a low cupboard, which Nellie had plainly used as added barricade, back into place. "You've seen them?" she said.

"I have that. Ugly brutes." Nellie frowned at the sounds of slapping against the door.

They both braced against the cupboard. An almost futile gesture, Georgi felt, against any attempt to force a way through. They leaned thus for a minute or more, but the expected attack did not come.

Nellie held a finger to her lips and beckoned Georgi to her parlour. There were no lamps lit, but a fire glowed in the grate gave sufficient ambience. They stood side by side, a few paces from the window, and gazed out into the street. Little enough to be seen beyond a half-dozen shapes wandering to and fro. Georgi's instinct had been correct. More creatures had indeed been summoned by their dying brethren.

A few minutes later they had vanished back into the gloom from whence they came.

"Not very bright are they," Nellie observed. "You're safe s'long as you stay in. They don't come out of a day time. Least ways they didn't 'afore."

Georgi stared at her, unable to believe her implication. "You've seen them before?"

Nellie nodded. "Once. Back in the Great War. We 'ad two weeks of bad fogs. They came up into the dock."

"And so…"

"Fire. They can't abide it." She was grinning, and Georgi had nothing but admiration for this stoic matron. Nellies's gaze shifted to the package poking from the capacious pocket of Georgi's coat. "That my supper?" She snatched it up before Georgi could reply and waved it under her nose. "You want some?" she asked.

Georgi shook her head. Even if she had eaten she was sure the meal had to be all the old woman would have that day. Nellie trotted over to the fire and crouched on the fire guard stool to unwrap her meal releasing a tantalising aroma of fried fish and greasy chips into the room. Forsaking plate or silverware she ate it straight down from the newspaper The silence was broken by crackling of the fire and the slapping of Nellie's toothless gums.

Georgi went to the window, standing to one side so that her outline could not be framed against the fire, and peered into the gloom. Nothing to see now. She returned to the fire and hunkered down on her heels to warm her hands.

Nellie paused in her chomping, greasy fingers half way to her lips. "Ain't eaten proper today," she mumbled around the fish pieces. "Nor yesterday neither. Not been out there since Friday night. I'm not so fast as I was."

"Understandable. But Nellie, when it happened before how come nobody heard anything about it?"

"The War Office hushed it up. Didn't want any panic. People had enough to think about without havin' sea monsters runnin' about the place." She scooped up the last scraps of batter, licked her fingers noisily, and then screwed the paper tight before adding it to the fire.

It flared briefly, a waft of burning fish belching into the room and Georgi felt slightly nauseous. Nellie was possessed of a cast iron constitution in view of what roamed the street just yards away from her home.

"Our department knew?" I said.

"Of course they did. Sent a lorry load of squaddies with flame throwers to clear them out. They've never been back before today. But then we haven't had many soupers quite so bad as this one since then."

"Still, we must let the Ministry know," she muttered.

"Oh, they know."

"How can you tell?"

"No flares out. They always puts flares down—least until people get home from work. Of course I'm only guessing, mind, but have you seen any flares?"

Georgi thought about it and realised the old woman could well be right. There had been flares laid at junctions on the south side of the river, but none to be seen since she had surfaced near the Gardens a short while ago.

Nellie was watching her face and as realisation dawned on Georgi's features, allowed herself a self-righteous nod.

"If they know, how is it they don't stop people coming across?" Georgi asked.

Nellie picked at Georgi's great coat. "You are military. They thought you was going to join the clean-up crews."

That made sense. Georgi huffed a little. "So what was so important I needed to come tonight?"

"Bit late," Nellie replied. "They're already here." She got to her feet and picked up a slim white envelope from the mantle. "I thought Brady would just send a messenger boy." She turned her head slightly to look at Georgi over her shoulder. "'Course if he had I'd never have got my supper."

"I would have been here earlier if I hadn't been hanging around for two hours on another job that never happened. The whole evening's been just crammed with jelly beans."

"And not goin' to get any better," Nellie replied. "You tell that Tamesis when you see her, 'Not yet'."

"How did you know?" Georgi gaped, lost for words.

Nellie only waved a hand at the small table to the right of the fire draped in velveteen cloth scattered with tarot cards. "Give you two guesses. Just tell for me."

"All right. But…" A pounding from the rear of the building cut off any other reply. "We must leave." Georgi muttered. "If we can get to the tunnel we shall be safe. I saw none of them on the south bank."

Nellie laughed sharply. "And how d'you think the north end of the tunnel got blown up'n the dome didn't?"

There it was again, that razor mind. "Hadn't thought about it," Georgi mumbled. "But I have friends that side. I was supposed to me meeting her this evening but…"

"She never turned up? An' you think it's safe? Two 'n' two child. Always has made four." She eyed Georgi up and down. "All down to that scamp Tammy. She'll be out stalking these buggers I'll be bound. Say what you like, but she's never bin one to shirk."

"You know Tamesis?"

"I do. A cousin of a sort."

"Ah. So who are you? Really I mean."

Nellie shrugged, and the decades melted from her face, leaving a slender dark haired woman of no more than thirty in her place. "I was called Nehalennia, before I retired. Well maybe not retired, but there's not so much call for me these days. Telegraphs an' wireless an' airplanes. But your Colonel Brady gives an old lady some dignity. And I've got all this."

Georgi regarded her with what she hoped was a lack of surprise, and wondered if Brady knew who she was. What she was. She looked at the shabby surroundings and puffed out her cheeks. If he knew then this place had to be of Nellie's choosing. And there was a lot here that she was too ignorant of for comfort. "Indeed." There was a small silence as she digested the notion. This ageless, and as it turned out beautiful, woman was goddess of the northern sea. A deity. She had known Nellie was somehow special. But a goddess. She was also wondering why she needed to have busted a gut getting here to feed her when she was doubtless more than able to feed herself.

As if reading thoughts passing behind Georgi's eyes like a stockbroker read tickertape Nellie added, "I may not be as ancient as I like to look, but nor am I as young as I was. I need help now and then. I am happy here by the water. And I am still kept busy between here and Amsterdam. Lot of ships. Lot of work." She waved at Georgi with a grin. "You're a fit lass. All you have to do is keep out in the open, and don't fire unless you have to."

"I don't need guns." Georgi held her hand palm out toward the grate and sent a lazy jet of cold fire at the burning coals, making them blacken and chill for a moment.

"Fancy," Nellie observed. She stepped close to Georgi and stared into her eyes.

The fetid room shimmered and the yalps of the creatures outside were suddenly crying of gulls. The smell of fish that of brine and tarred planking. Her hands ached and her vision filled with the green and blue of waves washing over her head, Georgi staggered back a pace. "What are you doing…" she began.

"I would save that fire for emergencies," Nellie replied. "You will need it. Now you should go."

"I can't leave you here alone," Georgi said. "It would not be right."

Nellie only laughed and waved a hand at the left over torches. "You saw what I am, yet you still believe what you see now. Things are often not what they appear. Now. The weather will turn tonight. Big storm brewin'. And then these things will be gone. Young Tamesis'll look by some time."

"That could be days!"

"Yes. It could." She grinned. "I'll be right as kittens in here. I got enough nutty slack for a week. I'll keep warm."

"But food?"

"I'll cope. Now go. If I'm wrong. And the Colonel don't know what's goin' on?" The London drawl returned to the woman's voice as her face settled back into haggard lines, "We'll neither of us survive in 'ere for long." She gazed at Georgi, a half smile on her lips and glitter in her eyes that was not all down to firelight. "A message for young Tamesis when you see her. Tell her *she's not ready yet.*"

"Who isn't?"

The old woman smirked. "Just tell her. *She's not ready yet.* Have you got that?"

Georgi nodded. "Yes, but…"

"Good. Now it is time you were not here."

Still Georgi hesitated. To leave an elderly woman alone ran against all logic and honour, and she knew Nellie was right. Every attempt to get back to the south bank and raise an alarm should be made, and she herself in her current guise was very unlikely to succeed, or, indeed to survive in that endeavour. But the crafty old dear was hiding something. She looked back at the window. There was nothing visible through the windows but mustard-tinted mist. Perhaps it was innate optimism on Georgi's part but it seemed a little less dense. She could only hope.

Reading thoughts once again, Nellie hobbled into the kitchen and returned with a pillow case from her ironing which she tore out and folded into a long strip. "Here." She reached up to tie around Georgi's nose and mouth. Her cool touch sent a shudder through the younger woman. "That'll do," she said. "Least ways until you get down to the tunnel."

Unable to speak through the layers of cotton, Georgi replied by way of a hug. She had not the slightest idea what had happened here, or for the entire evening. But she had learned not to question too deeply. They shifted the cupboard and she peeked into the alley. All seemed clear. A final thumbs up to Nellie and the young agent slipped out into the contaminated night; pausing only to ensure the door had properly closed, and to hear the bolts being shot home once more.

At the end of the passage she paused again. There seemed not to be any movement, or any of the alien cries in the immediate vicinity, though she heard a distant croaked chorus, and a strangled and very human scream from the direction of the dock. That at least confirmed her decision to head back for the tunnel and not go in search of a phone anywhere on the dock side, as had crossed her mind.

Georgi made her cautious way back to the junction and the telephone box bathed in the muted light of a street lamp. Or where it had been. Currently it was a ruin, torn asunder like some dolls house toy, and across the kerb lay the torn clothes and half eaten body of a young soldier. She shuddered at the thought it was he and not the light which had attracted attention on her outward journey. His presence here, however, told her at least that there were military patrols, albeit fighting a losing campaign, it seemed. She looked back the way she had come and considered backtracking. Nellie would be alone, and vulnerable. Except she would not. The Deep Ones were powerful, but not immortal. If she were being stalked once again then far better not to lead the enemy to the old woman's door. Plus—deity. If anyone should be able to defend themselves against Deep Ones it would be a sea goddess. She wondered again why she was doing this.

A double yip-yalp, close on her heels, decided her against doubling back. She backed into safety of unlit nocturne, reaching for her revolver in case it were required, and skirted her way around the tragedy. Somewhere over toward the Ropewalks there was a crescendo of gargling cries and gun fire. A dim flare of luminescence, followed by screams both human and other. Nearby a yalp and the slap of unshod, splayed feet pattered toward the sounds and she saw one of the barbarous wretches loping through the cone of lamp light, slowing only briefly to glance at the dead soldier before surging away to the east of her into the open swathes of the Mudshute.

She flipped her duffel hood up to hide the white of the cotton face binding, lest the gleam of it gave her away, and trotted as lightly as she was able toward Manchester Road. It was just a few minutes walk, but concentrating on following the kerb whilst listening out for the creatures made it seem like a mile and more. She was close to where the No.56 had stopped, and could see the lambency of both the bus and street lamp beneath which it was parked, when she heard that gut-juddering whisper of wet feet on cement. There was none of the calling that she had come to associate with these dire umbrae; and that in its self gave rise to concern. It seemed to Georgi that, like submarines and scrapyard dogs, they were to be feared the most when running silent.

She could just make out a wall running parallel with the kerb and stepped across, all the while listening for all that a small life was worth

A scraping from the section of road that she had just traversed was close and echoing from two sources. More than one creature on her trail, proving they did, then, hunt in packs; like the true predators they were proving to be.

Holding breath to a trickle she listened and waited. One set of feet pattered on past to her left, until a faint outline, a shadow, showed between her and the silent vehicle. And, almost imperceptible, a tenuous hint, a ruffle of movement from the right. So close, almost within touching distance. She was being hunted and that the figure showing itself so carelessly against the only available illumination was a feint.

Georgi immolated the movement and had them roar flaming defiance at saw-toothed mouth and talon-tipped paws. The creature dove once again and she parried, firing at the creatures face once, twice, exploding its eyeball in a spray of dull ichor. The creature stumbled back, clutching at its head and howling to a moon that no Londoner had seen for a week. She fired again and it fell, face forward, unmoving. Even Nellie's makeshift mask could not keep out the stench of rotting fish and of burning. She gagged. Her eyes, already watering from the foul air, wept under the fresh assault.

Soggy footsteps and staccato yaps from its compatriot as it hastened to aid. She pocketed the gun and laid down a swathes of blue fire in blind arcs. Her attacker drew back before it ever came within her sphere. Still the injured creature howled, and from along the street more of them answered.

She had to reach the tunnel soon or perish. She sidled along the wall, keeping the twin flames moving all the while, until the edifice fell away on a bend. She ran. Behind her were many feet, running also.

Slip, slap, slip.

Yip, yalp, yap.

She dared not turn, certain those execrable fiends were close enough to touch, certain that the fire she had sent against them also drew them like moths. She wished she had more shells for the trusty Webberley. She would rather pit hot lead against the *Promethean bane* any day, though on that day she knew without it she would have shared the fate of that pitiable corpse at the telephone box. In addition her arcane weaponry was effective, but limited by her own energy.

It could not be far to the North Entrance to the tunnel now. Fewer than a hundred yards. The faint lustre atop of the entry turret was emerging through the haze. From behind her came the slap of webbed feet and frenetic yarlping of the beasts.

The doors were showing as dark rectangles in the ochre mists and were firmly locked, no matter how she rattled and tugged at the handle.

"Help! Help me. Open the doors, in the name of all that's holy, save me!" She hammered her fists against the doors and screamed for someone, anyone, to open up.

She turned to meet the approaching assailants, holding out her aching hand, swishing rapidly depleting fire back and for. She could not last out for much longer. And when her energy failed she would be at the mercy of this uncanny mob.

Georgi kicked back at the doors, still screaming for succour. Jabbing and feinting with fast diminishing flame.

There was a noise of metal against metal, and a welter of light, and a roaring conflagration of cold fire was projected past her; singing her hair and coat as it blasted through the opening, searing her opponents in a rattle and hiss of scorching skin, like trout under a griddle pan, and leaving little behind it beyond a noisome stench.

A muffled voice shouted to her. Hands grasped her and hauled me into the dome. The doors clanged shut and Georgi was shivering in the company of Tamesis.

"Are you all right?" she asked.

Georgi nodded, "I will be," she replied. "That was— interesting."

"Yes, wasn't it." The Goddess glanced at the doors that shuddered and pulsed under the onslaught of our attackers. "You're alone?"

"Yes. Nellie would not leave. She knew this was coming didn't she."

"Not entirely. When we sent word to Brady we only had a vague rumour. Things got out of hand rather more quickly than we had imagined. But Brady knows now, and it will be brought under control before dawn."

"I hope so. I am not keen to tangle with those chaps again." She frowned. The night had been one of the strangest, and she had known a lot of weird. "Nellie gave me a message," she said. "No idea what she meant but she said *not yet*."

"Nehalennia said that?"

"She did. And she wouldn't leave. Said she was safe in her home."

"So she is. Don't let that wily old lady disguise fool you. She has a lot more power against these creatures than either of us."

"So why?"

Tamesis shrugged. "We could not have had a better testing if we had planned it," she replied.

"So not ready means what?"

"She meant you child. You are not ready yet. Lud's city will need its warrior in the decades to come."

"Decades." She laughed without any hint of humour, glancing down at the circle of scales around her finger. "Yes, of course. But how do I get ready? And what in hell for?"

"You are kin." Tamesis chuckled, shaking her head. "Have you not realised that yet? You are to take your place along side us. But the old woman is correct. You are not ready as yet—but when the time arrives? You shall be."

✗

FRAGILE

Lucy A. Snyder

H_1N_1 is such a tiny thing
a wee spiked ball slipping
quiet into cells to sabotage
our sticky machinery. Heat
kills it, as does alcohol. Hard
to imagine this slight particle
stirs so fierce a cellular storm,
wreaks such expensive misery,
clogs lungs, stops hearts, slaying
blooming youths and aged abuelas
faster than the cruelest brutal army.

BIRTH

M. Stern

The dream, since the first time he'd had it, was always accompanied by a sensation of scalding on his back. And like no other dream he'd had, it possessed a tangibility—one which had led him to explore the ways in which it was also unlike other dreams. Now he saw it all for the hundredth or thousandth time in his mind's eye:

The stone room packed with black-hooded men; the stinking air vibrating with their growling, grunting chants.

The caged captives, rendered wretched and filthy in the corners, shrieking their counterpoint to the chants as leprous slaves busily released vermin through the bars, and casual sadists in different state of undress and inebriation poked and prodded and creatively tortured and humiliated them, giggling.

The statuesque, musclebound centurions who lined the walls who he knew—in a dream's way of knowing—had sat at the table of the bloodthirsty boy Emperor Elagabalus, who had traded the ancient artifact to the Believers for a barter of blood and a promise of chaos.

The book with its arcane instructions on the podium before him; the flickering candle light in the chamber splitting unnaturally around the book as it somehow threw its shadow backwards in mid-air. The mirror image of his own face standing before the hooded figures at the podium, wearing an insanely ornamented headpiece. A single, thin line of sludgy brown residue dripping down his chin.

The Cheshire cat grin on his face changing abruptly to a look of uncertainty, then severe concern. The deep gurgling of his stomach that seemed to make the room rattle. And the stampede that ensued as the dark prayers and ululations shred the mettle of the onlookers—who shrieked at the sight of the man who had stood at the podium; who let out thick gurgles and deformed like a balloon with the air being sucked out.

And when it was over, there was the thing again—flopping and meandering dumbly around in the muck of liquefied bone and flesh, rank blended secretions and viscera. The brown, slimy amphibious thing with its wilted, asymmetrical fins, and with a sad longing in its anomalously beautiful, human blue eyes which were set in the sides of its slimy, grotesque form.

He knew—as one knows in a dream—that rather than germinating, it would return to its chrysalis.

He woke up.

At age eight, the dream had been a horror. At 16, a warning. At 26, a guidepost. And now at 36, as the throbbing of the underground alcove in ancient Syria dissolved into the furious pounding of his own heart, it was a story of a mistake soon to be corrected.

His eyes looked left and right. A smile flit to his face.

* * * *

"Hey there, yep—yep, hello there everybody out there in Internet Land," said the jovial man in a window on Alexander's laptop screen; the microphone finally kicking in after a few seconds of mouthed silences. "Yep, welcome everyone out there in cyberspace—does anyone still say that? Cyberspace? On your social media, your mediums, wherever you are—"

The man looked slightly down from the camera, his eyes tracking over a stream of incoming messages on his own computer monitor.

"I'm happy to have you here; happy to have you join me," he said. "In fact, I love you out there, guys and girls—you loyal members of the Bowelcano Army—and yes even you, FittiDiaperDeathSquad, I love you and I appreciate your support even though no, I will not as you have requested, *go fuck myself.* I am thrilled to have every one of you beautiful people out there watching today's *live*streamed episode of *You Send It, I Eat It.*"

The room Alexander sat in—as he watched the webcast of the social celebrity who called himself Rex Vesuvius—smelled like age-old cigarette smoke supercooled by an air conditioner broken to having only two settings; off and polar. The only factor that appeared to prevent any given room from having its door kicked in was the lack of guests to do the kicking.

It had been an abrupt transition in degree of comfort for Alexander. Through last week he'd been in a hotel so lavish its rooms had their own waterfalls and its swimming pools had their own swimming pools. Now, after a few international stopovers on a route mapped to match the countries with the most easily-greased customs agent, he was here in a motel in Bumblefuck, Nebraska alongside the highway.

"First off we've got something from Frank Gundemeyer from Amarillo, Texas," Rex said on-screen. "Frank writes, *my great-grandfather was sort of a hoarder and while we were cleaning out his house I found this—a box of original banana crème Twinkies from the 1940s. I guess I could have sold it on eBay but I thought I would be doing the world a disservice if I didn't send it to you. If you can determine that it won't kill you, I look forward to watching you eat it. Keep up the good work.* And yes folks, I have determined with no small amount of internet research over the past ten minutes that I should be safe…"

Alexander grinned. Despite having what others described as a superb memory, one memory that evaded him was how he'd stumbled onto Rex Vesuvius's *You Send It, I Eat It*. It seemed as though there had never been a time when he hadn't known the Rex's knuckleheaded antics.

While there were certainly plenty of shows on cable television that specialized in exotic eating, Alexander was almost entranced by *You Send It*'s willingness to take it far beyond the point where mainstream connoisseurship ended. Rex had unintentionally poisoned himself at least three times in the past four years. He'd consumed not just strange delicacies, but on occasion insects and other animals that weren't eaten anywhere—as well as research chemicals, cleaning supplies, small electronics, wood and a slew of other things the human body hadn't been created to consume.

Alexander had probably put in too much thought about why these sorts of things drew such massive audiences. On some level, he imagined that it spoke to a perverse human desire to want to see the ante upped on the spectacle of someone else's self-sacrifice—Rex Vesuvius; Gladiator of the Outrageous. On another level, though, there was the thrill of seeing Rex's almost celebratory indifference to consequences. It hinted at a sublimely Dionysian disdain for life's limits, or a skepticism about the relationship between cause and effect dating back to Pyrrho.

Alexander's phone vibrated. At the sound of the alarm, he inhaled and exhaled deeply. Dragging his USB mouse, he pulled Rex's window up to the top right corner of his screen and pulled up a bank of browser tabs he'd been working on earlier. He clicked through a few truncated titles, like *Strange Natur* and *World's Weirdest Ani* until he reached the window he needed, and clicked in the textbox where he'd been editing.

Recognizable by its distinctively human-like eyes, the Selk'nam Mudskipper *Is an amphibian commonly found in the* …

Alexander switched to another window, scrolled down and nodding at a confirmed fact, switched back and continued typing.

…*lagoons* of Tierra del Fuego. *Once consumed as a delicacy by indigenous tribes in the region, the animal is today widely thought of as an invasive pest due to its parasitic relationship with commercial fish and other aquatic life.*

Clicking back to Rex, he saw a sight that had grown familiar since he'd stumbled onto this strange niche of DIY internet media—a man vomiting into a trash can.

Watching this on-screen illustration of where Western culture had arrived made him think about his ever-so-brief encounter with Sergei—and what the Russian would make of the decadence, if you could even call it that. Sergei would probably call it the beginning of the end.

* * * *

"You must be Sergei," Alexander said to the two guests who stood outside the door of his room, high up on the 50th floor of the Dubai hotel. "What do you say, friends? Want to have a drink?"

The hulking, bald man Alexander had presumed to be Sergei and the smaller, fidgety fellow in a track suit next to him were about what he had expected. He ushered them in as he noticed them squinting against the sun, which seemed as though it could scald through the window. He shuffled across the massive suite in his pink bunny slippers and pulled the giant plush drapes closed.

Then pulling an unmarked bottle and three shot glasses from a cupboard, he turned with a glance that silently repeated the offer. Sergei whispered something in the ear of the man in the track suit, who Alexander gathered spoke at least two languages, neither of them English. The man got an exaggerated look like he'd stepped in something foul, and responded.

"Says he doesn't drink the alcohol," Sergei translated. "His mother— she would never forgive him."

"You?" Alexander said.

Sergei took the bottle, pulled out the cork from the top and gave it a sniff.

"My mother would not forgive me if I said no," he said.

Alexander placed two of the shot glasses on the table as the man in the track suit sat in a chair in the corner and fiddled with his smartphone. Alexander handed the bottle to Sergei, who poured one shot and pushed it towards him. Alexander hesitated.

"Ah!" he said after a moment. "Right. You Russians never pour your own shots. Bad luck or bad manners or something. Embarrassed myself at a wedding once."

Alexander filled up Sergei's glass and they toasted and knocked them back, locking eyes with the stone-faced, iron-throated indifference to the grain alcohol's burn each knew was critical to doing business respectably.

"So the item in question," Alexander said.

"Is here."

"What do you think of it?"

Sergei eyed him suspiciously.

"Is ugly," he finally said. "Ugly like hell. Like devil."

Alexander snorted a laugh.

"And your friend?"

"He has special relationship with it," Sergei said. "Had it up his *zhopa* from Mossul to Ankara."

The man in the chair must have caught the zing. He stormed toward the taller man with one accusing finger leading and the other fist cocked behind him.

Alexander coughed loudly through the commotion, cocked his ear and pointed up as if he was listening for distant music.

"I'd advise that everyone stay cool," Alexander said. "This room is rigged to monitor heart rates and some other environmental metrics. If the AI recognizes any impending violence, well—"

He pointed at the two men, who now had laser pointer targets on their chests.

Beeping from an unseen source pulsed in the silence.

If the two had been frozen, they froze harder—hands up, Sergei urging acquiescence to his partner with his eyes.

"Amazing what you can find on the internet these days," he said. "Very easy to put together. It's just loaded up with tranquilizer darts, I promise— but you know, you never can be too careful in these matters."

The beeping stopped, the two lasers faded.

Sergei let out a huge belly laugh while his partner, scowling, returned to the chair in the corner.

"You do business like Russian, motherfucker!" Sergei said, reaching to pour Alexander another shot. "I like it. You deserve your ugly statue."

Sergei pointed to the man in the track suit. He looked up from the phone he'd just returned to, clearly irritated, picked up the briefcase and carried it over to Sergei.

Sergei placed it on the table, entered a combination, popped the sturdy lock and opened the briefcase. He threw aside the stacks of papers and the book therein, then took a small tool from his pocket and dug into the lining of the briefcase. He removed the briefcase's false back, revealing the artifact; an eight-inch long eel-like creature that looked like it could have been carved from off-yellow limestone. There were gems in place of the eyes, and it was mounted on a small stone stand.

Alexander's heart raced. He reached, not for the statue, but past it. He grabbed the book that sat atop the papers that had fallen from the briefcase—a hardcover with no dust jacket which on the spine read, simply, Гомер.

"Odyssey or Iliad?" Alexander said as he scrutinized the outside of the book.

Sergei looked perplexed.

"You understand Russian?"

"I know the Cyrillic alphabet," Alexander said. "Enough to know names. You're a fan of the classics?"

"Important to have culture," Sergei said. "I think that nobody does too much today under intellectualism. Everything is this—virtual. People play the video game. They play the computer. Nobody reads the book. So, life? Nobody understands. Nobody appreciates."

Sergei pressed the mock lining back into the briefcase as he spoke, then tossed the stacks of dummy papers back in. He reached for the book in Alexander's hand.

"But you are American scientist, no? Such literature is a little spiritual for you. No calculations. Not useful to make car fly to moon. Or make faster computer to play better video game."

"I don't draw such distinctions," Alexander said. "Learning is learning. Homer's as important as anything. Homer might be more important. Who do you think he was? Have you thought about it?"

"A Greek," Sergei said. "Probably nice guy."

"Someone writing 700 or 800 years before the height of the Roman Empire," Alexander said. "About events that may have happened a thousand years before that. His words transferred and copied and recopied, no-doubt imperfectly, from scroll to codex; from language to language. Who was he? Did he believe that gods walked the earth alongside men? Did he *see* them? Was he trying to tell us something? Does whatever he was trying to tell us remain pertinent? Did the people he was writing about exist? Were they anything like the characters in that book? Was Homer ever an individual person, or was he many different people working together? Or working separately? We'll never know.

"The simplest things are unknowable to us, Sergei. We are misled and we mislead at every step. Our own senses lie to us. The words we read betray us. The ones we write do not convey our meaning. The gulf between what we know and what we think we know is near infinite."

"This does not seem to me the opinion of scientist," Sergei said. "In science you have right, you have wrong."

"The real forefront of scientific study, if you ask me, is where things are quite the opposite," Alexander said. "Where the scientific method is an outmoded heuristic, not a hard and fast rule, because it's impossible to test a hypothesis without changing the outcome."

"I do not understand quite what you are trying to say, my friend."

"Sometimes it's better not to know," he said.

Sergei's partner looked up from his phone for the first time in a while and yelled something in Russian. Sergei yelled something back. Then he sighed.

The lumbering Russian tossed the book in the briefcase, lurched slightly to the left as he stood up straight, and quickly righted himself. He was receiving what Alexander assumed were reprimands from his partner which the big man brushed off with a hand gesture.

As Sergei turned to leave, the smaller man already one foot out the door, Alexander could see the Russian was searching for a thread through the cryptic conversation. Drunkenly in the silence, Sergei said:

"Riddles. This is not like the scientist, I don't think. This is more of like the mystic, no?"

Those familiar dream images flashed in Alexander's mind's eye: His doppelganger cult priest wearing the ornate crown atop his head. Following his interpretations of the arcane instructions in the strangely-shadowed book that was his birthright. The brown amphibious being, vile save its captivating eyes, to which the instructions pertained. The moment of miscalculation.

"You could say it runs in the family," Alexander said.

* * * *

Alexander's childhood had been a happy one—truly, thoroughly, even uncommonly happy. With the exception of that one day, one single experience that stuck out in his memory as such a bizarre anomaly. It had started with the eight-year-old boy's parent-teacher conference—one he'd gotten the gist of despite not being present; one he could almost hear in the voice of his fourth-grade teacher, Mrs. Price:

"Your son, Mrs. Ollis, is *very* creative," Ms. Price had said. "So much so that he has trouble concentrating. He's always telling the other students stories. Me too—sometimes things he seems to truly believe. Not that I think that there's necessarily the need to get the counselor involved. He's imaginative, and I believe that's good. Not all teachers do Mrs. Ollis but I certainly see the value of a strong imagination. And with what they've got on television these days, the He-Man and these sorts of things—Hmm."

"But ... but Mrs. Ollis, Alexander said something in class the other day that did make me quite concerned about where he's getting certain messages. He said, 'my mommy has an old book, it's so old that it's older than even,'—(and this is where I am getting a little concerned, Mrs. Ollis)— 'it's older than even Jesus Christ, and we can't throw it away, because it just comes back. We can't burn it or bury it or anything, we just have to keep it. And if you shine a light on it, it eats the light right up.' Is there something going on, maybe, at home that the school should know about?"

Alexander was sitting in front of the television watching Thundercats when his mother flew in the door, an anxiety and an anger in the opening of the door that caused him to spring up. He was clad in pajamas and frozen like in headlights—a frenzy in his mother's eyes he'd never seen before bearing down on him.

And a sensation of off-ness when the door flew open, like there was something subtly different, un-verifiably shifted, about every object in the room.

The look in his mother's eyes, though, was verifiable.

"Alex," she said. "Did you say something about a book to the people at school?"

And he racked his brain, digging, trying to remember, because at that age things just spill out—it seemed as possible to him that he'd said something as that he hadn't.

"I don't ... know?"

This was the first and only time he'd ever wanted to run from her.

"What's the one rule in this house, Alex?"

"I don't—"

"What is the one rule in my house?"

"That I'm never supposed to mention the—"

He felt his mother yank him upwards. His neck jerked back. Shocks of light burst before his eyes and his head hurt, and he shrieked. A deep, primordial, unhinged cry. His head throbbed. And he screamed a gargling, choking scream through tears and snot.

Alexander could barely see—just the haze of bright lights as he was dragged to the kitchen, and he realized that his panicked screams were matched by his mother's furious ones.

His shirt was tugged up over his head, and he heard:

You made me do this!

And then he felt the boiling water on his back. He had been kneeling and collapsed flat. He was hyperventilating, and turned on his side and was kicking wildly, trying to make the scalding ache stop.

Why? He sobbed.

The lights went out.

There was never any discussion of any of it again. And like most scars incurred in childhood, when the world is small and each such shakeup seems so significant, the wounds on his back wore heavily on his mind at first, then faded as time passed and his world expanded, growing as forgotten as the stories of how they came to be there.

But the dream he began having that night only grew more real as he grew older.

* * * *

"With all due respect, Alexander, let me see if I understand the implications of what you're saying here," said Dr. Anders Kane, chair of the physics department, standing before the microphone in the center of the room.

There was a rumble of assent across the University's conference room.

Alexander saw the professors and other doctoral students that made up the audience of about 40 engage in a collective nervous release. He'd sort of expected it. He had, after all, written the thesis. He knew that most of the professors in the various departments he'd been working in were skeptical to say the least—in fact he'd expected that Kane had been planning whatever he was going to say here now for some time. Alexander knew that to Kane, this entire project was not only unworthy of scholarly consideration, but filled with claims so questionable that it demanded the public humiliation of its author.

A few people whispered to one another. A snicker ran across a face or two. A fellow in the back massaged his temples theatrically and folded his arms.

"What you are saying is that if I had no idea what an apple was—if I were raised in a society without apples, and then someone gave me an apple, not telling me what it was, and I ate it," Kane thought for a second. "That the apple would somehow *understand* that I was ignorant of—what you call its 'nature,' on a quantum level. And so my experience of eating it would be *different* from someone else's, based on—*how the apple felt about me?*"

There was hushed laughter.

"It's instructive that you chose the apple to illustrate the point, Dr. Kane," Alexander responded. "I think it's no coincidence that some of our oldest and most familiar stories deal with this specific dilemma—of knowledge or lack thereof as it pertains to an object like an *apple*. Eve, remember, in Genesis, is misled about the *nature* of the apple that she consumes. She is deceived by the serpent. In fact there are some—what you might call esoteric—interpretations of this parable that speak directly to that. They indicate that perhaps what the story is trying to tell us not about good and evil, but about our observation of objects and the physical responses we provoke—on what we now understand to be the quantum level. In fact if we leap ahead in theological history to the ritual of transubstantiation, we see—"

Alexander's microphone squealed briefly with feedback and he jerked back from it, waving slight apologies at the crowd.

"Mr. Ollis," Dr. Kane said, "I find it unbelievable that you have been able to reach this point in this institution, in this department, pursuing this type of absurdity and calling it scholarship. This is not the comp. lit department, Mr. Ollis. We do *science* here. We do not debate confused, conceptually unsound metaphysics like a bunch of benighted 2nd century Neoplatonists. If I had an apple right now, I would throw it at you."

Dr. Kane walked away from the microphone as the audience chatter began again. Kane took a few steps away, then turned back and said:

"Would the fact that I just told you it was coming change how it felt when it hit you?"

Dr. Kane stormed out.

"Any more questions?" Alexander said.

Dr. Aniella Barsuk, associate professor and quantum physics wunderkind, approached the microphone.

"You must intend to conduct some sort of experiment to give credence to these bold assertions," Dr. Barsuk said. "What would such an experiment look like?"

"I have good reason to believe that I will someday demonstrate, without question, that the principle I have described is at work in the natural world," Alexander said.

"I don't think you know what 'reason' means," Dr. Barsuk replied.

"Then I have faith."

Alexander's microphone squealed.

* * * *

"But hey, that's why I do this folks—for science. We'll never know unless I try it. And thank you, user *JeanClaudeVanDoucheBag* for telling that I'm the *man*, I appreciate it—and *you* are the man for donating that $5. In fact everyone out there in the Bowelcano Army is the man—whether you're man or woman, and especially if you send a few bucks my way here or on Patreon."

Alexander walked into the bathroom and placed his palms on the sink, resting his weight.

On the floor were the remnants of the statue—if it could be considered that—which yesterday he had smashed with a hammer. Inside he had found what the book had promised. A thin black, desiccated worm-like thing, nearly eight inches long with two puckered, empty blind eye sockets at one end.

He had thrown on the scalding hot shower, grinning and gritting his teeth with the streams slashing at his naked back and the thing at his feet. He had performed the rites of reanimation the book described.

Now, as he considered the sludgy brown residue ringing the bathtub, a sensation of elation nearly floored him. Things were in motion.

He heard from the computer speakers in the other room:

"And so ladies and gentlemen I give you, the—Selk'nam, is that is? Sorry if I didn't pronounce that quite right folks, the Selk'nam Mudskipper. And Wikipedia tells me. let's see,"

While the Mudskipper was reputedly eaten alive for a number of ritualistic practices by indigenous tribes, there are no known peoples currently who eat the amphibian—generally considered an invasive species—for either ritual or sustenance.

"No known peoples?" Rex said. "Well now there's going to be one peoples. People. Persons. Am I using the royal 'we,' here now? Send a message if you think we're going to start a trend here of eating Selk'nam Mudskippers."

As soon as Alexander began to hear that Wikipedia entry read aloud— the one he had written himself, based on sources he had also, earlier, written himself—he was on his way out the door.

Alexander, bounding out of the room, saw on the screen Rex Vesuvius locked in a strange side-eyed stare-down with the awkward creature's watery, entrancingly sympathetic and quite human eyes, as it sat quivering dumbly.

* * * *

The reputation for rural Nebraska being the kind of place where people never locked their doors was borne out as Alexander rushed across the street from the motel, threw open the front door of the house to which he'd yesterday delivered a package, and rushed down the basement stairs.

"And it's—you know guys," Rex said, "It's not—it's actually not bad!"

Alexander saw the brown thing oozing and hissing and struggling as Rex gripped and chewed it, the slick goop of its innards splattering like chocolate pudding.

"It tastes, you're not going to believe me, like marshmallows. That's exactly what—hold on—"

Rex gulped down the eyeballs and sucked the remnants off of his fingers. He then spun to face the stranger who had barreled into his home. Rex looked on dreamily, as if only dimly aware of Alexander's presence. His eyes were then suddenly, wildly senile—watery and bloodshot with confusion. Alexander could tell that his unexpected presence in the basement was insignificant in the midst of the strange sensory onslaught Rex was undoubtedly experiencing.

"What?" Rex said to Alexander. "What *is* it?"

Alexander nodded.

"You can't know," he whispered. "But you will."

Alexander turned his back on the scene—the first half of which he'd seen so many times in his mind's eye. He heard uncontrollable belching, then a howling scream, the gurgling; the collapsing.

And then there was something new. *Light.*

A bright purple light that colored the room, near-blinded Alexander even with his eyes averted. Arms folded, head bowed—tears began not to pour, but to squirt from his eyes.

As the light went dim, he heard a cool, smooth voice that registered, synaesthetically, as being same purple as the light. The sense-disrupting voice asked:

מדוע

Alexander turned and faced Her.

She stood, taller than Alexander, amid the grizzly cast-offs of the broken human pupa from which she had torn forth, slick with red like a child after birth. Her body was sleek but motherly and her arms hugged her large, full breasts. Her wings behind her twitched and shivered and flapped off hunks of gristle. Her facial features displayed the preternatural beauty of a being beyond human understanding—austere, strong, created along the lines of a more perfect geometry than the dim shadow that is the human one.

And those eyes, the same blue eyes that had bulged ugly from the sockets of the form to which she'd been banished, were now set perfectly in the angelic face and stared, glassy, icy and soft, at Alexander.

At the beauty, Alexander's mind began to unravel. He grinned like a dumb child and went knock-kneed and scratched the back of his head awkwardly.

She asked the question again—this time at a shriek that grew louder, then louder, until the room, then the world, flexed like it was drawn on an acetate sheet that someone was bending.

The bright foolish smile spread further on Alexander's face. Tears of blood poured from his eyes. He ejaculated two or three times in rapid succession and acknowledged it with only vague grinning embarrassment. And as his mind turned to a slurry, he felt the satisfied awareness that he'd done what he was meant to do.

Alexander had awoken the sisters of the Nephilim, the ones who walked and ruled the earth before man, whose own brothers had wiped their names even from myth—about whom no writings had remained except in one tome. Now they would awaken and stretch their wings.

Outside, the sky darkened. And as She sat down on the floor, wings stretching behind her, knees pulled up near her chest, Alexander crawled instinctively to her.

She cradled him in her arms and Her quiet tears ran onto his face and rinsed it as he nursed at her teat; Mother of a new world to come.

SPECTRES UNTOLD
Maxwell I. Gold

A long time ago, when stars were young
There was a place, that in firmaments hung;
So high above where darkness lies
And the light comes to die.
It's there in dreams, where memories fade,
Unreachable cliffs, next to swampy glades.
A realm aloft inside my mind,
Where one day, the truth I'll find.

Along a path, I wandered so,
Into this place, where dreams daren't go.
Alone I walked, under burning skies,
Until upon a glade, did I espy,
An endless field stretched on and on;
Where a tall dark tower, lay off the horizon.
Its shadow hung in the glow of the morning,
Like a ghostly spectre, eternally warning.

To that tower I fearfully walked,
As the shadow behind me crept and stalked.
Past the glade and its youthful presence,
Under the stars and their leaking phosphorescence.
High above the tower stood,
In marbled frame and horrid good.
Upon its door, I stood and waited,
Where I read its warning, unabated.

"Beware the spectres, ghosts untold,
Reactionary haunts of old.
They lurk in shadows and creep in darkness,
And twist our minds, most heartless."
The warning read, quite odd and queer,
Though I ignored it with a simple jeer.
The door was tall, massive, and ancient.
I pressed its hinge open, inside what waited;
Passed wholly dark, and moist spaces,
Immense vaulted ceilings that loomed high in places.

Inside I found what struck me true,
A piece of history that seemed new.
Time then sang an ode to me,
Of how things will never again be.
"The stars will cry and gates will crack,
Behind their latches, they'll never go back."
The atrium was large and empty,
With corridors winding madly.

Through endless pathways and curling arches,
The insides were as mysterious as the darkness.
Still I wondered, how this tower remained,
As a fixture in a world unchanged.
There were no markers or remnants there,
Or beacons bright, just ancient and bare.
Was this place as timeless as,
The world it sat, in aghast.

No other people walked the halls,
Of the great stone tower or made a call.
The world undone and lost to all,
But the tower remained, after the fall.
Still inside I walked along,
The endless halls that song their song,
"Beware the spectres, ghosts untold,
Reactionary haunts of old.
They lurk in shadows and creep in darkness,
To twist our minds, the most heartless."

I heard the song, as it mimicked,
The ancient warning, its haunting limerick.
What were these ghosts, spirits untold,
Who sought to damn the world of old?
I struggled in vein to comprehend,
And hoped I'd find out in the end;
What reactionary plight unfurled,
To reign such chaos on this world.
And condemn the stars in waning pity,
By deeds so horrid, a cosmic misanthropy.

So on I went, into the dark,

Despite the warnings, from gaunts that hark.
Until I came to a winding stairwell,
WHERE IT TOOK ME, TIME WOULD TELL.
IT CURLED ALONG THE SPIRE WITH EASE,
A BOUNDLESS TREK, THAT DID LITTLE TO PLEASE.
PAST GRAY STONE STEPS, AND STAINED-GLASS SKIES,
SUCH WANTON BEAUTY NEVER PIERCED MY EYES.

HIGHER I CLIMBED ON THOSE GRAY STONE STEPS,
AS THE TOWER DECAYED AND SHADOWS CREPT.
THE STAINED-GLASS SKIES CRACKED APART,
AND ITS INSIDES WEPT, DOWN TO ITS MARBLED HEART.
THERE SEEMED TO BE NO END IN SIGHT,
ON THIS WINDING PATH, MY INFINITE PLIGHT.
UNTIL I REACHED ITS SUMMIT PEAK,
WHEREUPON A DOOR DID CREAK.

TALL AND MOLDED, WITH TIME'S SCARS,
THE ANCIENT GATE WAS THEIRS AND OURS;
A WAY TO STOP THESE HAUNTS UNTOLD,
BUT TO NO AVAIL COULD IT HOLD.
THE RUSTED LETTERS, BROWN AND GROTESQUE,
READ THOSE WORDS AS I CLUTCHED MY BREAST.
"BEWARE THE SPRECTRES, GHOSTS UNTOLD,
REACTIONARY HAUNTS OF OLD.
BEYOND THIS WAY, IT IS NOT CLEAR,
BUT IT IS CERTAIN, OUR END WE FEAR."

THOSE SPECTRES HAUNT MY MEMORY FOREVER,
REACTIONARY SHADES, IN GRUESOME SPLENDOR.
WHEREUPON THESE STEPS I STAND,
FROZEN IN PLACE, AFRAID TO DEMAND;
FOR AN ANSWER OF HOW OR WHY,
DOOMED TO WAIT, UNTIL THE STARS WILL CRY.

A LONG TIME AGO, WHEN STARS WERE YOUNG
THERE WAS A PLACE, THAT IN FIRMAMENTS HUNG;
SO HIGH ABOVE WHERE DARKNESS LIES
AND THE LIGHT COMES TO DIE.
IT'S THERE IN DREAMS, WHERE MEMORIES FADE,
UNREACHABLE CLIFFS, NEXT TO SWAMPY GLADES.
A REALM ALOFT INSIDE MY MIND,
WHERE MAYBE ONE DAY, THE TRUTH I'LL FIND.

✡

BELLADONNA'S KISS
Ashley Dioses

Her purple petals sway,
And ever do I stray
Anear her–she, I say,
Dims asphodel.
And like a serpent's hiss,
The Belladonna's kiss
Brings dwale I will dismiss–
How cruel, her spell.

AMONG THE FALLEN
Ann K. Schwader

The sun mends nothing. Only nightfall holds
what healing may remain to us who wait
with broken pinions, just beyond that veil
so few acknowledge. Fallen from our own
mythology, forgotten now by those
whose fear & faith created it, we fade
to footnotes. To the moonlight that prevails
upon our darkness. In this long Almost
of exile, we remember heaven's wars,
but never we fought for—or the cost
of one small rock. We vowed to reign in hell
& landed here. Immortal, soul-maimed, torn
to shadows, we drift whispering till dawn
dispels what few illusions we have left.

(after Elinor Wylie)

OKIKO'S DOLL
Stefano Frigieri

Translation by Amanda Blee

Dolls are very precious in Japanese animism: they are the faithful companions of little girls all throughout their childhood, protecting them by attracting bad luck and storing it inside themselves.

To help girls face the inevitable separation from their dolls, collective funerals are organised on designated days of the year, during which the girls face the pain of separation, sharing it with others. This way, the dolls also finally find peace, taking all the evil they collected during their lifetime, kept locked away inside, with them on their last journey.

* * * *

On an altar inside the Mannenjin temple in Hokkaido, lies a small shrine, almost buried beneath flowers, small origami animals, incense sticks and baskets of fresh fruit and toys.

Here you have the distinct feeling of standing before something important, something that commands respect and veneration.

But the atmosphere, heavy with the strange tension that is transmitted to whoever enters the temple, quickly transforms those feelings into fear.

Inside the shrine lies a small doll with long black hair, dressed in old-fashioned clothing, now faded by time.

It seems strange to associate such a huge demonstration of devotion to something that is not a religious image, but there is something incredible about that doll: its silky hair has been growing for almost seventy years, as if it were the hair of a living person, but how and why it keeps on growing is still an enigma.

A monk is assigned to take care of the doll's hair. He washes and combs it, and trims it with loving care, keeping it tidy, always ready to be admired and venerated by the numerous and frequent visitors.

When I went to see it, I came out of the temple feeling strangely uncomfortable.

The doll doesn't look particularly sweet. There's nothing about her that inspires tenderness or kindness. The deep cracks on her face resemble wrinkles; her eyes are small, cold distant globes, that observe the pilgrims as if they don't even exist, as if she were the only real thing in a fictitious world.

The long-haired doll did not have a funeral like her doll-companions. She was kept there, perhaps as a warning, or perhaps as a sign of something far more important. And I wanted to know her story.

After years of research, I was able to reconstruct part of what had happened, the rest I deduced.

This strange and terrible story is the result.

* * * *

Ayao, was a sweet little girl who lived in a village in southern Hokkaido.

Her father was a fisherman and every day he faced the hardships and hidden dangers of the sea to give his wife and daughter the best life possible.

Ayao's mother contributed to the family's meager income by weaving vegetable and fruit baskets, which left her hands cracked and had ruined her eyesight.

Above all, they tried to make sure their beloved daughter wanted for nothing but, however much they tried, however many sacrifices they made, their modest financial resources meant they were unable to satisfy all of Ayao's requests for the toys and playthings which, at her age, seemed more important than food and clothing.

Her classmates were aware of this and every day they would wave their beautiful dolls in her face with practiced cruelty.

Ayao owned very few things: a few animals made from sacking stuffed with straw, with two stitches for eyes, a pinwheel and a ball made from cloth.

Her classmates constantly made fun of her, saying she smelled of fish.

At first, Ayao had tried to wash herself thoroughly every day, scrubbing at her skin with stiff-bristled brushes until it hurt.

But there was nothing she could do. They still said she smelled.

In the end, she gave up. She clutched her stuffed dog, worn threadbare by the passing of time, close to her chest, and suffered in silence.

One of these girls was Okiko. She had a beautiful doll with long black hair, that her brother had bought her at a market in Sapporo a few months earlier, and she never missed the chance to show her off with pride and satisfaction.

Ayao was fascinated by it but, only when Okiko was distracted, did she dare reach out and touch it

She grew sad and angry. Every day she returned home and begged her father to buy her a doll, always receiving a kind but firm refusal.

Until, after yet more pleas, accompanied by copious tears, her father gave in and decided he had to do something.

There was barely enough money for food, so he decided to make the doll himself. Taking advantage of the bad weather that prevented him from going out fishing, he set to work, and after a week, his efforts paid off. His little masterpiece was finished.

The result was a delightful little kokeshi doll in smooth white wood. He'd painted a brightly colored dress on its cylindrical body with the paint he used for his boat, and on its round little head he had painted black hair, colored ribbons, narrow eyes and a smiling red mouth.

As soon as it was finished, he held it out in front of him and solemnly asked it to protect his daughter then, confident that his plea had been heard, he handed it over to Ayao with a satisfied smile.

Finally, the little girl was happy. Now she could proudly show off her tiny but incredibly precious doll to the others.

Which she did, and for a while everything seemed to be going well.

She had called the doll Maruo and never missed a chance to proudly show her off to her classmates who, finally, began to regard her with respect, almost envy.

All except one: Okiko.

She couldn't stand the annoying little brat, and she liked her even less now she dared give herself airs and graces and look down on her and her beautiful doll.

One morning, the inevitable happened.

Okiko was mad at the whole world. Perhaps she had been scolded or had argued with her sister. The fact was, she was looking for a victim, someone to take her anger out on, and she found Ayao, playing with her treasured little doll.

She walked over, determined to teach her a lesson. Maliciously, Okiko snatched the doll away from her. 'This isn't a doll,' she announced. 'Just an ugly piece of wood. It's only good for lighting the fire!' and she abruptly tossed Maruo into the flames.

Ayao was paralyzed, speechless. But not one tear fell from her huge eyes, frozen in shock.

She watched in silence as her doll burned then, still silent, turned and made her way home, cold tears finally streaking down her hot, furious face.

Okiko watched as she slowly walked away, never once looking back. She'd been expecting screams and shouts but in the end all she got was silence.

A woman who entered the room when she heard the voices of the other girls, who had seen what had happened and were unsure whether to laugh or cry, hadn't dared stop Ayao.

Okiko was scolded bitterly but it was too late: the tragedy had happened. The damage was done.

When Ayao arrived home, she immediately locked herself in her room, without saying anything to her mother.

* * * *

Next morning, Ayao got up as if nothing had happened, prepared her own breakfast, got dressed and left.

Her mother, exhausted after a sleepless night of intense work, was happy to let her go.

When she arrived at the school gates, however, she stopped and thought for a moment, then turned confidently towards the fields. She wandered a little, her small blue bookbag bouncing on her thin shoulders with every step, her small braids dancing in the air like the antennas of an ant, alert to everything around her. She seemed calm, as if she had already forgotten the unpleasantness of the previous day, but thousands of horrible thoughts swirled around inside her head.

It was a beautiful day in late February and the sun brought with it the promise of a spring full of warmth and light.

Ayao spent the morning sitting by the river, thinking and playing with the grass and the insects.

The real reason for her apparent calm was that she had replaced her sadness with purpose and one thought buzzed relentlessly in her mind, leaving her no time for tears and pain.

When it was time to go back for lunch, she decided to stop by the village temple.

She couldn't explain why, just that something had told her to do it.

She stood at the entrance, admiring the imposing red columns, the intricate beams and the pitched roof adorned with fantastic figures: writhing, colorful dragons, strange creatures with menacing fangs, severe old men with long white beards, their arms outstretched, as if they were pointing at her.

Everything was so immense, so enormous and mysterious, that she suddenly felt out of place: a small helpless creature in a hard, hostile world.

Suddenly all the sadness that she had been ignoring came crashing down on her.

Almost as if in answer to her gloomy thoughts, she caught sight of an object glistening in the sunshine. It was a small, dusty daruma doll, watching her with a resolute scowl from the nearby pebbles.

She picked it up and dusted it off. The red that she had glimpsed beneath the patina of dirt was now revealed it all its crimson glory. The dark outline highlighted the stylised face, the lightly sketched moustache and the two blank eyes, waiting to be drawn.

Ayao knew exactly what it was. It was a spherical head without a body that represented the spirit of the Buddha.

She also knew, because her mother had taught her, that if you painted in one of the eyes, you could make a wish. You could only paint in the other eye, however, when your wish was granted.

She noticed that the daruma's eyes were still white. No one had painted them yet. It seemed like it was just waiting for her to make her wish.

She put the doll down on the ground and it wobbled for a moment, making a faint creaking sound in the dust.

Ayao was determined to take home that little miracle sent by fate.

Before anyone could intervene and stop her, she hid the daruma under her dress and quickly ran home.

She spent the afternoon sitting, staring at it, wondering what to ask. Then suddenly, everything became clear. She knew exactly how to use the daruma to achieve her goal.

Now it all seemed so easy.

* * * *

Next morning, Ayao woke up earlier than usual, ate a hearty breakfast and went to school.

When she reached the large room where the girls usually played, she immediately headed for Okiko, her eyes serious and resolute, her hands deep in her pockets.

The girl was sitting down, engrossed in combing her doll's long black hair. When she saw her coming, fearing that Ayao wanted to hit her in revenge for what she had done, she raised her hands to protect herself.

Ayao looked at Okiko and smiled. She pulled the daruma and a pencil out of her pocket and quickly drew a black dot in the doll's left eye and held it in front of Okiko, right in her face, her lips tight, her eyes narrowed in intense concentration.

She held the doll still, while the other girl gazed at her in amazement then, after several seconds of silence, she announced, 'There, that's what I want!'

Then she turned and left, without saying another word.

Okiko sat there, motionless, watching her leave then, sensing that something was wrong, looked down at her doll. One look at those small glass eyes, staring back at her, and her hand began to tremble. Perhaps from fear, that awful brat had given her a terrible fright, or perhaps because the doll was moving on its own.

Whatever it was, the doll's beautiful black hair began to flutter in the air, as if ruffled by an unknown breeze.

Okiko stared at her doll until there was nothing left of her mind. A nothing as cold and solid as stone.

Everyone rushed to help, but she never moved, not even once.

Her eyes were glued to the doll, which was now as lifeless as her, staring back in the exact same way.

It was as if they had become one and the same.

Okiko was carried home and laid out on her bed, but in all that time she never reacted in any way.

Only when they tried to take the doll from her, did she put up such strenuous resistance that they were forced to give up for fear of harming her.

She had absolutely no interest in anything that happened around her. The only thing she did was cling to her doll and gaze into its eyes.

Okiko remained like that, immobile, for the rest of her short life.

When she died, slowly and without even a whimper, as if she had finally surrendered to some mysterious evil, her father ordered that she be buried together with her doll.

Her mother objected, however: she was convinced, with a certainty she was unable to explain, that somewhere inside that inanimate object, her daughter was still alive. Till her last moment, her eyes had remained glued to the doll's, as if transmitting the light from her own eyes to those of the doll.

Eyes that had refused to close, even when life had left her. Eyes that were so wide and still they seemed made of glass.

They had to force her fingers, almost breaking them, to prise the doll from her desperate grip.

Okiko's parents decided to preserve it inside a shrine and place it on an altar inside their own home.

Every day, her mother spoke to the doll as if she were talking to her daughter.

She continued to speak to her until the end, without even the slightest doubt.

From that moment on, day after day, the little doll's hair began to grow, and to this day, almost fifty years later, it is still growing.

Tests carried out later confirmed that the long black hair, trimmed regularly by the monk at the temple, is alive and unequivocally human.

In itself, the story of Okiko's doll is pretty terrible. One of those stories that stays in the back of your mind, only to reappear one day, waking you screaming in the middle of the night.

Unfortunately, that wasn't the end of the story.

* * * *

For two weeks, Ayao waited patiently for the right moment.

It finally arrived on March 3rd, the day of Hinamatsuri.

On this day, in a splendid setting, against a backdrop of peach blossom, female children and their dolls are celebrated in a ceremony that prays for their continued health and happiness.

The dolls are carried down to the local square and paraded in front of everyone or displayed in front of houses or in neat rows on improvised shelves inside temples, where they are honoured like tiny divinities.

When Ayao announced she wanted to go, her mother felt she couldn't refuse, probably thinking it would help her get over the death of her friend.

She had watched as Ayao sobbed for two whole days, holding the daruma tightly in her arms, but when the girl was alone, all she did was frown, staring into the doll's empty eye, her lips contracted.

From the way she insisted, her mother understood that it was a very important day for her daughter and, though she was very busy, she agreed to accompany her.

When she realised the girl no longer had her kokeshi, she asked where it was.

The girl told her she had lost it.

She was surprised at her calmness: her daughter had pleaded and suffered so much before receiving it!

She was even more surprised when she saw the small, round daruma clutched firmly in her daughter's small hands.

However, she had preferred not to ask anything else.

The little doll was now perfectly clean, resplendent in its red, gold, black and white colors.

As they walked towards the village square, Ayao all dressed up in the only good dress she owned, her mother finally found the courage to ask where she had found it, but all she got in reply was a candid and disarming smile.

Then she noticed that Ayao had only drawn in one of the doll's eyes and, remembering the legend, she understood that the wish, obviously made by her daughter, had yet to come true.

Perhaps that was why they were there.

It didn't occur to her to ask anything else. After all, why worry? Ayao was happy and it looked like it was going to be a truly beautiful day.

They had set off towards the centre of the village early in the morning, under a beautiful, cloudless blue sky.

Colored garlands were strung from rooftops and through the branches of the trees and on every corner were stalls, on which stood sparkling pitchers of amazake, baskets of savoury snacks, trays of various colored treats, bouquets of flowers and small, twirling pinwheels.

On large, tiered platforms covered in red velvet were long rows of dolls, sumptuously dressed as noble women, courtesans and empresses.

The square was packed with people, young and old, parents and children. In pride of place, however, were the girls with their dolls, dressed, as tradition required, identically.

With every step, Ayao turned her head, gazing ecstatically at the wonderful world around her.

However, she hadn't forgotten her real reason for being there, and her eyes were searchlights as she scrutinized the crowd. In her hand she held the daruma, which turned with every step like a diviner's rod. Then she saw them, joking among themselves, dressed exactly like the dolls they held proudly in their arms, smiling and happy as if they had already forgotten all the pain and suffering for the fate of their little friend.

They were her classmates: Oren, who always pulled her hair, Kako, who had once pushed her over, making her skin her knee, Maya, who laughed whenever she walked past - just laughed, and perhaps that's what hurt the most.

She dropped her mother's hand and walked quietly over to the group of girls, who were now howling with laughter.

She pointed the daruma straight at them, just for a few seconds. They didn't even notice she was there.

Then she turned, joined her mother, and resumed her stroll.

Wherever she went, whenever she saw a girl holding a doll, whether she knew her or not, she walked up to her, raised the daruma, then walked away again.

Her mother watched, uncomprehending.

Suddenly, the screams began, at first barely distinguishable from the loud chatter of the crowd.

They were isolated at first, becoming more numerous and more acute until it hurt her ears: desperate screams that sounded like the roar of a rushing river that had broken its banks and was sweeping through the village.

As her mother looked around in amazement, Ayao continued her terrible mission.

Undaunted, unhesitating.

Then, when the whole village was in chaos, and the people around them had lost all control, running around mindlessly, the girl turned around, a satisfied expression on her face, and serenely walked back to her mother, who stood there, lost, her hands clasped to her ears trying to block out the absurd noise, and whispered calmly, 'Shall we go?'

The woman looked down at her daughter and saw that, while in one hand she was holding a doll dressed in a beautiful emerald green dress, which she must have found somewhere, in her other hand she still held the daruma, which now had two, perfectly drawn eyes.

* * * *

I arrived in the village intent on finding out how the story ended.

I was sent to see the old temple caretaker, who had been fifteen at the time, and was the only person left who had witnessed the events.

He confirmed that what I'd read in newspapers from the time was true and that his fellow villagers had taken it upon themselves to keep the story alive over the years, retelling it whenever they got the chance, making sure no one forgot what had happened.

It had become a kind of local legend, which also served as a warning never to let it happen again.

They understood what had happened: something had been transferred from the girls to their dolls. Something important, the loss of which had isolated them from the world and transformed them into inert creatures: their vital essence.

They didn't know how, and they certainly didn't know why. All they knew was, the dolls had become the girls' only link to reality.

Perhaps, their parents had thought, the only way to destroy that evil bond and purify the dolls, was to confine them to a sacred place.

So that is what they had done.

Unfortunately, the caretaker told me, lowering his eyes to avoid meeting mine, it hadn't been as successful as they had hoped.

After a few seconds, during which I preferred to leave him alone with his thoughts, he raised his head, his gaze far away in a distant time, and told me what had become of the girls.

Over time, some had recovered their sanity while others had been lost forever.

'No one has ever understood why all this happened. The only thing we're sure of is that whatever is hidden inside the dolls is now in this temple, guarded and protected.'

With a long, bony finger he pointed to the sturdy chain and the large padlock which held the solid, painted wooden doors tightly closed. 'Yes,' he said, wiping his forehead with a huge handkerchief. 'The temple is closed. In the beginning, many years ago, we went inside to take offerings, something that might help, but then we gave up. None of us could stay in there for too long without the risk of going crazy. I can't explain it any other way. Try it for yourself, if you wish.'

He handed me a key.

I took it and stared at it for a few seconds as it sparkled in the midday sun.

I glanced around me, not knowing what to do.

Everything had been kept in working order: the perfectly polished chain, the huge, well-oiled padlock.

At the entrance stood three rows of small candles, surrounded by flowers and images of the Buddha.

In the yellowish grass, I spotted a small jizo, a large hat protecting its head from the sun. Moss had transformed its cheerful, serene smile into a grimace of pain.

Strips of paper bearing Taoist prayers of protection were hung above the doors.

I placed my hands on the heavy wooden door and leaned in close to listen.

What I heard, against the backdrop of the old caretaker's anxious sighs as he watched me, rubbing his wrinkled hands together, was nothing. Simply nothing.

But it was a concrete, solid, compact nothingness.

Something that penetrated my soul, found its dead center then began to dig, making a noise that was a combination of anguished screams and desperate cries. Something that, in only a few seconds, became unbearable.

I snatched my hands away from the rough wooden door with a shiver of horror and fear, wondering what it would be like to enter that place.

I gave the key back to the caretaker and walked away without saying a single word.

From the corner of my eye, I saw him quickly hide it in the folds of his robe, his back curved as if crushed by an enormous weight.

* * * *

Even today, when I remember that horrible sensation and see the distant, empty eyes of the doll with long black hair inside the shrine, staring out at the nothing that surrounds it, I imagine what lies behind those two small pieces of glass, what hell they are hiding.

Then I fall to my knees and pray, pray with all my might.

HEATSEEKER
Tim Curran

1

The screaming brought them.

They came running through the narrow passages in their green terrain suits—Wells, Sarrasin, and Gill—kicking up clouds of pink Martian dust. Screaming wasn't something you heard much in the immense, dead desolation of Mars, but once you heard it, you would never forget it.

Bouncing through winding corridors in low gravity, trying to stay on their feet, they climbed over hoses and bumped their helmets on pipes and tripped over heaps of rubble. This was the reality of subsurface mining on an alien world: weird gravity and crowding.

The screaming echoed through their headsets, shrill and deranged, the agonized sound of an animal being tortured to death. By the time they reached #4 Compressor Shack, it had stopped.

And the silence that followed was somehow worse.

Like hearing footsteps coming at you in a dark, empty house, then hearing nothing.

They stopped running once they entered the high cavern where the shack and maintenance sheds were housed.

Sarrasin was the first one into the shack. "Dientz!" he cried out, his voice modulated through both internal and external speakers. "Dientz! Royer! Jesus Christ, where the hell are you guys?"

"Out here," Gill said. "Out here."

Dientz was over near the entrance to an intake shaft, crouching there, rocking back and forth on his heels, gloved fists pressed to the bubble of his helmet. His face looked yellow and slack. His shiny green insulated jumpsuit was spattered with something dark like he'd been sprayed with ink.

"Dientz!" Sarrasin said as he raced over there. "Where's Royer? What the hell gives—"

But then he saw the same thing that made Gill and Wells turn away.

Royer was right there by Dientz.

Sarrasin could see fragments of his terrain suit, except now it was shredded and torn, dipped in red.

"Oh, Jesus," he said.

That about covered it. Royer looked like about 200 pounds of red, well-marbled meat that had been caught in an ice auger, sucked in and spit out the other end. He was splashed over the walls of the cavern and down the intake shaft a good ten feet. Bits of him hung like stalactites from the roof overhead, fifteen feet up. Like some kind of sick joke, one of his boots was dangling from a lip of rock above...a knob of bone spilling a red icicle.

Sarrasin wanted to be sick, but he didn't dare.

He just kept looking at the remains, amazed at how most of Royer's anatomy was still connected, spread out maybe thirty feet, but still connected. Some of him was in the shaft, some of him was hanging from the cavern wall, and some of him was spilled underfoot, yet linked by muscle and tendon and nerve ganglia as if he'd been full of springs and had exploded. One of his hands, still in the glove, twitched once or twice and went still. His blood was everywhere, crystallized in the subzero temperatures like rubies.

Deintz got to his feet and nearly fell over. "I heard him scream...I came running out...then he hit me, Royer fucking hit me..."

Gill grabbed him by the arm. "Hit you with what? What the hell do you mean?"

Deintz kept shaking his head inside his helmet. "I was hit *with* him. I saw a big shadow...something huge, something fast jumping around... and then Royer...oh Christ, Royer...he...what was left of him...*slammed into me...*"

They got it then, all of them, though they didn't understand a thing. Deintz stumbled about in a tight little circle, moving from Sarrasin to Gill to Wells and they each in turn backed away from him. Maybe it was what he was splattered with and maybe it was something else. He began to sob, then to gasp. He went down to his knees and frantically tried to pop the plastic bubble of his helmet, which would expose him to the frigid, poisonous atmosphere.

Sarrasin and Gill took hold of him so he couldn't break the seal. The atmospheric pressure of the red planet would have boiled away the moisture in his sinuses, eyes, mouth, and lungs...if the massive decompression didn't kill him first.

His lunch came out in a steaming gush, splattering the inside of his face bubble with vomit. He gagged and coughed, making choking sounds.

"Goddamn idiot," Gill said, her mouth pulled into a scowl.

They took him back into the shack and sealed the airlock, decompressed. Then they all took their helmets off, helped Dientz clean up.

It took some time for him to come out of it and when he did, he just kept looking at them with wide, glazed eyes like he was drunk. But he wasn't drunk.

Wells kept shaking his head. He looked over at Sarrasin. "What was he trying to do, boss? You puke in your helmet for chrissake, you never take that bubble off. Was he trying to kill himself or what?"

Gill said, "Maybe you saw what he saw, you'd wanna kill yourself, too."

2

Fifteen minutes later, sipping a mug of hot coffee, Dientz started to talk. "It was like I said…just a blur, a big shadow or something. Whatever it was, it was already finished with Royer by the time I got there. It wasn't my fault. It wasn't any of it my fault. There wasn't nothing I could do."

"Course not," Gill told him, but it almost sounded like she didn't mean it.

"What did you see?" Sarrasin asked. "Just take your time. You were in the shack, you heard that screaming on your set, you got suited up and went through the airlock…what then?"

"Just like I said," Dientz told them. "Just that blur, a shadow or something sliding around and then he slammed into me, Royer slammed into me, knocked me flat. Next thing I know, he's…well, he was all like you saw. Then you guys were there."

Wells and Gill looked at each other.

"That's it?" Sarrasin said.

"That's it."

Sarrasin didn't like it. He believed every word Dientz told him. Something had happened, something terrible, but as to what that really was, who could say? Royer had been slaughtered. But how and by what?

"You quit looking at me like that, Wells," Dientz said.

"Like what?"

"Like what, he says. You been looking at me like that ever since we got into the shack, since I came around. I know what you're thinking, I know what's going on in that mind of yours, but you listen to me, you sonofabitch, there wasn't anything I could do. It wasn't my fault."

"Never said it was."

"You telling me you're not thinking it?" Dientz set his coffee down. There was something in his eyes. Before it had been fear, shock, and revulsion. Now it was murder. "Royer was my friend. Not like you. He was good, he was decent. He cared about people. He wasn't an asshole like you, always saying shit behind peoples' backs."

Wells turned away. "Oh, shut the hell up."

"All right," Sarrasin said. "Everyone just settle down."

Gill wasn't saying anything; she was just watching.

Dientz pounded a fist on the table. "It's not me, boss, it's Wells. That dirty sonofabitch. He's acting like I killed Royer. Like I'd do something like that."

"Well, did you?" Wells put to him, then shook his head. "No, I'm figuring something came out of the tunnels and went after Royer. And you just pissed your pants and let it happen, scared shitless."

"Fuck you!"

Dientz was small, but wiry, and he launched himself right at Wells. And Wells was grinning, waiting for it. But Sarrasin and Gill got in-between them, breaking them apart like a couple mouthy drunks ready to go at it over a football game.

"Knock it off! Both of you!" Sarrasin shouted. "We can't afford this candyass shit! There's too much on the line here! Now both of you act your fucking ages because I'm not in the mood for this crap. We got a dead man out there and I wanna find out how he died. They'll be back to pick us up in two days and I want some answers by then. You boys with me on that? Good. Because you start in again and I'll crack both your heads together."

He meant what he was saying and they all knew it. Nobody said anything for a time.

"Get suited up," Sarrasin told them. "We're going back out there."

He figured it was the best thing for all considered. In here, in the normal gravity, those two could make mincemeat of each other, but out in the low gravity, they couldn't do much but dance around. The terrain suits they all wore were weighted to compensate for the low Martian gravity. You could move around fine in them, do anything you could on Earth, but if you tried running or fighting, anything really physical, you'd just bounce around comically. You could grab a 200-pound man and toss him thirty feet, but he'd just bounce. You couldn't really hurt him. There was no impact, just a lot of silly bouncing and hopping.

Suits and helmets on, they moved into the airlock, crowded shoulder to shoulder in there.

"You can wait in here if you want," Sarrasin told Dientz.

"No way," he said. "I'm going with you."

"Well, try not to piss yourself," Wells said.

"What did I tell you?" Sarrasin said to him.

The atmosphere in the airlock decompressed with a hiss and they stepped out into the cavern. Though nobody really wanted to, they went over to the body. They were all glad they couldn't smell through the helmets, because they'd gotten a good whiff of Dientz' suit in the shack and all that blood had smelled raw and savage. Just plain bad.

"You sure you saw something?" Sarrasin said. "A shape?"

Dientz shrugged. "I think so...I don't know. It happened too fast."

Sarrasin just sighed. "Could have been just about anything. Maybe Royer hit some kind of weird gas, maybe there was an explosion."

It sounded weak and nobody was buying it, not even Sarrasin. But he was in charge here, he had to keep everyone's head level. He had to feed them bullshit even if he knew it was an out and out lie. Because the idea of a monster running around down in the shafts, well, that wouldn't do at all.

"Explosion," Wells said, laughing dryly in his throat. "I like that. That's good. Take a long look at Royce, boss, weren't no explosion that did this. Look at that trauma, will ya? Look at those wounds…looks like somebody took a goddamn scythe after him."

Everybody was thinking it, but nobody was saying it, so Gill did. She said it in a whisper, but they all heard her. "Heatseeker," she said.

Sarrasin just shook his head. "C'mon, Gill, that's an urban legend. There is no such thing. Just talk."

"What about that crew they found in Sarvis Valley?" Wells pointed out. "They were gutted like this."

"Stop that," Sarrasin said.

But Wells shook his head. "Not about to, boss. Not now. Something got those men. You know it, I know it. The Company knows it. Only no one wants to talk about it."

Sarvis Valley was three klicks over the next rise, topside, and everyone there knew it.

"That business was all eighteen years ago. There was no evidence then and there's none now. Use your head." Sarrasin had been waiting for this. Oh yes. It was only a matter of time. "Just drop it. Last thing we need here, people, are ghost stories."

Mars was full of them.

You hung around the edges of the colonies or the far-flung outposts, you could hear stories that would turn your hair white, make you afraid to step outside at night. There were tales of Martian ghosts prowling the deserts, dead intelligences that could possess a man and make him kill himself. Crazy shit about dead Martian cities full of monsters and entire colonies that had vanished, things that scratched at your door in the dead of night and ancient voices that would call you to your death like sirens. The Heatseeker was just another one, a story passed around from the early days of exploration. The favorite Martian boogeyman. Anytime somebody went missing, the Heatseeker was resurrected.

But Wells was not pacified. "I'm thinking the Heatseeker ain't a ghost, boss. But something else. Something…something with big goddamned claws. And it's hunting us."

"Knock it off. You're acting like a kid afraid of the dark."

"I am afraid, boss."

And what could Sarrasin say to that?

"That's all bullshit, right?" Dientz said like he needed to believe it.

"Sure it is. No evidence whatsoever."

Gill motioned them towards a down of pink sand across the way. It was illuminated by her exterior LEDs. "How's this for evidence? It fit the bill?"

Pressed down in the soft sand was a grotesque print. Several of them, in fact. They were diamond-shaped, about five inches from tip to tip, with four smaller indentations spaced evenly around them. Like some sort of weird alien foot had been set down, one with spurs coming off it.

Gill said, "What leaves a track like that?"

"I know," Wells said. "It's some of that weird gas."

Sarrasin ignored him, studied the print. He was thinking maybe something had been set down there—a lot of somethings, because there were quite a few prints—but deep in the barren wastes of his soul, he knew better.

This was it.

This was the spoor of the beast.

The Heatseeker.

3

The real crazy thing is, it should have been a milk run.

The sort of thing they could have done with their eyes closed. Sarrasin and the others formed part of a large maintenance crew that bopped around the extensive, endless canyon system of the Tharsis Bulge performing general upkeep on a string of propellant factories and subsurface ore refineries, all completely automated. These installations were vital to man's existence on the Red Planet. The factories processed propellant from the raw carbon dioxide of the Martian atmosphere which was used to power the outgoing spacecraft for the long flights back to Earth. The refineries refined iron ore on-site to be used in composite metals for building, construction, just about anything. Everything was metal on Mars. With the lack of free oxygen in the atmosphere, nothing corroded.

So that was the deal. Sarrasin's team had been dropped off at the Rift Valley Refinery for a few days' work. The hovercraft would pick them up in 48 hours. All they had to do was make their checks, charge the batteries, blow out the lines, the usual.

And now this.

Royer was dead, slaughtered, and everyone was getting panicky. The four survivors were alone, hopelessly alone. The nearest colony was New Providence, some 500 kilometers to the east. Sarrasin could have called for an early pick-up, but that would've been a big deal. The hovercraft ran on tight, inflexible schedules like everything on Mars. If one of them had to divert a few hundred miles, it would mean some outpost wouldn't get their supplies or their relief team. There would be hell to pay and the bureaucracy would see to it that Sarrasin was never in charge of anything more challenging than a broom until he went back home in sixteen months.

But either way there was going to be hell to pay.

For there was something down in the mines with them.

Something that liked to kill.

4

"I can't stand this place," Dientz said as they stood watch just outside the maintenance conduit to Level #3 Substation. "I hate it here. I hate this whole goddamn place."

Gill just sighed. "Settle down, will ya? They'll be back to pick us up tomorrow afternoon. Just hang tight."

"I don't mean these mines, Gill. I mean this whole fucking planet. I hate it here. I just hate it. I hate the cold and these goddamned helmets. I hate the dust storms and the emptiness…I hate it all." He stood there in his terrain suit, peering around in his helmet with beady, watching eyes. "I grew up in Bayonne, you know? Goddamned New Jersey. I thought Bayonne was a shithole. But you know what? Bayonne's like fucking Palm Beach compared to this place."

Gill just shrugged, didn't bother arguing the point.

Sure, Mars was a hellhole. It was barren and desolate and goddamn spooky. But people kept making the trip same way they'd once kept making the trip to the Old West back on Earth. Why? Space, freedom, a new start…and money. Yeah, there was big money to be made on Mars. The mining companies were making a fortune and they needed everyone they could get. So in the last thirty years since the early manned expeditions, colonies had sprouted up quicker than mushrooms after a rain—New Philadelphia and New Chicago, New Atlanta and New Baltimore, New London and New Hamburg. Dozens and dozens of colonies, manned mining camps and automated installations, research outposts and you name it.

People came to Mars because they could make as much money in a year or two as they could make in a lifetime back home.

That's why Gill was there.

That's why they were all there, except for the labcoat johnnies and bugheads who actually liked Mars.

It had been nearly twelve hours now since Royer's death. Sarrasin didn't want to call for an early pick-up and Wells was riding him hard about that. Sarrasin had called it all into the Company and they agreed with him—wait it out. Not good. On the other hand, Sarrasin *had* issued particle blasters to everyone so at least they could defend themselves. That and a lot of amphetamines, enough to keep them all wired until pick-up came.

Dientz kept pacing around, kicking up dust. Now and then he'd stop dead, listen, then shake his head. "No, nothing. I thought I heard…never mind," he'd say, just about driving Gill nuts with the repetition of it all.

Gill was with him because Sarrasin didn't like the idea of Dientz and Wells being around each other, especially when they were carrying blasters. So they were down here on #3 at the substation which powered most of the levels and Sarrasin was with Wells up on #2, going through the motions of maintaining ore crunchers. When that was done with, Sarrasin said, they could all hide out in the shack until the hovercraft got there.

Dientz said, "You…you think that Heatseeker is real, Gill? You think there is such a thing?"

"You tell me," she said. "You saw what took Royce. Not me."

"I…I don't know what I saw."

Gill aimed her blaster down the conduit shaft, the halogen light fixed to it lighting up the tunnel for forty feet. "Maybe there's a Heatseeker and maybe not. I don't know. Something got Royer, though."

"No life on Mars," Dientz said.

That's what they always said before man got there. No life on Mars. Of course, that was bullshit. There weren't any little green men stalking around, of course, but there was life. In the early days of exploration, hydrobot ice corers had drilled through the ice caps and found huge lakes beneath them, lakes warmed by geothermal energy. The water was full of microbes and protozoa, things like primitive sponges, echinoderms, and bryozoa, not much else. Down deep in the natural limestone caves, lots of weird toadstools and fungi were found growing, colonial organisms like jellyfish living in streams polluted by methane and sulfur dioxides.

So there was life, just not any large terrestrial forms.

But the fossil record of the Red Planet was very rich. At one time, the surface had been teeming with life. There had been extensive river systems and floodplains that fed lush plant life, supported a variety of Martian invertebrates—flatworms and gastropods, mollusks and bizarre moss animals. An incredible variety of arthropods: creatures like crabs and spiders, beetles and pillbugs, locusts almost as large as dogs.

But all those were long gone.

And none of them had been as large as what Dientz had claimed to have seen…or glimpsed. There were ruined cities in the desert, but no remains or evidence of who or what had built them. The most recent had been abandoned at least 30,000 years, if not much longer. The general consensus was that they were built by some great extraterrestrial civilization that had seeded much of this part of the galaxy during Earth's prehistory and then died off.

So, no Martians.

No intelligent Martians.

Nothing smart and nothing large enough to tear a man apart. So what then? What had gotten Royer? Was it the mythical Heatseeker that was rumored to be a surviving Martian predator from a long-dead race? Or was it something else? A remnant of what built those cities? Some nightmare still defending its turf?

It was really hard to say.

Mars was a place of secrets and it would take centuries of looking before every spook from every moldering casket was dragged out and every skeleton was shaken out of every closet.

"You believe any of that stuff about those colonies that vanished?" Dientz asked. "You hear lots of things about that. Down south they were, I heard."

"Who knows?" Gill said.

She knew about them, of course. The one you heard most about was a place called New Salem—appropriately named—where some 200 members of an early research team just up and vanished. New Salem carried the same connotation in Mars folklore as the Mary Celeste or the Roanoke Colony in Virginia did back on Earth. Twenty-seven years ago, it was. Back then, it took almost six months to make the hop out to Mars and this with a gravity assist. When New Salem hadn't been heard from in three months, a rescue mission was sent and they found nothing, just a lot of empty domes and buildings, but no people. Whatever had happened, legend said, it happened fast because it looked like everyone had just stepped out...food on tables, beds slept in, nothing missing or moved. Through the years New Salem had become the focus of ghost stories and conspiracy theories. It was located down in the Southern Highlands, but there wasn't anything within a thousand miles of it these days. And maybe that said something about the truth of that matter.

"Yeah, those mining companies, they own everything and everyone," Dientz said. "Anytime something weird happens, they cover it up. Hey, you ever hear about that wrecked ship they found in the ice up north? Well, it wasn't one of ours. About as close to a flying saucer as you could—"

"Shut up," Gill told him.

"What?"

Gill grabbed his shoulder. "Listen."

They stood there shivering in their suits, trying not to breathe or make a sound, just listening over their external mics. For a moment there was nothing and Dientz was all set to get back to his tales of flying saucers and frost ghosts, but then...well, then they both heard it.

Singing.

At least, that's what it kind of sounded like...a high, melodic singing or humming, very shrill, rising and falling and echoing. It was weird and unearthly. It made something pull tight in Gill's stomach, made gooseflesh ride up her spine and settle at her throat. It stopped, then started again. It had a strange, almost feminine caliber to it, like some morbid Irish funeral dirge as sung by keening locusts.

"Let's get out of here," Dientz breathed. "Man, I don't.. I don't like the sound of that."

"Quiet," Gill told him.

The singing—if that's what it was—was getting neither closer nor farther away. Whatever it was coming from seemed stationary. They waited there, trembling, listening to it and thinking that it sounded like the Sirens of Greek Mythology calling them to their deaths or the high and evil-sweet voice of a wraith echoing from a haunted house or a tomb. They did not know what it could be, only that it was alien and macabre. To Gill it sounded almost melancholy and deranged, like the voice of that woman from Poe who'd been buried alive and escaped, her mind shattered.

"C'mon," she said. "It's coming from down that tunnel. We got our blasters."

Dientz pulled away from her. "No! I'm not going down there! Are you out of your fucking mind? Can't you hear it? Can't you *feel* it? It's not right, it's horrible...Jesus, Gill, it sounds like a voice from a grave..."

Gill stood there. Dientz was right. Completely right. Nothing that could sing like that was remotely human or remotely sane. Yet, she was compelled to follow that voice, to seek it out, to see what could possibly be making it. "Then wait here because I'm going."

"No! No! You can't...you can't go in there! You can't leave me alone!"

"Then come with me," Gill said.

The tunnel led up to a pump house. There was nothing else up there but a lot of rudimentary tunnels the engineers had never finished, some old and unsafe cave networks.

Dientz was shaking so badly he thought he might fall out of his suit. "I'm calling Sarrasin! You're out of your fucking head! I'm calling him! You hear me? I'm calling him!"

"So call him," Gill said and slipped into the tunnel.

The blackness swallowed her and then Dientz was alone. He could see the retreating glow of her helmet LEDs bobbing away into the darkness. The singing had stopped, but now it had started again, shriller, more rhythmic, more insistent than ever it seemed.

Dientz stood there unsurely. Funny, but that voice made him want to go into the tunnel, too. You listened and kept listening, it sort of wrapped something warm and fuzzy around your brain and you stopped thinking about how terrible it sounded, how morose and off-key and eldritch. You started thinking it sounded kind of nice. Like a lullaby your mother might have sung you to sleep with in your crib. Sweet and loving and—

Oh, Christ, oh my God.

Dientz nearly cried out, because he'd been walking towards the tunnel just as Gill had. He'd actually been letting that voice get into his head where it had settled warm and comforting, spinning webs through his mind.

He stepped back and away.

There was a ping at his headset which meant he was about to receive a communication.

"Gill!" he said. "Gill! Listen to me! You gotta come back, you gotta come back right now."

"Dientz, come into the tunnel," Gill said, very calmly. "You have to see this! This is incredible, this is really incredible…"

She said something else, but Dientz couldn't pick it up because the singing was blaring, blotting out everything else. He kept trying to get a hold of her, but it was useless. He shut the channel off and kept his exterior mic open.

The singing was very loud, echoing and shrilling.

And then there was a ping again and Gill came on, screaming and shouting in pure terror.

Dientz made a frantic call to Sarrasin.

He could hear things echoing from the tunnel now…wet, meaty sounds like a carcass being cut apart. Splashing sounds, but no more screaming. Then it all ended with a piercing roaring sound that echoed away and died.

Then there was nothing but silence.

Silence.

Dientz went down on his knees, sobbing and praying and waiting for death to find him, too.

But it didn't.

Sarrasin and Wells found him.

"Where's Gill?" Sarrasin said, yanking him to his feet and shaking him. "Where the fuck is Gill?"

"She went up that tunnel," Dientz said in a shallow, scratchy voice. "Went up that tunnel, following that singing, that beautiful singing."

"What the hell is he talking about?" Wells wanted to know.

But Dientz just nodded, like he was hearing something they couldn't. "That Heatseeker, boss…she's a female…she's a female…and she likes to sing…"

5

They were tracking her now.

They were going to bring her to ground or die trying. Sarrasin himself led the way up the tunnel after Gill. Dientz was right behind him. Wells was taking up the back door. Wells didn't care about Mars or the Company or any of that high happy shit, he just wanted to bag what was killing people. He saw nothing beyond that.

"Funny," he said to Dientz, "how every time we leave you alone with somebody, they get killed."

Dientz stopped. "What you mean by that?"

"Just curious, is all."

"Listen, you sonofabitch—"

"Shut up," Sarrasin told them. "I'm sick of both of you. Just plain sick of the bickering. Yeah, every time Dientz gets alone with somebody, they die. What of it? Could have been you or me that bitch went after, too. She tries to get us alone, Wells. She found Royer by himself and then she got Gill away from Dientz. That's how she operates and that's why we're not separating anymore."

"You're the boss," Wells said.

"Damn right I am."

Dientz said, "We should just make for the surface, wait for pick-up."

"It's pitch black up there, dumbass," Wells said. "You think she couldn't take us up there, too?"

"The habitat. The emergency habitat. If we can get there..."

Wells laughed with derision. "*If, if if*...she'll never let us get that far."

Dientz didn't argue and Sarrasin was glad of that. One more pussy-ass suggestion from him and Sarrasin figured he'd cold-cock him and stake him out as bait for what they hunted...and what hunted them.

"No more talking," Sarrasin told them. "We're getting up to the fork now."

They could all see it in the lights strung from the tunnel roof. One passage led to the pump house, the other wound off into the mountain itself into a labyrinth of ancient caves and half-finished tunnels that had been abandoned years before. Sarrasin knew why they'd been abandoned. He would have never admitted it to the others, but he knew, all right. Ten years before, the engineers were going to put in a new boiler system. The diggers cut about a quarter mile of new passages and broke into an ancient system of limestone caves. And that was like some kind of catalyst, because in the next two days, six men were killed, ripped apart like Royer. Two others just went missing. None of this was common knowledge. The truth of the matter was sealed up tightly in the Company's files and there it would stay.

Anyway, that's why the new tunnels were only half-finished. Word had it a few had even been collapsed on purpose. So the digger crew had been attacked by this creature ten years ago, same way the surveying team had been gutted in the Sarvis Valley eight years before that. And now this.

The bitch definitely liked to kill, but it wasn't like you could set your watch by her. She just came and went without rhyme or reason every now and then like a bad storm.

Sarrasin cut off into the right tunnel at the fork. The signs said it was dangerous past this point, unsafe, but they kept on. No lights now either. Only their helmet lamps to guide them.

They followed Gill's tracks.

Her boot prints were easy to see in the undisturbed sand which was very fine like that of a beach, red and pink and sparkling with mica. The helmet LEDs were splashing light onto the rough-hewn walls, creating wild leaping shadows.

"I don't like this," Dientz said.

"Shut the hell up," Wells told him.

Ten minutes into the passage, it broke off into three separate runs. The one to the far left, Sarrasin knew, just circled back into itself and the middle one was a dead end. He led them into the right channel, following Gill's footprints. The passage was getting narrow now like a spider hole, so tight in some places his shoulders brushed rock to either side.

Gill's footprints stopped.

The sand was disturbed like a whirlwind had blown through there. Blood was everywhere, a great splatter marking the spot where she had been attacked. It was frozen into crystals.

"Where's her body?" Wells wanted to know.

But that was obvious. There was a crystallized blood path before them, drag ruts. The bitch had dragged her off. Swallowing, Sarrasin led them on. Nobody was saying a thing, not even Dientz. They kept moving, the shadows jumping and the tunnel turning this way and then that. To a man, they couldn't shake the idea that they were being watched.

The tunnel began to break into the old caves. Offshoots ran to the left and right, some of them big enough to drive a sand rover through and others you would have had to navigate on your belly.

Sarrasin was still following the drag marks. The blood was very spotty now, a few drops here and there and he figured Gill was dead before she reached this point.

There was a sudden arc of light like one of the helmets had spun in a crazy circle. Sarrasin heard what he thought was a grunting sound. He stopped and swung around.

There was nobody behind Dientz.

No Wells.

Dientz started losing it right away. "Pick us off one by one, that's what she's going to do, Sarrasin! You played right into her hands! Oh, that's great, that's just fucking great!"

"Stop it!" Sarrasin told him. "You want out? You had your fill? Then take a fucking hike or just shut up!"

Dientz said nothing.

Sarrasin backtracked, but it was hard to say where Wells had disappeared to. There was some blood on one of the walls, but he could have been yanked into any of a half-dozen passages.

This was it then, he knew. They either hunted that bitch down and killed her or she killed them. Regardless, it would have been just as dangerous to turn back now as to go forward. Like slipping a noose around your throat and kicking out the stool, there was just no turning back.

The passage split again and this made Sarrasin stop.

"What?" Dientz said. "My God, what now?"

Sarrasin didn't answer at first, he had to be sure. Then he was. "Look, Dientz. That tunnel to the right…it's new. It didn't used to be there, I'm sure of it."

It was tall and narrow, more of a cleft through the rock than anything else. The floor was littered with detritus, lots of loose rocks and scattered pebbles. The walls looked as if they'd been cut with axes and picks. Sarrasin went in there, not caring now if Deintz was behind him or not. The drag marks were still evident and now they led into a low grotto that he had to crouch to get into. It was maybe thirty-feet wide in there. Once you got inside, the roof opened up into a wide cylindrical shaft that disappeared up into the blackness. Sarrasin put the lights of his helmet and blaster up there, but it just went up and up. He crouched, waiting for the Heatseeker to drop down on him like a spider.

But nothing happened.

Swallowing down something thick in his throat, he looked back once and Dientz was still with him.

First thing they saw were lots of odd-shaped boulders that looked as if they'd fallen from the roof overhead. Next thing was what was left of Gill. They could only see her legs—she'd been driven into the ground like post. You couldn't say where her suit began and her flesh left off.

But that wasn't all.

Ancient elliptical depressions were carved into the walls, dozens of them. They led right up the shaft as far as their lights would reach. They were half-filled with sand and debris now, but they looked oddly like the honeycombed cells of a beehive. Most were still occupied.

Occupied by dead things.

They went over to them, not afraid really, because there was no possible way the things were alive. They were curled-up and horribly withered, leathery brown creatures about four-feet in length that reminded Sarrasin of katydids. Maybe they weren't insects exactly, but something like insects. Arthropods. Their thoraxes were ribbed, short and shriveled limbs branching out into triple-pronged appendages. Something like a narrow stalk rose from the thorax, looked like it was made of vertebrae, with a tear-drop shaped pod at the end, gigantic hollows where no less than three eyes might have once been. They had too many limbs to count, bundles of whip-like things that might have been feelers.

Looking at them, desiccated and mummified, it was hard to say whether they stood or crawled.

"I can't stand looking at them," Dientz said.

And for once, Sarrasin agreed with him. Rawboned and wiry and multi-limbed with horny, chitinous shells and too many anatomical adaptations you couldn't begin to guess at, they were about as alien as anything he could imagine. Seeing them alive, seeing them moving, it would have been almost too much for the human mind. They were repulsive and hideous; you wanted to step on them.

Yet, his curiosity got the better of him☐he panned his light up and found more of the creatures interred above. These were larger, maybe adult forms, but just as withered and brown and crumbling. They looked somewhat like Earth mantises.

Dientz began to giggle, then he began to laugh…a dry and wizened laughter that was scratching and broken. The sound of a human mind emptying itself. "You know what this is, don't you?" he said. "Don't you, Sarrasin?"

"How could I?" Sarrasin said.

"This place," Dientz said, motioning around with his light and then jabbing one of the insects with his blaster so that a limb fell off, "this place is a burial chamber. These hills we've been tunneling into are probably part of some huge cemetery, some sacred burial ground. All these years we've been desecrating it."

He was out of his head.

He had to be out of his head.

But that didn't make him wrong. Rift and Sarvis Valleys were probably part of some sort of great Martian necropolis and men had been violating it ever since they arrived on Mars like dogs searching for bones. And the Heatseeker? Some caretaker, some survival that should have died out eons ago, but kept living, probably demented even by Martian standards, doing the only thing she could do…grieving her race. Probably hibernating for long periods of time, then waking up, pissed-off, and taking invading humans as sacrifice to the memory of her species.

His skin crawling, Sarrasin thought: *I'm in command here. I can't crack up. I can't let myself crack up.*

Dientz was out of his mind now and Sarrasin was close at his heels. He led him back out into the tunnel, nearly dragging him.

"Get a hold of yourself," he told him.

"I'm okay," Dientz said, but his eyes were wide and glassy and mad through his helmet bubble.

"C'mon," Sarrasin said. "Let's get the fuck out of this crypt."

6

The idea of escape, of making for the surface slapped Dientz out of it. Whatever had been holding him, squeezing his mind flat, it let go now. He could do this. He could make the run with Sarrasin. He wouldn't lock up. He'd keep going.

Down the tunnel they went.

Death waited in any of the passages and spider holes arching off to either side. Dientz was sweating rivers in his terrain suit. He held his blaster tightly and anything so much as breathed, he was wasting it. If that was a man, so be it.

"We're going to make it," he told Sarrasin because he had the oddest sense that Sarrasin was beginning to unravel. He wasn't saying a thing; he was just waiting for the shit to fly. "We're going to get out of here and that bitch can't stop us."

"Sure," Sarrasin said.

No hope, no optimism left. Sarrasin, who was always so confident and sure of himself, always standing on sure ground, he had died now. What was left was a man that was sure of nothing, that dared hope for nothing, that saw his death coming and did not shrink from it. Fatalistic.

Dientz didn't like this new Sarrasin. He was not in charge, he was not leading from the front. He had folded-up psychologically and there was nothing left but flesh and blood, nothing at all.

Dientz knew what he was feeling, what had taken possession of him. It had gotten him, too, but he'd managed to shrug it off. Had to. Because when you started thinking that way, your luck ran out and you wore a target on your back and fate was all ready to stuff an apple in your mouth and roast your ass over the hottest fire in hell.

"When we get back," he heard himself say, "when they pick us up, Sarrasin…what's the first thing you want to do?"

"Shut up," Sarrasin snapped.

"What?"

"Shhh!"

They were stopped now and Dientz didn't like it. Forward momentum was what he needed, hesitation like this made all the bad things start crawling through him again. The paranoia and dread, the absolute fear. Sarrasin seemed to be listening, but Dientz heard nothing. Saw nothing. But he was feeling *everything*. There was simply no getting around what his nerve ganglia was telegraphing right up his spine…the sense that they were in incredible danger, that something was following them, shadowing them like a leopard in the jungle. Something patient and malevolent and deadly as poison. He could feel it watching them, studying them, deciding which of them it would bring down first. And when it did, it would be to maximize the utmost terror in the other. Because that's how the Heatseeker worked— it could smell fear, it could taste fear, and it knew exactly how to use fear.

The Heatseeker was so close, Dientz was certain he could smell it, as impossible as that was…gray, moldering, the stink of shrouds and bones.

Closer and closer still.

We're going to die, he thought then. *We won't make it out of here.*

And they wouldn't; he was certain of it. Just as certain as he had been that they would make it five minutes before. The mind was funny, wasn't it? It was like a green tree limb: you put too much pressure on it and it either snapped or it sprang back, swinging and swinging. That was what had happened to his mind.

The only reason we're not dead yet is because that bitch isn't ready to take us. She wants us more afraid, she wants to push us to the brink of madness. She'll be satisfied with nothing less.

Dientz was shaking badly now and Sarrasin was frozen into place. They did not speak and they did not move. Dientz knew they had to and right now. He opened his mouth to say so and then a shrill, insane screaming began to echo around them, coming from behind them or ahead of them, maybe from the mouths of all those other passages. It rose and fell, fragmented, and then started again.

He felt something like a sucking wind rush through him at the sound of it. He wanted to giggle, he wanted to cry, he wanted to scream along with it. He was going mad and he didn't see what he could possibly do to stop it.

The screaming came again, filling the tunnels and bouncing around until it was not a single scream, but a dozen. And then it rose to a strident, inhuman pitch and became the hysterical voice of Gill: "*Help me! Somebody help me! Please dear God don't let her touch me don't let her touch me!*"

Sarrasin tensed, turning in circles, trying to find where it was coming from. "We've…we've got to help her. That's what we've got to do."

"Are you crazy?" Dientz said. "That's not Gill! It can't be Gill!"

But it sure sounded like her. And about five seconds after it ended, it started again…only this time it wasn't just Gill, it was Royer, too, and Wells. They were screaming and screeching, begging for help, begging for Dientz and Sarrasin to help them before *she* hurt them anymore.

Dientz just stood there, breathing so fast he was hyperventilating. The sound of those screaming voices had locked him up inside…dear God, the suffering, the torture, the absolute pain. It sounded like they were being skinned. And Sarrasin? He was completely unhinged. Moving first this way, then that. Stopping, starting, aiming his blaster here, then there.

Finally he grabbed hold of Dientz's arm. "We've got to help them! We've got to go to them!"

Dientz yanked his arm away. "They're dead, Sarrasin! They're all dead! You know they're dead!"

"Then who? Who's calling us, dammit! Who in the fuck is calling for us?"

"She is," Dientz said.

But that wasn't good enough for Sarrasin. He shoved Dientz and Dientz went airborne in that low gravity, bounced off a wall and thudded gently to the ground. By the time he was on his feet, Sarrasin was already gone. He caught a brief glimpse of his helmet lights bobbing up a passage and then disappearing.

"Sarrasin!" Dientz called through his mic, but it was pointless.

She wanted to separate them and now she had.

Dientz went after him, entering the darkened tunnel. It was cramped and close in there, the floor rising along a gentle incline. He had to find Sarrasin before she did, but he knew he wouldn't. And it was about that time that Sarrasin screamed. It was loud and piercing and short. There was a wet ripping sound, a thudding and cleaving noise like Sarrasin had been split lengthwise by an axe.

And then something was bumping down the tunnel from above.

Sarrasin's helmet.

It was crushed and battered, sprayed with frozen blood And his head was still in it.

Dientz ran.

7

He could not remember much of his flight, only that he kept going until he was at the power substation. It was shut down and all the lights were off. And Dientz had been a maintenance tech long enough to know it wasn't a mechanical or electrical failure.

It was the Heatseeker.

She'd doubled back and did something.

She didn't need the light—she hunted by body heat, hence her name.

He began running, trying stay on his feet. The turbolift was just ahead. If he could get in there, it would shoot up to the surface and there wasn't shit she could do to stop it.

He ran maybe twenty feet, felt something big pass by him. He went down in a crouch and fired random shots with his blaster. Bolts of blue light vaporized rocks with explosions of smoke and sparks.

He got to his feet, started running again and something hit him in the back, put him face down in the sparkling orange sand. Screaming, he got back up and then something grabbed his left ankle and flung him. He bounced from one wall to the next, spun head over heels and rolled to a stop.

His helmet LEDs threw grotesque shadows of him in every direction. He sensed movement and brought up his blaster and something whipped into him like a tree branch and the blaster was snatched from his hands. He caught a glimpse of a black, spurred foreleg thick around as a fencepost.

Then he was crawling, whimpering and mumbling, but crawling, making for the turbolift.

Something grabbed his ankle again and threw him back down the tunnel.

Hopeless, it was completely hopeless. She was toying with him like a cat with a mouse.

Sobbing, his mind torn open in a bleeding gash, he fell onto his back, gasping for air.

And there she was.

The Heatseeker.

She was clinging to the roof of the passage like some immense and glistening insect, a mantis set with serrated, irregular plates that moved independently of each other. She was not an insect exactly, but a surreal version of one, too long and too thin, spindly and spidery, limbs jointed by spiked balls, body segments joined by what looked like threaded screws. She was a bug welded together out of odds and ends from a metal scrap yard…pistons and pipes, iron frames and corrugated steel.

Dientz didn't bother being afraid. He was beyond that now. He just looked at her and felt an almost surly sense of calm. "Got me, have you?" he said to her.

She just clung there, making a sort of trilling sound that his mic picked up, watching him with three huge liquid green eyes that were slit yellow like cat's pupils. She was composed of an elongated, narrow body with dozens and dozens of wiry, hooked limbs. They were all moving like knitting needles and threshers and scythes. Glacial eyes studied him with grim, malefic amusement from atop a curling stalk shaped almost like a question mark, but longer than a man's leg.

So this was the Heatseeker, eh?

Every bit as awful as anything Dientz could have imagined. Maybe worse.

Just beneath those globular eyes, there was something like a proboscis, long and black and oily. As he watched, it split open, revealing a wicked, saw-toothed mouth, more jelly dripping from it, gouts of steam blowing from the channel of her throat.

Dientz sat up slowly, waiting for her claws and her teeth. He felt something rising inside him. Something sure and immovable. "No, you silly bitch," he said, popping the seal on his helmet bubble and feeling the bitter cold. "I won't make it that easy on you."

Then he let Mars have him.

And was dead almost before she got to him.

✗

WITCH'S BARROW
Chad Hensley

Upon a shadowed, cragged cave mountain
Bizarre inhuman skeletal grasping sconces
Hold flaming torches before glowing fountain.
Above- a monstrous, hinged door mumbles responses

With dozens of carved mouths full of honed fangs.
Rotting red carpet- giant tongue unrolls;
Leads to enormous stalactites where hangs
Winged, green goblins sleeping over trolls.

She stands near, in a kitchen full of brooms,
Twitching carved parts and bloody sharp, big knife:
The cauldron cooks, steaming black noxious fumes;
A brewing spell delaying afterlife.

She smiles sharp teeth and sings a cackling song,
Knowing her evil lasts not very long.

✗

THE LIBRARIAN
Sharon L. Cullars

"Will it hurt much?" the woman standing before Aja asked. Approximately twenty-five, five foot seven, nine stones more or less from the look of her, the applicant ostensibly would be an easy transfer.

"You'll be asleep during the whole process, so you shouldn't register any discomfort," Aja assured her. "Monitors will measure your brain waves during the transfer and we'll be able to track for any anomalies so we can do any necessary corrections if needed."

"Corrections?" the woman asked nervously. She raised a forefinger to her parched lips, nibbled at a black-painted nail with crooked teeth.

"Nothing to worry about, Ms...." Aja paused, looked down at the application lying on the table before her. "Ms. Calendar. Just know that hundreds have gone through the process without any adverse consequences. So far, we haven't lost anyone so you needn't worry."

"Just call me Jerri," the young woman said. "Look, it's not that I'm nervous or anything like that. Well maybe just a little. I mean most of my friends have already gone over so I guess there's nothing to be afraid of, right?"

"Jerri, trust me, there is nothing to worry about. The procedure is one hundred percent safe. Wouldn't you say those are decent odds?"

Jerri nodded, uncertainty still playing across her face as Aja handed her the completed paperwork she would need to submit to Division One on the upper level of the library.

"Go down this aisle to the bank of elevators and take the one on the right to the fourth floor. There you'll be processed for the transfer."

Another uncertain nod before the woman took the aisle as instructed.

Aja had encountered a number of wary applicants, many of whom were apprehensive about a procedure that was only slightly over a year old. But given the alternative, many were more than willing to risk the foibles of the new technology. What awaited them here was much worse.

She rose from her seat, straightened a pile of applications sitting on the right of the wooden desk. Everything had to be in its place if things were to go smoothly.

Aja heard the receding footsteps moving along the mosaic-tiled floor. The sound was muffled; most likely the woman wore sneakers. Aja had heard hundreds of shoes walk that same path, their owners seeking a better existence.

For the moment, Aja stood alone amid the bookcases that lined the aisles and walls of the library. The structures stood like silent sentries, imposing in their numbers that stretched into the infinity of the long halls of the library. Shelves and shelves held every book ever written by humans throughout the centuries. Ideas translated into words and pictures that conveyed the supremacy and baseness of mankind, a contradiction not confounding given the complexity of the human soul.

Aja walked the length of one bookcase, glancing at the offerings housed on its shelves. She stopped when her eyes spied the familiar spine: *Mortem Ignobiles*. Though she was not versed in Latin, she knew the title translated to *Ignoble Death*. It stood apart from the other books simply because of the beauty of its covering and spine. She pulled it from its place, held it as she had many times before. The front of the book depicted elegantly dressed skeletons, their bony hands interlaced as they moved in a circle, reminiscent of some *Danse Macabre* It spoke of horror, exquisitely showcased. Within its pages was a tale of a demon's obsession to destroy the love of two innocent youths through measures sadistic and of course, demonic. In the end, the death was not of their mortal bodies, but their immortal souls.

Since Aja had first laid eyes on the tome, she'd been mesmerized by it. Even though she could not read the language, she'd asked Mrs. Thorne, the head librarian, about the book's contents. Mrs. Thorne, knowing several languages including Latin, had easily translated the story for Aja.

Once Aja heard the ending, an idea began germinating in the back of her mind, a series of thoughts coalescing to form a plan inspired by need, fed by hatred.

Down the corridor, toward the entrance came the sound of someone entering the building. Another applicant. Or rather, a traveler, one of the brave souls willing to withstand the tyranny that had been thrust on them, who refused to bow, though their heads were bloodied, their very existence threatened. Sadly, there were those who'd already capitulated to their situation.

The woman walked toward Aja as Aja reached her seat at the librarian's desk. This one was older than the previous applicant, probably forty or so. Her weight looked to be approximately twenty stones. Although the transfer wouldn't be difficult, it might be tricky nonetheless.

She looked as unsure as Jerri had been, her eyes nervously glancing at the shelves of books behind Aja before settling on a spot just above Aja's nose.

"Is this…where I come to…" the woman stumbled over her words.

"To transfer?" Aja filled in the missing request. "Yes, and you would be…"

"Francis…Francis Taversham. I want to join my husband, if you please."

Aja retrieved the request form with the required information from the inbox. She had already been cleared through the first stage of the process, so all that was left to do was send her to Division One, which she promptly did.

Another echo down the hall leading toward the elevators.

And yet, another applicant headed towards the desk.

To all appearances, should anyone be observing, the transaction between librarian and patron was an ordinary exchange of information, concluding with the librarian directing the reader to the specific aisle, the requested tome.

But in reality nothing was ordinary now.

Hell had descended to earth and heaven was nowhere to be found. The invading demons had taken a more pernicious form than those depicted in books, more horrific than the pictures displayed in *Mortem Ignobiles*. No horned brows or prehensile tails.

The whole earth was inundated with the alien creatures, most topping eight feet, their dermis simultaneously scaled and viscous, their gaping maws edged with serrated teeth of iron, their appetites insatiable for flesh. Mortals had become hardly more than morsel bits for the invaders.

A number of humans had escaped, taking to the mountains, every expanse of wooded areas, the deepest caverns. Eventually they were sought out, some found. Those not immediately devoured were herded and kept like cattle.

Most of the cities, towns and villages around the globe had already fallen, their borders open, their skies vulnerable. A millennium ago, New Chicago rose, the brainchild of far-seeing architects who anticipated that maybe enemies would not attack from adjoining lands, but from adjoining skies. The planners girded the city's borders with a gate of impenetrable steel and glass which reached into the clouds. An electromagnetic field hovered above the city, allowing in the gamma rays necessary for plant growth but shielding the city from anything less innocuous. The water systems allowed a self-sustaining ecosystem. Through the centuries, the descendants of that first generation had grown and prospered in all areas, especially technology.

And now that technology would save them as there was a breach. The gate was beginning to falter and could no longer protect those inside.

Some had chosen to fight just outside the gate hoping to forestall the inevitable, including her brother Ryan and their father. They had been among those who had stood against the invaders, their biotech weaponry the only leverage they had against the monsters. Neither her brother or father had survived. Aja soothed her soul with the thought that they were now reunited with her mother, somewhere beyond this existence.

Soon, a queue began to form at her desk as more 'travelers' arrived. She perused through their applications, sent them to the fourth floor, to their salvation.

A disgruntled looking man with disheveled white hair and a map of grooves etching his face stood at her desk.

"I don't believe in all this new-fangled tech. Man wasn't meant to be translated," he said.

"You can stay and fight," Aja said. "Understand, the translations are not compulsory. You're free to change your mind."

She could see the conflict in his face. He was of an age to remember the last war that raged nearly sixty years before. Men and women had fought side by side in defending their neighbor cities, refusing to vow allegiance to the Djann and his tyrannical forces. Running then would have been an act of cowardice; it wasn't so now. Fighting was a certain death and that death would be in vain.

He did a slow nod.

"I'll stay. We'll show those godforsaken monsters that humans can give just as good as they get."

She smiled. "Yes, you'll show them," she said without irony. They both knew he would die once the invaders crossed into New Chicago. At this moment, the monsters were ranged around the gate, their electron phasers cutting through the glass and steel that were supposed to be impenetrable. The library was the only recourse to certain death.

The old man gave her a final nod and walked back to the library doors, exited to his destiny.

One after another, men, women, children, some in groups, in families, some standing alone, gave their names, took their pre-submitted applications to the upper floor of the library. For those who did not fit the requisite criteria for the translator, either because of health issues or other anomalies, Aja sadly turned them away. Being a librarian in this case was holding life and death in her hands.

Hours passed but she did not tire through the processing. The translations had to be completed as soon as possible. The administration had pinpointed the exact hour when the gate would be fully breached and that hour was just past sunset. The horrors suffered by those in other cities, other countries, would finally befall the citizens of New Chicago. They would become food or slaves. Or die fighting.

Aja and the other processors had only gotten word late last week. Though she'd initially panicked, she'd known what she had to do and had set to work the very next day, she and the others receiving and processing applications, keeping everything in order. After all, they were librarians and scientists. Disorder was chaos.

Right now, her mind was numb with it all. But just beneath the numbness was expectation. And after the long line that was replicated in every library in the city had shortened to just a few souls, she spotted the one she'd known would be in line. He was not one to stand ground and fight. Or stop and help the woman whose car he'd hit and totaled with his vehicle. A year ago, he'd run away just as he was running now. Her mother had died only hours after she was injured; the attending doctor had told her father that her mother might have survived if she'd received timely help. But she'd lain on a dark road, undiscovered for hours.

"Yes, my name is Jackson Quivers," he announced with a measure of arrogance. But then he was the CEO of one of the largest employers in New Chicago. He looked at her blankly and she realized he didn't recognize her from the several court sessions that had ultimately found him not guilty due to a technicality.

But Aja could never forget that face: the stern brow, the humorless blue eyes, the thin lips, his expression that of a man in a hurry. Just as he'd been in a hurry that night on the dark road where he'd left her dying mother.

"Yes, Mr. Quivers. I've assigned you a special translation. I think you'll be pleased," she said as she handed him the application pre-filled with all of his vitals.

"I've always wanted to go on a Jules Verne adventure," he said.

A half smile curved up those lips, allowing a smattering of teeth to show through. They were as discolored as she remembered them.

She'd already spoken with Hendrickson who was presently manning the translator. He would know where to send Mr. Jackson Quivers. Although initially hesitant, Hendrickson had finally nodded his acquiescence. He too had lost a mother, knew the void it left.

She fought back a tear. There was no time for that. But in her heart, she spoke to her mother. *I'll be joining you soon.*

When the last applicant had left her desk, she stood and walked to lock the library doors then leaned her back against the brass metal, sighed with weariness.

A small smile played on her lips as she thought of what she and the others had accomplished during that last week.

Yes, the literature of the world would have new characters, some in the backdrop of well known scenes. Some playing more pivotal roles, changing plotlines. On a street in Digne, Jerri might be witness as Jean Valjean is turned away by an innkeeper. And the young woman, now appropriately attired for that time in history, might offer the man solace. That was the book Jerri had personally chosen to be translated into. And she would live her eternity as a new player in the travails of *Les Miserables*.

As for Mrs. Traversham, she would be running along the moors, calling for Heathcliff. Undoubtedly, the man would not answer as Cathy would forever be his love. But at least Mrs. Traversham would have the opportunity to try.

So much better than being a midday meal or kept like a herded animal, yoked and worked to near death.

Aja walked the familiar path to the familiar aisle, picked out the familiar tome. She opened to a random page, flip forward, looking for the sign.

And though she didn't understand Latin (yes, a failing for a librarian), she recognized the name now included in the text of the horrific book. Jackson Quivers.

Strangely, his translation to *20,000 Leagues Under the Sea* did not take place.

She imagined his screams as he ran from demons similar to the ones he had escaped here.

She heard the opening of elevator doors, the sound of steps along the mosaic floor. She replaced the book and walked toward them.

Stan Hendrickson stood near her desk, his six-foot plus height dwarfing that of Leila Downey, Curtis Smithson and Luann Wi.

They turned to her as she approached. On their faces, of various ages and colors, was the same expression. The weariness of long hours of work, the satisfaction of having fulfilled their duties, and mingled in, the defiance they would need.

There would be no salvation for them. They had manned the translator to help the others escape. They had not chosen escape for themselves.

After all they were the librarians. It was their duty to protect the treasures contained in every vellum that sat on the endless shelves. The monsters would not be interested in paper and leather. They only came for flesh.

Those who were translated would be safe for eternity, the eternities they had chosen for themselves.

The sun was descending and soon darkness would blanket the city. The automatic city lights that usually blazed would not come on this night. The city administrators had decided that. The invaders would have to scavenger in the inky blackness of an unrepentant night.

Within minutes, Aja heard a booming crash indicating the gate had finally been breached.

Thunderous steps were soon followed by the screams of those who had chosen not to be translated. Aja imagined the elderly man who'd decided to stay and fight standing in a darkened street, impervious to his fear, defiantly looking up into the maws that would descend to swallow him whole.

Dying as courageously as he must have lived.

In the dim lights of the library, she made her way to the cabinet on the wall behind the librarian's desk, where each of them at a time had sat and tended to the literary needs of their citizens.

She pulled out the biotech weaponry that would only delay the inevitable. The weapons had been gathered for this day, this moment.

Even though they didn't stand a chance, they would go down fighting.

She handed each of the librarians a weapon and they walked to the door, standing sentry. Soon the metal doors boomed as a mammoth force rammed against them. It would only be a matter of seconds.

She would be with her family soon. Hopefully, there was something on the other side of death, another kind of translation.

The creature that stepped through the ravaged door was as horrible as she'd heard from accounts.

His scales gleamed under the dim lights.

On cue, the librarians raised their weapons, their last action as protectors of the books of New Chicago.

✗

THE THIRD OBSCENITY
Frederick J Mayer

"Child of the universe, no less than the trees
and the stars; you have a right to be here."

—Desiderata

Fidelity conjoined psychic twins onscene
there be obscenely unspoken Third
Fluid silhouette darkly mirror Asiatic
rapturous shadow fold at inner corner
Fertility macabre odd beauty sybaritic

Buried within Jeju's Mount Halla bowels
there Korean Tcho Tcho worship
Blasphemy fecund protean's own desiderata
sacred quincunx blood so great siblings shun Her
But dice entre las piernas;1 vagina dentata.

✗

DREAM WARRIORS (1) TEAM SPIRIT

D.C. Lozar

From the side of the pool, a bevy of young girls, swimsuits glistening under folded arms, watched as Jenna tore through the water. Her breast-stroke was a thing of power and practiced ease, and her body moved with the grace of a mermaid. Hitting the far wall, gasping, she pulled herself out of the pool as her coach, a heavyset woman, clicked her thumb down on the stopwatch.

"The school record," announced Mrs. Plata as she marked the time down on her water-stained clipboard. "Fantastic."

The class watched, admiration and jealousy cascading across their sunburnt cheeks, as Jenna lifted herself into her wheelchair and toweled off.

She didn't look up. "Thanks."

Behind her, perched on the upmost bleacher-seat, a bearded man lowered his phone and glared at the swimmers. The mid-day sun bounced off the aluminum benches. Sweat stains clung like exploded tomatoes to his armpits.

Mrs. Plata walked slowly down the row of shivering girls, her sneakers squeaking softly on the wet cement. She clicked her tongue in disappointment. "In twenty years, I've never seen a weaker freshman team."

The girls hung their heads. Hesitantly, one raised a hand.

"No excuses!" Mrs. Plata swatted at the hand with her clipboard. "If she can do that, you can do better."

Someone sniffled.

"Normally, I would train you myself, but the varsity team needs me this month. Instead, Jenna is going to be your student coach. Do you have questions?" She waited, watching their expressions for signs of dissent. There were none. "Good."

Mrs. Plata leaned down so only Jenna could hear her whisper. "A strong team needs a strong leader."

"Right." Jenna took the clipboard, her expression stern.

"Don't let them slack off," warned the coach as she made her way toward the school's indoor pool, where the varsity girls trained. "They're your responsibility now."

"All right, girls. Time to get wet," Jenna barked. "Now!"

In mass, the twenty young women dove into the pool. Water splattered the hot cement and Jenna's withered calves. A moment later, heads broke the surface, turned, and waited expectantly.

"Dog-paddle," she ordered. "No legs."

Groaning, the team complied. Jenna glanced down at the clipboard, checking off each girl's name on the attendance roster. She came to her own and smiled at her time. She hadn't even been trying. Looking up, she watched as a thin, bookish recruit named Hope sank below the surface.

The girl didn't reappear.

Annoyed, Jenna waited, but no one noticed. "Great."

Behind her, the man in the bleachers got to his feet.

Jenna folded her towel and placed it on the ground. Calmly, she set her clipboard down and rolled forward. She could see the wavering outline of Hope's body at the bottom of the pool.

Her dive hardly made a splash as she entered the dazzlingly clear underwater world. Great strokes brought her to where Hope clawed vainly at the water, her eyes wide with growing alarm.

Jenna clutched the drowning girl's hair with one hand and swam to the surface with her other. Her legs were useless, but her hips pivoted smoothly against the water's resistance, and they rose.

Breaking the surface, Jenna was thankful the team had finally noticed the emergency. Dozens of hands took Hope, and Jenna swam back to her chair, exhausted.

The man from the bleachers, Derek Broadmoor, helped the girls pull Hope from the pool. Kneeling over his daughter as she coughed up water, his lips tight with disappointment, he scolded her. "I told you not to eat so much before practice."

Hope looked away in embarrassment. "Sorry, Dad."

"She almost drowned." Jenna rolled up. "We should get her to the nurse."

"She's fine." Derek gave Jenna a sideways glance. His words were slow and measured. "She...had...a...cramp."

A searing pain blossomed in the skin beneath Jenna's chin. Startled, her hand flew to her neck, covering the tattooed ankh that rested at the base of her throat. "Excuse me."

Steam rose from between Jenna's fingers as she moved away from the crowd. The heat diminished as she retreated, but she could feel the flames flickering against her palm, the devilish itch in her throat begging for release.

Something had triggered her key.

Glancing over her shoulder, she watched Derek pull out his phone.

Recording video, as Hope staggering to her feet, he clapped her on the back.

"Brush it off, honey. Back in the water."

* * * *

The cafeteria bustled with students carrying trays of processed goo and carbonated drinks. In the far back corner, three unlikely friends spoke in hushed tones.

"It hurt like I was being branded or something." Jenna's fingers massaged her tattoo. "But, now it's back to normal."

Michael, dressed in a Letterman's jacket and jeans, and his younger brother, Eric, struggled to hear over the cacophony of lunchroom chatter.

Eric, adjusting his glasses, swallowed hard. "So, this is our first one."

"Are you sure?" Michael bit his lower lip. "Maybe you swallowed too much water or something."

Jenna shook her head. "I don't like this any more than you, but Marina said the King in Yellow would be after us, and I think this guy's been infected."

"With a lurker," agreed Eric, clenching his small fists.

"My key went off because I was too close to him. Did either of you feel anything?"

The brothers glance down at their necks. The ankhs tattooed on their skin were identical to Jenna's. They shook their heads.

"Right," said Jenna, disappointed. "Well, I did. So we need to destroy it."

"Maybe we should watch the guy first," suggested Michael, his eyes drifting up as a crew of six hulking jocks walk toward them. "You know, to see what he's all about before we make our move. We'll—"

The jocks' leader, Tommy, had a slender blond under each arm. He waved at Michael. "Hey. The coach wants us on the field early today."

"I'll be there." Michael took an apple from his tray and stuffed it into his backpack. "I'm just finishing up."

Tommy shrugged and walked on. "Drop the losers, man. They're holding you back."

Michael stood up.

"Say something," Jenna hissed under her breath, her eyes flashing with hatred at Tommy. "Anything."

Clueless, Michael ruffled Eric's hair. "See if you can get the dad's address off the net. We'll track him down tonight and see if he's infected."

"The longer we wait, the tougher it'll get." Jenna took a large bite of her ham-and-cheese sandwich. "I say we do it now."

Michael pretended not to hear her. "Stay away from the pool unless one of us is around. It's not safe."

"Whatever." Jenna glared up at him.

"Ignore him," said Eric as they watched Michael hurry to catch up with Tommy. "What's the girl's name?"

"Hope Broadmoor."

Eric pulled out his phone and began searching.

* * * *

Michael parked his rusted 1963 Ford Maverick across the street from the hardware store Derek Broadmoor entered. Scrunched down, squinting to see in the waning moonlight, the three friends were tired and bored.

Michael shifted positions, arching his back. "This is dumb."

Eric yawned. "Sorry, Jenna, but he hasn't done anything interesting all night, and I have a test tomorrow."

"Hush." Through the shop's display window, Jenna watched Derek collect an armful of supplies before heading toward the cashier. "Can you see what he's buying?"

"Probably shaving cream and donuts." Michael cracked his neck. "Did you know Tommy's dating Nicky and Jenny at the same time? That's crazy right? I mean, they both know."

"Just look," growled Jenna. "He's up to something."

Derek walked out of the store with two brown bags. Glancing up and down the darkened street, he made his way to his car.

"Shit. I can't see what it is," said Jenna, her jaw set. "We're going to have to follow him."

"No, we're not." The ankh on Michael's neck glowed a deep blue as he stuck his arm outside the car's window. "Watch this."

"Michael, don't," spat Jenna. "Only if it's an emergency."

Michael's hand turned semi-transparent, ghost-like, and extended like a pseudopod of air across the road. The nearly invisible tentacle wrapped around Derek's legs and tripped him.

Stumbling, their suspect dropped his bags and cursed as he chased after the spilled contents—dozens of spray-paint cans.

"Why does he need so much paint?" Michael's voice deepened with concern. "No one needs that much."

"The guy is smarter than I thought." Eric clicked his tongue in appreciation. "They're flammable, under pressure, hard to trace. He's building a bomb."

Jenna turned on Michael. "I told you. There's a lurker in his head."

They watched as Derek gathered his cans and threw them into the back seat of his car. Jumping inside, he sped away, his tires shrieking.

Rematerializing his hand, finally convinced, Michael slid the Maverick's key into the ignition. He revved the engine. "We need to talk to Marina."

* * * *

The rusted Maverick pulled up to the wrought iron gate outside the Marlow Dream Institute, and Michael punched his code into the security box. The ivy-encrusted gate swung open, and they drove up the meandering driveway, through a tunnel of overhanging pines, to their home.

The Institute once belonged to an eminent Hollywood producer who sold it for pennies when the FBI nailed him for money laundering. Michael and Eric's parents bought it, renovated it, hired therapists, and opened the world's first virtual psychotherapy program. Joe Marlow, the boys' father, developed the technique by fitting nanobots with magnetic neuro-transducers and then injecting them into a gel mask. Patients wore the masks while they slept, and the nanobots recorded their brainwaves, converted them to visual images, and then replayed their TV-style dreams the next day. Only the wealthiest clientele could afford such therapy, but they paid well, and so the Marlow family had been happy.

The accident that allowed the nanobots to escape the masks woke the King in Yellow and his lurkers, and transformed the children into Dream Warriors had closed the Institute forever.

Now, where once stood a marvelous gem of architectural glory, there was only a dark foreboding mansion that the townspeople refused to speak of in anything above a whisper.

Sneaking into the house through the back door, the three wove their way down the numerous abandoned hallways until they came to the observation window that looked into the lab.

Jenna peeked inside and saw that Dr. Marlow, surrounded by robotic arms and hundreds of glowing plastic tubes, was turned away from the glass. She nodded to the boys and rolled past the window unseen.

Crouching low, Michael and Eric followed.

On the other side, the three faced each other outside their respective rooms.

"It's early, let's meet at the trailer park. She's probably still at home," said Eric.

Jenna nodded. "Twenty minutes."

"Night." Michael turned and entered his room. The walls and dressers overflowed with football paraphernalia and trophies. He left his dirty clothes in a pile on the floor and changed into a pair of shorts and T-shirt. Flopping into his unmade bed with a sigh of exhaustion, he closed his eyes.

In stark contrast to Michael's, alphabetically arranged books and journals cover every surface area of Eric's room. Upon entering, he moved to his immaculate desk and opened several textbooks. Flipping through the pages, speed-reading, he absorbed their contents in minutes. Satisfied, he turned on every light in the room and lay down in bed, fully dressed, and closed his eyes.

Jenna transferred from her chair to her bed. Crammed with heavy-metal posters, an electric guitar, and unwashed clothes, the room radiated her personality. Dressed in dark pajamas, hair loose, she clapped her hands to turn the lights off and closed her eyes.

Simultaneously, each child raised their fingers to the black tattoos under their necks. A spectrum of eldritch light radiated from behind their closed eyes, and their ankhs glowed with iridescent power.

* * * *

A cluster of translucent women hung laundry on the lines outside their ramshackle trailer homes while stealing glances at the dusky gray sky, trying to judge if it would rain. Sitting around a rickety card table erected between the houses, a group of bleary-eyed men played cards with hands as see-through as their wives. A group of ghost boys danced around a bonfire made from splintered furniture, tree limbs, and dry grass. Embers rose like angry fireflies from the blaze as gasses squealed with furious delight as they escaped the wood.

Then, something about the fire changed, deepened and grew, so that it billowed outward and caused the youngsters to leap back with singed hair and skin. The yellow flames rose and swirled together, mixing in with the dark smoke, before forming the shape of a young girl with eyes of amber. Her skin glowed, iridescent and hypnotic, while the burning strands of her hair snapped at the air like furious snakes.

"You shouldn't play with fire," said Jenna with the silky smooth voice of a woman.

Screaming, the transparent boys scampered away.

Jenna stepped out of the pile of black ashes at her feet and let the flames that enveloped her upper torso go out. She wore the same dark pajamas she'd gone to bed in, but rather than the withered lower extremities of her waking life; she stood on glass-smooth legs of living flame. She stretched, savoring the strength she felt in the dreaming.

A catcall whistle interrupted her, and she looked up to find the men who had been playing poker staring at her with appreciation. She walked toward them, her right hand blazing into flames. "What did you just do?"

The ground beneath the gambler's table exploded upward, throwing the players on their backs. Stepping up through the Earth, gravel raining down from his massive shoulders, a giant with stone skin and emerald eyes coughed apologetically.

The men ran, scattering behind oil drums and old car frames.

"Sorry," said Eric with a baritone voice so profound the ground shook. Spotting Jenna, he grinned and caught up with her in two enormous strides. They walked together down the street.

Neither Jenna nor Eric were transparent, a malady attributable to dreamers but not to those who were awake in their dreams.

"It's not far," said Eric as huge boulders and massive sheets of dirt fell off his frame to reveal the boy beneath. He wore the street clothes he'd worn to bed. Ahead, an older trailer with a fenced yard filled with weeds greeted them.

Jenna pointed out the light behind a curtained window. "She's still home."

They pushed open a knee-high gate and walked onto Marina's property.

A transparent, barrel-chested dog rose from behind a discarded tire. It issued a low growl.

"Do you think it's friendly?" Eric moved toward the animal.

It rushed at him, foam dripping from its mouth, and lunged for his throat.

"Sorry, puppy," said a hollow voice from nowhere. "We don't have time to play."

Suspended in mid-leap, the dog gnashed its teeth as it began to spin in slow circles. The speed of rotation increased as Michael, little more than an outline, materialized with folded arms. His jet-blue eyes sparkled.

"Thanks." Eric swallowed. His hands moved away from his neck. "Who said dogs don't dream?"

Gently, Michael lowered the now whimpering animal to the ground. It stumbled back to its hiding place behind the tire. "I don't know. He's kind of cute."

"Focus, boys," said Jenna as she walked past them. She knocked on Marina's aluminum door and waited. No one answered.

"Marina!" shouted Michael. "Are you in there?"

"Maybe she's asleep," suggested Eric.

"Funny," said Jenna with a scowl. "Should we go in and look?"

"I wouldn't recommend that," said a woman's voice from behind them.

The three spun to find Marina perched in the branches of a twisted oak tree. Her dark swirling robes, more clotted darkness than clothing, shifted over her pale skin like a living creature. Using a spoon, she peeled an apple as she regarded them with eyes of sparkling silver. "There are things in there that will hurt you if I'm not around."

Jenna stepped forward. "We found a lurker."

"Did you?"

"Yeah," Michael nodded sagely. "He's trying to build a bomb."

Marina fell out of the tree; her body twisted like a cat's, and she landed in a practiced crouch. Deliberately, she scooped out three sections of her apple and gave one to each child. "Not everything is as it seems. The King in Yellow is a master of disguises, of games. Don't..."

She clutched her shoulder, the apple falling, forgotten, to disappear into the weeds. Gently, pulling back her flowing robe, she examined the yellow stain on her forearm with revulsion.

Jenna reached for her. "Does it hurt?"

Michael watched Marina, wary. "It looks bigger."

"It feels good." Marina bit her lip, and a thin line of blood ran down her chin. "Do not underestimate him. His mark...is...addictive."

"I'm sorry," said Eric, his voice betraying his annoyance, "but can't you tell us anything that might help?"

Marina shook her head as she moved past them to her trailer. The hinges on her thin door piped as she entered its shadowed interior. "Don't eat the apples."

The children looked down at the scalloped sections of fruit she'd given them to find black serpents crawling out of the cores of each. The snakes' sticky diamond heads reared back.

All three flung the apples away.

* * * *

Jenna stood over the pool, her eyes trained on the swimmers as they raced toward her. The lead girl touched the wall, her final stroke as smooth as cream. The whistle between Jenna's lips blew shrilly as she jotted down the time. "Good job, Rebecca. That was a solid run."

Rebecca smiled proudly as she climbed, dripping, out of the water to be joined by her teammates seconds later. Soon, there was only one splashing figure left in the water. Awkward, gasping for air, Hope flopped onto her back at Jenna's feet.

"Yes!" Derek yelled from his customary place in the stands. He was recording everything with his phone. "Way to go, honey!"

Jenna moaned as she watched Hope's father punch the air, living vicariously through his daughter's limited abilities. "Alright, everyone. That was good. I want ten more freestyle laps. Work on your form."

The girls dove back into the water as Jenna addressed Hope. "Can I talk to you for a minute?"

Struggling to her feet, the young girl forced a smile. "Sure, Coach."

"I'm not going to put you in the meet this weekend."

Hope's eyes darted to her father. She looked scared. "He's going to be upset."

"I just don't think you're ready. Maybe in a couple of months…"

"Months? You can't do that to me!" Hope spoke loudly enough for Derek to hear. Then, leaning forward, she continued in a pleading whisper. "Listen, Coach. I know I'm no good, but if I don't compete he'll—"

Jenna cut her off. "I'm sorry. I've got to do what's best for the team. I've decided."

In tears, Hope ran for the lockers only to be intercepted by Derek as he stomped down the bleachers.

Her father held her in place. Their conversation was hushed, but Derek glared at Jenna as Hope's explanation trailed off.

Fuming, he stormed toward the indoor pools where Coach Plata was training the varsity swimmers.

* * * *

Jenna and Michael's gruff argument broke the library's habitual silence. Ignoring them, Eric focused his attention on the three books open in front of him.

"…And the coach said I had to let her compete," sputtered Jenna. "Just because he's a member of the school board, he thinks he can push people around."

"That's why I don't want you alone with him," said Michael. "Either Eric or I—"

Jenna beat the armrests of her chair. "I told you, I don't need to be babysat. Besides, all you're doing is sitting around and waiting for something to happen. We should be going after him right now, catch it by surprise."

"Think about it, Jenna. We can't just power on and blast him. There are people around. He's dangerous."

Jenna seethed. "That's the point."

Eric cleared his throat. "I've got my test next period, guys. Can we talk about this later."

Both Michael and Jenna hissed at him, "No!"

"The next time he gets in my way I'm taking him out." Spinning her chair, Jenna ran her wheel over Michael's foot as she left. "Alone."

Yelping, Michael bounced on his good foot.

"Wimp," sang Jenna as she vanished down an aisle.

Nursing his foot, Michael sat down next to Eric. "You've got a free period during Jenna's swim practice tomorrow. Can you keep an eye on her?"

Eric sighed. "If I say yes, will you go away and let me finish cramming?"

"Done." Michael's ankh glowed, and he vanished. "Just remember keep your distance. I don't want Jenna or the lurker to know you're there."

* * * *

Sitting in the bleachers behind Derek, Eric watched the girls swim with a pair of binoculars. Every few minutes, he lowered the glasses and took notes on a yellow legal pad.

Annoyed, Derek glanced back at him. "What are you doing?"

"I'm watching the practice. Same as you."

"Don't you have class?"

"Don't you have work?"

Derek's ground his teeth. "That's my girl down there. I'm here to support her."

Eric tightened the focus on the binoculars. "You mean the cute one. I've been watching her…"

Derek's eyes darkened as his fingers curled into fists.

"…She's got real talent. No doubt about it, she's going to be someone."

Derek relaxed. "You think so?"

"I'm sure of it." Lowering the binoculars, Eric extended his hand. "Rob Underwood. I'm doing an article for the school paper."

Derek beamed with pride as he shook Eric's hand. "She works harder than any of the others. You should see her dive."

They sat for a moment, silently watching the swimmers together. The afternoon sun glimmering on the water.

"Say," said Eric, cautiously. "Do you think I could interview your daughter?"

Jenna noticed the pair as they walked down the bleachers. Her hand went to her throat as her eyes flashed with amber light.

Water splashed onto the deck as her girls pulled themselves out of the water. They were finished with practice. Toweling off, Hope broke from the other girls to join her father.

Jenna bit her lower lip. She needed to keep it together. "Good work this week, girls. Tomorrow's the meet, and I want one hundred and ten percent from each of you. Go home. Get some rest and be here on time."

Cheerfully, the girls headed for the lockers.

Jenna uncovered her neck and steam escaped between her fingers. Waving it away, she rolled over to where Derek, Eric, and Hope were talking.

"I thought I told you to stay away." Jenna glared at Eric. "I can handle this."

Eric beamed at her. "Just doing my job, Coach. The paper needs an article on fresh new talent, and I think I've found the one."

Hope turned bright red.

"Paper?" Jenna struggled to contain her anger.

Eric turned his back to her as he shook Derek's hand. "So, it's decided.

I'll meet both of you in the school gym at six tonight—"

"Get...out...of...here." Jenna spat the words.

Eric glanced at her. "Is she always like that?"

"Always." Derek scowled. "It's a surprise Hope is doing as well as she is given the pressure she's under."

Jenna spun her chair and wheeled away. "Hope. Lockers. Now!"

"Yes, Coach." Hope's feet slapped the wet pavement as she ran to catch up.

"We'll talk tonight," said Derek to Eric before lowering his voice. "But don't finish your article until after the swim meet. I've got something big planned for tomorrow night, and I want you to see it."

At the back of the locker room, surrounded by the chatter of girls changing and gossiping, Jenna studied Hope. "Be honest with me. Do you want to be here or is your father making you do this?"

Hope watched her teammates pack up. She shivered, her voice betraying her growing apprehension. "I'm going to look like a complete fool, aren't I?"

"Don't worry how you look," said Jenna. "You should be doing this because you like it. It's supposed to be fun."

Hope's eyes snapped up to meet Jenna's. "For who? He's driving me crazy. He's making me look like I'm a... He keeps coming to practice... Everyone's laughing at me...or feeling sad for me because I'm such a loser."

"Listen, Hope." Jenna bit her lower lip, considering how to proceed. "Maybe I can help... I could show you a few tricks. You won't win, but you might not be the last to finish. Can you sneak out tonight?"

"What?" Hope stared at her. "Like without him knowing?"

"Yeah." Jenna met Hope's eyes. "Do the interview with your dad, then say you're tired and go to bed early. Meet me here at midnight."

"Okay."

"But don't tell anyone. Especially, your dad."

Hope nodded.

* * * *

Except for a half-a-dozen discarded basketballs and Eric, the gym was abandon. The orange light of the setting sun shone through the rectangular windows near the rafters. Eric glanced around, picked up a ball, and mumbled calculations before tossing it.

The shot was from half-court, and it swished through the hoop.

He picked up another ball and duplicated the same incredible shot.

"You're good." Hope stepped out of the shadows near the door.

Startled, Eric spun to find her dressed in a simple white dress with glasses. She was pretty. "You're early."

She smiled at him. "You should go out for the team."

Eric blushed. "My health insurance isn't that good. Besides, it's not that hard. It's all about the trajectory. You just have to work out the distance, height, and coefficient of gravity. Anyone can do it."

Hope moved to join him. "Can I try?"

Eric glanced at the empty door. "Where's your dad? I thought he was coming with you."

"He wasn't feeling well." Hope took the ball from his hands. "It's alright I came be myself, isn't it?"

"Yeah." Left alone with a girl, Eric mumbled. "Sure. No problem."

Hope moved in front of him and lifted the ball. She aimed. "Show me."

Eric reached around her to reposition her hands. "The basket is ten feet off the ground, and we're forty-three feet away. So, you have to raise your arms a bit more."

"Like this?" Seductively, Hope backed into him.

Eric's neck stiffened with a searing pain as his ankh ignited with green flame. Instinctively, his hands rose to cover the glowing tattoo.

Hope's elbow slammed into his solar plexus, knocking the air out of him and sending him to the floor. She lifted the basketball over her head, the whites of her eyes replaced by black pearls. "The King in Yellow sends his regards, thief."

Eric was too slow to stop her blow. His skull rebounded off the ball and into the floor with a crack that echoed around the gym.

Hope knelt next to Eric's unconscious form and smiled. Lovingly, she moved a lock of hair out of his eyes. Then, looking toward the gym's far door, she yelled. "Help! Someone come quick!"

Hope had arrived before either boy and watched from the gloom as Michael hid in the hallway armed with a bat. They had planned on ambushing her father, so it was only fair that she had found a way to turn the tables.

Michael rushed into the gym, his bat raised.

Hoped looked up from Eric's side, her features desperate. "Help him."

"What happened?" Michael dropped the bat and ran to his brother's side.

Backing up, pretending to make room for Michael, Hope explained. "I don't know. We were just talking, and then he kind of fainted."

Michael shook Eric. "Hey, Buddy. Wake up."

Calmly, Hope retrieved the bat.

Michael's hands came away from the back of Eric's head bloody. Just then, his ankh ignited with a blue flame. He turned on Hope. "What are you?"

The bat hit Michael in the side of the head, and he went down.

Hope giggled. "Sweet dreams, little Princes."

* * * *

A yellow taxi pulled up to the school, and the diver got out to retrieve Jenna's wheelchair from his trunk. Unfolding it on the passenger side, he waited for her to transfer. "It's the middle of the night, Miss. You sure you want me to leave you here?"

"I'll be fine." Jenna gave him a reassuring smile. "I'm meeting someone. Thanks, though."

Popping a wheelie, she rolled her chair toward the school's outer gate. She unlocked the padlock with her student coach key and left the gate open. If Jenna were lucky, Derek would follow his daughter, and she could end this charade.

The school grounds were quiet, pitch-black, and deserted. Jenna took a deep breath. This was her favorite time of the day. She rounded a corner and saw all the lights over the pool were on, and there was someone swimming.

She edged closer and found Hope doing laps.

Jenna rolled over to the edge of the pool. "How'd you get in?"

"Never left," said Hope. "I've been practicing all night."

Jenna looked up at the empty stands. "What about your dad?"

"I slipped cough syrup into his coffee. He'll be out all night."

Jenna nodded, admiring the girl's initiative. She pulled off her shirt and sweat pants to reveal the swimsuit beneath. "We'll work quickly. I want you to get some sleep before the meet."

"Great." Hope watched her eagerly. "What was it you wanted to show me?"

"You've got good form, Hope. But you're hesitating, almost pulling back at the end of each stroke. You need to even them out."

Hope frowned. "My dad says I'm doing it right."

"Your dad is a complete—" Jenna bit her lip on seeing Hope's face. "Just try it, okay? Make each move flow into the next."

Hope dog-paddled backward, her arms whacking the water. "Better?"

"No." Jenna shook her head. "I'll show you."

Locking her chair, Jenna fell forward into the water. A moment later, she surfaced.

Hope pulled herself out of the pool, her lips pulling back into a wicked smile. "I'll be able to see better from up here."

* * * *

A single naked light bulb hung over Michael and Eric. The boys were tied back-to-back in the Janitor's closet.

Eric moaned with pain, shook his head and took in his surroundings. Straining his neck, he recognizes his brother's clothing and profile. "Hey, Mike. Wake up!"

Michael stirred but his motions are slow and placid. "Man. I've got the worst headache...What hit me?"

"More like whom." Eric pulled on his ropes. "The King put a lurker in Hope, not her dad."

Michael tightened his chest, trying to break the bounds, and failed. "She's going after Jenna. Get us out of here."

Eric's ankh glowed, and the ropes disintegrated. "Done."

Michael shot a tentacle of air at the locked door. The blast took it off its hinges. "She's going to try and catch Jenna off guard, lure her someplace she feels safe."

They looked at each other. "The pool."

* * * *

Jenna finished another lap and looked up at Hope. "Are you getting it?"

Hope's eyes turned ebony as she smiled back. "Don't worry, Coach. I know just what to do."

Steam rose from Jenna's ankh as her throat went to it. Understanding, she flipped and swam toward her chair.

Leisurely, Hope lifted her palms and the water around Jenna began to swirl in a snug circle, a whirlpool. Clawed liquid digits rose from the water to grab at Jenna's shoulders and hands. "I think it's my turn to teach you something."

Jenna wriggled against the living waves, but the powerful hands dragged her down. She hit back, the ankh on her neck flaming and then extinguishing beneath the water. Bubbles of air escaped her screaming lungs.

Hope stood on the edge of the pool and laughed.

Furious, Jenna broke free and swam to the surface only to meet an invisible barrier, a patina of water as thick as a sheet of ice over the pool. She pounded against it, the precious air in her lungs escaping.

Hope folded her arms over her chest and watched with growing satisfaction. "Thief."

The ground shook and threw Hope off her feet.

Extending like a knife, a mammoth pillar of cement grew from the pool's floor to rupture the clotted water on its surface. Jenna hugged the column, her body smoldering with growing rage even as she coughed up the water she'd swallowed.

Hope got to her feet and turned to find Eric crouched in the field beyond the bleachers, his hands stuffed into the muddy grass, his eyes glowing a deep green.

Jenna heaved herself to the edge of the pillar and stared down at Hope. "That was not very nice, lurker."

The pillar, directed by Eric, twisted unnaturally so it could deposit Jenna in her chair.

Hope's black eyes blazed with fury. "None of you deserve your powers! You took it from the King. Return your ankhs, or he will drive you mad."

Hope extended her arm, and a tidal wave of water rose as a massive fist. It hung in the air, a liquid sledgehammer, before crashing down on Jenna with colossal force.

The wave receded to reveal Jenna, unharmed inside a protective half-dome of air. "Thanks."

"She's a vicious little bugger," said Michael, the blue glow of his eyes being the only hint of where to find the outline of his body.

Jenna's hands burst into flame. "We need to get inside her head, fight it on its turf."

Apprehensive, Hope edged toward the pool.

"She needs the water," warned Eric. "Stop her."

Hope lunged forward.

A jet of fire shot out of Jenna's arms as if they were twin flamethrowers to form a massive wall between Hope and the pool.

Hope faltered and backed up.

Eric raced forward and tackled her, his unarmored human form barely heavy enough to keep her on the ground.

Jenna and Michael approached as their ankhs pulsing with ethereal light.

Jenna leaned forward, Michael knelt down, and Eric grunted as he tried to keep Hope from escaping. Simultaneously, they placed their hands on the girl's forehead.

A white light enveloped them.

* * * *

They woke on a midnight beach in another world, the dreaming world, and thunderclouds and lightning filled the sky above their heads.

Eric, Jenna, and Michael, each with glowing ankhs, stood to face the monstrous-water-creature, the pure form of Hope's lurker, as it took shape in the sea. Below it, lay Hope's semi-transparent body. The girl was unconscious, dreaming.

The lurker was a fisherman's nightmare, a swirling dark mass with triple rows of jagged teeth set in a tentacled canine face. Oily-black eyes that led to mindless oblivion leered down at them as the creature's suckered arms tapered to needle-sharp points. The King in Yellow's minion spoke. "Thieves."

Flames blossomed over Jenna as she rose into the air, her amber eyes like white-hot torches against the sinister sky. "Leave her alone."

The lurker cackled wetly. "Make me."

The blast of molten flame Jenna threw at the monster vaporized half its face and arm. Seconds later, the damage was repaired from the endless ocean feeding the beast.

Rocks flew across the sand, covering Eric in a giant's armor. Four times larger, eyes glowing with an emerald light, he slammed his fists into the beach. A deep crevice split the ground. The land broke apart, lifting up like the edges of an imaginably large towel to form massive walls of Earth. "Bad lurker."

The walls smashed shut, annihilating the minion.

Moments later, the sea mist congealed back into the creature's terrifying form, only larger and thicker than before.

Blades of air spiraled out of Michael's arms, Frisbee-shaped weapons with paper-thin edges, to shred the beast into thousands of jiggling globules. Seconds later, they gelled back together.

"We can't hurt it," complained Michael.

"That's why," said Jenna, pointing down at Hope.

Twin ropes of brackish water extended like tubers from the lurker's side to the girl's wrists.

"It's feeding off of her," said Eric, lumbering forward. "We have to separate them."

"Not so fast." The lurker's toothy mouth grinned. "Don't I get a turn?"

It raised its arms, and paired columns of water rocketed out of the ocean to knock Jenna and Michael from the sky. The liquid doused Jenna's flame while the speed of the attack caught Michael off guard, flinging him into a palm tree. He dropped to the beach in his human form.

The lurker turned to face Eric. It swung a clawed hand at him, and the ocean rushed up the channel Eric's initial attack had made in the sand. The ground became quicksand, and Eric sunk into it.

Lightning flashed, and a dark rain began to fall.

No longer threatened, the lurker's body washed away into the sea. A fluid shape, no larger than a boy, walked up the beach to where Hope lay. The shimmering abomination knelt over the girl and unhinged its terrible jaw.

"No." Jenna crawled toward the lurker, her fingers tearing up great chunks of sand as she inched forward. "That's my student."

The lurker inhaled, and Hope's astral form moved toward its throat like smoke drawn to a vacuum. Putrid saliva the color of rotting seaweed dripped from between the minion's teeth as it began to swallow its prey.

Hope's face contorted with pain.

"No!" Jenna's body reignited like a kerosene-soaked bonfire, her expression crackling with vengeful energy as she rose back into the air. Narrow beams of flame extended from her amber eyes to slice through the cords connecting the lurker to Hope. Jenna sent another massive discharge into the creature's chest. It reeled back into the ocean.

"Turn it down, Jenna." Michael shook his head and, cringing from the heat Jenna was giving off. "It's too much!"

The sand beneath Jenna's feet glowed red hot, melting into a disc of glass as she rose into the air like a vengeful sun. Her voice boomed with mounting fear. "I can't control it!"

The ocean split open, and the lurker, now the size of a mountain, rose up to meet her. Roaring, it swung a suckered arm.

"Come at me!" Jenna flew at the titan, her body vibrating with effort as her powers neared super-nova. The forces collided and the ground shook with a detonation that thundered throughout the dreaming.

The smoke cleared, and neither Jenna nor the lurker appeared touched.

Jenna looked at Michael, desperate. "I'm going to explode!"

Michael flew to Eric and used tentacles of air to draw his brother's rocky armor out of the sandy muck. "You can't do this alone, Jenna."

Eric's voice boomed. "Let us help you!"

The lurker's watery paw closed around Jenna's fireball. Squeezing, it tried to extinguish her.

Tears of fire dripped from her eyes to reflect like fireflies off the disc of glass she'd made in the sand. Her nostrils flared as she fought the constricting ocean. "I've got an idea. Can you isolate it?"

"Done." Michael flew at the lurker; his arms spread wide. He gestured with his hands, bending the reality that was the dream, and a hurricane formed around the monster. The winds pulled at the possessed water, lifting it out of the ocean.

Jenna called down. "Eric, I need sand."

Eric's stony fists hammered the beach, and six columns of sand rose to merge with Michael's winds.

Distracted, annoyed, the lurker released Jenna as it lashed at the walls of the waterspout.

Jenna sent a swath of heat at the swirling sand and water. The flame evaporated the lurker's body while melted the sand in the air into molten glass.

Michael worked with her, molding the steaming crystal sludge into a ball of glass around the lurker.

The lurker lunged vainly against its hollow paperweight prison as Michael lowered the sphere to the beach.

The children reverted to their human forms. Jenna's legs remained twin columns of flame as she walked with the boys to examine their captive.

The monster yowled at them, grinding its liquid teeth.

Drained, the three Dream Warriors shared high-fives.

Michael beamed. "Good work."

Hope's limp form shifted in the sand.

Jenna nodded. "Good teamwork."

* * * *

Scorched concrete and a half-empty pool met the children as they stepped back into reality. The first rays of sunlight fell across Hope's sleeping body.

"You sure the meet's today?" Eric brushed the dust from his shirt. "Cause I think they're going to notice this."

Jenna saw a figure moving carefully across the campus. Her eyes narrowed. "I have to go take care of something. Can you guys get Hope home and clean up this mess?"

Despite their fatigue, the boys nodded.

"And…" Jenna stared at her useless legs for a moment before looking up at her friends. "Thanks."

Embarrassed, collecting her street clothes, Jenna rolled away before they could respond.

She kept to the shadows, her wheels barely making a noise as she followed her prey. Finally, they came to a dumpster. The man climbed it and unzipped his backpack. Glancing around, Derek pulled out a dozen spray cans.

Curious, Jenna took out her phone and began to record.

Derek was talented. It took him less than ten minutes to have the majority of the gym wall covered with colorful graffiti.

Jenna coughed. "Hey, Mr. Broadmoor…"

Spinning around, shamefaced, Derek tried to hide the spray can behind his back. He squinted at the shadows. "Hey…Jenna."

Innocently, Jenna lowered her phone. "Not exactly the type of behavior I'd expect from a member of the school board."

Defeated, Derek slumped back against the freshly painted wall. "What do you want?"

Jenna grinned.

* * * *

The crowd cheered as Jenna's team struggled to maintain fifth place. Jenna sat, clipboard in hand, her body tense.

Derek occupied his usual spot in the stands and recorded everything, his eyes never left the pool. Behind him, in full view of the visiting teams, his graffiti wall read, "HOPE RULES."

Jenna nodded to Hope, and the young girl took her place on the edge of the pool. Her teammate reached the wall and Hope dove into the water.

Startlingly, she was liquid fast. With smooth strokes, Hope caught up with the opposing team, flipped and swam back. Free of the lurker, her mind once again her own, Hope's suppressed talent blossomed.

She touched the wall, having brought their team to forth place. Looking up at the scoreboard, she beamed at her time.

Hope pulled herself out of the water to receive the admiration and hugs of her peers.

The meet was over.

Derek walked down the stands, and his daughter ran to him.

"I got us forth place, Dad…" Hope hesitated. "Is that good enough?"

Jenna's amber eyes flashed at Derek as she evocatively pulled out her phone.

Derek met his daughter's gaze. "It's perfect, Hope."

Hope hugged her father.

"It really was a great job," said Derek sincerely. "I'm very proud of you."

Jenna looked up to find Michael and Eric standing on either side of her, enjoying the show.

"It looks like you won that battle," said Michael.

Jenna pulled an apple out of her backpack. Using a spoon, she scooped out a section and offered it to the boys.

Eric backed away, his hand raised in mock fear. "Not that hungry."

Michael grinned at the joke. "At least not for apples."

Jenna shrugged and took a bite. "Don't worry. I think we got rid of the all the bad parts."

They watched as Derek and Hope walked away.

Hope looked back at them and smiled.

* * * *

In the dreaming, the lurker's crystal globe hung from a rope. The cord was attached to the underside of a decomposing bridge and hung over a river of molten lava. Deep canyon walls rose from the glowing magma stream far below the Dream Warrior's prisoner.

Roaring with frustration, the lurker melted, reformed, and battered the smooth inner walls of its glass prison. The sphere rocked gently on its rope like a quartz pendulum.

Beneath the beast, ascending the crumbling path leading to the bridge, a figure in yellow cloaks climbed.

Softly, The King in Yellow chuckled.

BANG!
Chris Kuriata

Using his forefinger and thumb, the boy pointed an imaginary gun at the TV, taking dead aim at the newswoman standing before a green-screened map of the prairies.

"Bang!"

The babysitter, Laurie, watched astounded as the TV woman's clothing tore away. The white blouse and black skirt flew off into the wings of the studio as though attached to invisible wires, leaving her exposed for anyone to see.

Laurie fumbled for the remote control and switched to another channel, the easiest way of respecting the poor, now-naked woman's privacy. Laurie had never seen this young lady on the Weather Network before, so this might have been her first day on the job, her big chance to show what she could do. Her parents back home were probably watching, proud, rooting for her.

Why didn't the cameraman point away? Laurie thought. *Save her the humiliation?*

The boy moved his finger across the TV screen, leaving a thin scratch in the dust. Static crackled.

"Bang!"

This time, a man in a studio kitchen dropped his mixing bowl as his apron, chef whites, and tall starched hat flew off his body. Lucky for him, he had the counter to hide behind, where he ducked to retrieve his spilled bowl of batter.

Laurie kept the TV off until the boy's parents returned. They carried salmon and asparagus wrapped in tinfoil folded into the shape of a swan. They offered this high-class doggie bag to Laurie as a bonus for her babysitting. She accepted it gratefully, not wanting to hurt their feelings, even though she knew she would be tossing it into the garbage at home. She didn't care for fish.

"We had a quiet night," Laurie reported. The parents stood in the front hall, waiting for her to leave, in no mood for conversation.

"Wonderful."

"Watched some TV."

She studied their faces for a reaction, but neither parent appeared to be listening to a word she said as they slipped out of their coats, not even holding her eye contact.

"Great," the man said, reaching around Laurie to open the front door. "Good night."

She crossed the busy street, heading two blocks through the late evening to her bus stop. Judging by the parents' reaction, they knew nothing of their child's ability.

* * * *

On Saturday, Laurie took the boy to the park while his parents finished up "office things". Her knees grew sore from walking, and she rested on a bench while her charge frolicked in the sandpit with two other children.

While the new kids dug into the sand, curious to see how far down they could claw before hitting water or rock, the boy pointed his finger into the sky at a swooping bluebird.

"Bang!"

Laurie raised a hand to shield her eyes from the noon sun. Would all the bird's feathers come off, bursting in a big swarm? Would it tumble to the ground dead?

Nothing happened. The bird continued its arc, coming to rest in the branches of a tall oak, where it unloaded a beak full of plucked worms into its babies' mouths.

I guess he can only shoot people, Laurie thought. She worried the boy might point at one of the other children and say "Bang!", but he respectfully kept his finger holstered for the rest of the afternoon.

* * * *

Back at the house, the boy sat in the front door, watching the weekend traffic clog the street. This activity made Laurie feel sweet on him. Her own boy, Jesse, spent his childhood fascinated by cars. He took out huge books from the library filled with diagrams of disassembled engines, and he collected catalogues from all the dealerships. By the time he was in high school, he worked part-time at Kivell's mechanics. Jesse could identify a car's make just by the sound of its approaching engine. Had he lived, he would be in his early '40s today.

"You like the cars?"

The boy poked his finger into the door's screen, excitedly singling out an idling SUV, one so dark and imposing it looked militaristic.

"There was a big truck, even bigger than that one."

Since last week, Laurie only felt comfortable watching TV while the boy stayed out of the room. She knew she hadn't imagined what she'd seen, because the Weather Network issued an on-air apology.

"While we can't take back the unfortunate event that occurred on our broadcast, we do apologize, and rest assured, something like this will never happen again."

They fired that poor girl. Probably thought she did it as some kind of prank for attention.

Laurie wasn't sure what happened to the chef who caught the second blast from the boy's gun. Likely, he met the same fate.

Selfishly, the Weather Network's apology eased Laurie's mind. She considered the possibility what she'd witnessed hadn't really happened. Maybe she had grown doddering in her age, unable to tell the difference between dreams and real life. A terrifying thought.

The boy entered the living room sucking his thumb. Laurie quickly changed the channel. She felt responsible for making the TV a safe space, unwilling to put anyone else at risk of being humiliated and fired. She switched from the live news to an old game show. The program wasn't just a re-run, it was an antique, filmed over sixty years ago, back in the day when most people listened on the radio as only the wealthy owned television sets.

The boy pointed his finger at the TV screen. Laurie did not make a move to stop him, secure in the knowledge the boy could do no more damage than when he pointed his finger at that bird.

"Bang!"

On TV, the game show host's grey suit flew off. The studio audience shrieked, but unlike the weather girl or the chef, the ancient, black-and-white man did not cower or run off stage cupping his vulnerable bits. He placed his hands on his hips, pinching his cigar between his teeth at a defiant angle. Laurie knew she should shield her eyes, but she stared fascinated, realizing she had never seen this famous man without his glasses before. He looked older without them, less dignified.

"Now we break for a word from our sponsor," the game show host said. *"During which I'm sure our sponsor will want to have a word with me."*

* * * *

Laurie hated the computer pad her daughter bought her, distrusting the little camera in the centre of its forehead. According to the news, computer people could hack into her camera and use the lens to spy on her. While she couldn't imagine anyone was interested in looking at her, the possibility gave her the creeps.

She rested her fingertips over the blank Google screen for a good ten minutes, telling herself there was nothing wrong with what she wanted to see. This wasn't an invasion of privacy, this was different. She remembered a couple years back when all those movies stars had private pictures stolen and put onto the computer for any pervert to see. What astonished her most was the discovery otherwise normal people like her own daughter and son-and-law also looked at those photos, and more surprisingly, had no problem joking about them over dinner. Laurie would have hidden her head in shame if she's ever done such a terrible thing, invading other's privacy. It was unconscionable. Her son-in-law made a joke about one of the actresses having a messy face, and her daughter smacked his wrist and told him to watch himself. They didn't think Laurie knew what they were talking about, but of course she did. They were fooling themselves if they thought nothing dirty existed before their generation. For crying out loud, there were clay pots thousands of years old depicting the same things.

"Alright," Laurie muttered, and tapped her fingers across the screen, typing out:

GROUCHO MARX NAKED

Within 0.40 seconds, the first page of some 252,000 results came in.

"Oh my goodness."

She tapped the first link, bringing her to a still image from the game show re-run she just watched. Groucho in all his glory, a pixilated dot obscuring the area beneath his hairy navel.

As the first instance of televised nudity (male frontal, no less), the May 24th 1956 episode of *You Bet Your Life* was well documented. The discovery of a Kinescope copy in the early '80s proved it not to be an urban legend. Laurie found references to naked Groucho spread across dozens of articles, appearing on multiple lists of *TV's Most Famous Moments*.

Surely, Laurie should have heard about this before now. The first televised nudity? Especially under such bizarre circumstances. How could she have no memory of this?

Because I was the first person to see it, she thought. *This didn't happen until today.*

It didn't happen until the boy pointed his finger and said, "Bang!"

For the first time in years, Laurie couldn't fall asleep. Not with her tea, not with her pills. She lay awake until the break of dawn, her mind fizzing over like a glass of Alka-Seltzer, bubbling up ideas about what she ought to do next.

* * * *

After putting the boy's bedding into laundry, Laurie played the DVD she borrowed from the library. She held the boy in her lap, struggling to keep one arm around his midsection while the other fumbled to operate the remote control. The boy tried hiding under the bed all day, as though avoiding her.

"Let's get close to the TV now," Laurie said. "Bang?"

"Bang," the boy mumbled, but with his hands in his pocket, so no shot was fired.

Laurie took his hand and guided it close to the screen, wanting him to be ready.

"Are you going to say *Bang*?"

"Bang," the boy replied and grinned. Laurie hugged him tight, letting him know he was being a good boy. She didn't want him getting gun-shy when the time came. They would only have seconds.

On the TV screen, waving people lined a street. It was a parade. Not the kind with ornately decorated floats and Santa Claus coming at the end to throw candy. There was only one car in this parade people were interested in seeing. After the police motorcycles, came a long black car Laurie's son would have instantly identified as a converted Lincoln Continental. The top was open, and from the back, a man in a dark suit smiled and waved alongside his pink-jacketed wife.

"This was something very important," Laurie whispered into the boy's ear.

As the car rounded a corner, she made a gun out of her finger and pointed it at the TV.

"Bang!" she said, and nudged the boy. "Your turn. Go on."

The boy placed his finger on the TV screen, down near the corner, so she grabbed his hand and moved it onto of the head of the waving man.

"Bang!" the boy said.

The graininess of the 8mm footage made seeing exactly what happened next difficult. At the moment the man's suit flew out of the vehicle towards a pastoral knoll, the camera got real shaky, blurring the image, so thankfully for the man's modesty, you cannot see his nudity, but Laurie knew it was there. In the half second it took for Zapruder to refocus his camera, the Lincoln began speeding away. A secret service agent jumped onto the back of the car, throwing himself into the backseat to help Jackie Kennedy lay over top of the naked president to protect him from on-lookers while the car sped through the rest of the parade route. Oswald (or whoever) did not get off a single shot.

* * * *

Although the long day and bus ride home exhausted Laurie, she picked up her computer tablet to Facetime with her daughter.

"What do you remember about Kennedy?"

"From MTV?"

"Who? President Kennedy."

"Kennedy…" Her daughter's voice trailed off, as though she has been asked about one of the more obscure presidents, such as Garfield or Harrison. It took her a moment to find her bearings. "He was assassinated."

"Where?"

Long pause. "Um... God, why can't I remember this?"

Dallas. You know it's Dallas.

"I want to say... Washington?"

Although he escaped being shot in the head in Dallas, Kennedy still did not live to see the first manned space mission. Instead, he was shot through the heart by sniper fire on the lawn of the White House. After that, every other event fell into place; LBJ taking oath aboard Air Force One, Bobby's assassination at the hotel... Whoever the gunman was (Oswald?) they managed to escape this time. There was no slain cop and movie theatre arrest. Who shot President Kennedy remained a great mystery, something that after all this time could never be definitively solved.

But I know, Laurie thought. *I'll always know, because I had it changed.*

"Of course in Washington!" Laurie's daughter said. The famous new images flooded her mind; the blood splattered steps of the White House, the flag draped coffin being blessed by the visiting Pope... Images so vibrant and familiar, she was unaware she was remembering them for the first time.

Laurie couldn't let it go, not just yet. "What were you going to say first? Before Washington, where did you think?"

Her daughter laughed. "Nowhere. It just took me a second to remember. Brain fart."

* * * *

"This isn't working out."

After Laurie put the boy to bed, before the parents said goodnight with their customary grunt and minimal eye contact, they asked Laurie to come to the kitchen for a cup of coffee. Such a dramatic break from the last four month's routine could only be viewed as a bad sign.

Their kitchen was cold and silent like a mausoleum. The father slid a white envelope across the table towards Laurie. The paper looked woefully thin, only her regular wages, no severance to make up for any difficulties suffered by the sudden, unexpected loss of her job.

Laurie sipped bitter-tasting coffee from the parent's expensive French press she always felt too intimidated to use. The silver monstrosity looked like one of her son's beloved car engines standing upright on the counter. With so many parts, she'd have no idea how to clean the machine.

"Have I done something to displease you?"

All week long, she'd worried about the boy taking a negative effect from the TV she made him watch. She had no way of knowing what pointing his finger and saying, "Bang!" to president Kennedy might do to his psyche. Sure, all the boy's young, innocent eyes saw was a panicked car speeding the naked president away, but what happened to the world Laurie remembered? The one where the top of Kennedy's head exploded into a bloody miasma of shattered hopes? Laurie only had a passing familiarity with esoteric concepts like the Uncertainty Principal and parallel universes, but just as she believed every soul went somewhere, she also believed the changed past could not simply cease to have ever existed. Where did that chunk of time go?

She feared the boy absorbed that terrifying alternate reality into his mind. At night, he probably experienced those fatal shots through vivid nightmares, awaking covered in sweat, confused, calling in the dark for someone to comfort him.

What a terrible burden Laurie had placed on the boy. He was barely six. No wonder his parents wanted her gone.

"Is Trevor alright?" she asked, gulping more of the awful-tasting coffee as punishment, thinking of Socrates drinking hemlock.

"Hmmm?" the father asked, checking a message on his phone. "Trevor? Yeah, he's great. Another reason to do this now, before he grows attached."

Laurie felt relieved to know she hadn't scarred the boy, although she didn't one hundred percent trust his busy parent's ability to judge his wellbeing.

"May I see Trevor one last time before I go?"

The mother, who'd sat silent during the entire awkward coffee date finally spoke. She couldn't let her carefully planned passive-aggressiveness go to waste.

"Twenty dollars an hour is an awful lot."

"I'm sorry?"

"We've looked into other sitters. They charge a lot less than that. Makes you feel like you're being taken advantage of."

Laurie set down her coffee, unable to finish the grind-filled dregs at the bottom. Her gag reflex would vomit the cooled coffee back onto the table if she tried. She knew it.

"I'm sorry you feel that way, but…you placed the ad offering that wage."

"You didn't warn us we were overpaying. Comes off a little dishonest. Just saying."

Laurie sighed, taking the moment to decide how best to flatter this pair of self-absorbed idiots.

"I appreciate you entrusting me with this very special job. Looking after a boy as well-raised and gifted as Trevor is an absolute pleasure. I'd hate to give it up. We can certainly discuss reducing my wages to a level you feel is more fair."

Laurie might as well have spat the last of her coffee into the mother's face. At the offer of reduced rates, her eyes went cold, like marbles stuffed into a taxidermy reptile. Her expression turned to one Laurie had seen many times before, when a woman decides *I don't have to be nice to you anymore.*

"You think we're worried about money? It's trust. Besides, if we start paying you less, wouldn't you have to drop the quality of your service to compensate?"

"That's…only a very stupid person would think that way."

* * * *

Later, Laurie regretted her honesty. And her foolish pride. For the sake of winning a meaningless argument, she'd ensured she'd never see the boy point his cocked finger again. His parents were awful people, but surely groveling before them to stay on good terms was worth a hundred times over the value of having access to the boy's magic.

Magic. Laurie had never before used that word to describe the boy's ability. Frightened people seek protection for themselves, and there is no easier and stronger layer of protection than denial. But Laurie couldn't make herself play dumb any longer, not after seeing with her own eyes the pictures of Kennedy dying on the White House lawn. The boy possessed magic, no other word would do.

Her own son, Jesse, died stupidly, with his hands in his pocket, idly waiting on a street corner for the light to change when he was struck down from behind by a stolen car that had lost control during a police chase. She remembered after the funeral, being contacted by the owner of the car, who sobbed apologetically for reporting the theft after he left the vehicle idling outside St. Joseph's Deli, saying if he'd only known the future he would have waited for the car to turn up when the joy riders abandoned it. Still in shock, Laurie told the man her son undoubtedly identified the sound of his car's engine with such confidence he wouldn't have bothered to turn around to confirm.

Now, suppose there was a movie of Jesse standing on that street corner, one the boy could point his finger at and cause Jesse enough bewilderment and embarrassment he would jump into the bushes, out of the way of the speeding car? Wouldn't Laurie want someone to show that to the boy?

Sadly, no such movie existed. Laurie couldn't save her son, but she could try to save others. Waiting at the bus stop, the first drops of falling rain dampening her perm, Laurie accepted the grave responsibility of putting the boy's magic to use one more time.

Laurie's daughter was annoyed she rented a vehicle.

"I'll take you anywhere you want," she said after Laurie drove over for a visit. "You wasted money renting this…thing?"

Laurie knew her daughter's driving offer had less to do with altruism than control. Her daughter thought she was too old for driving, too prone to accident. Every time her daughter insisted she was "too old", Laurie wanted to remind her, *Honey, we're only nineteen years apart. You're going to be old as me before you know it.*

"Do you even still have your license?"

Of course she still had her license. She gave up her car not because of the Walmart parking lot accident, which was blown way out of proportion, nothing more than some scraped paint and few scared birds, but because of the gasoline expense and the realization she never went anywhere. Still, she kept the license renewed, because that was what responsible people did. She kept it renewed for situations just like this.

The reason I don't want your car is because that is how they are going to catch me. One of those surveillance cameras posted all over town will see the license plate and I'll be tracked down within an hour. Your car would be seized by the police because it was used in a crime, and they'd probably wind up pulling it apart or auctioning it off, so be thankful I did you this favour.

Of course, her daughter would not think of it as a favour. Laurie imagined the newspaper articles, her picture on the front page following her arrest, and her daughter's searing shame and embarrassment.

The thought got a small chuckle out of Laurie.

* * * *

Just as he'd done most weekends, the boy sat in the front door, poking his finger through the screen and watching the cars on the busy street.

The ridiculous vehicle Laurie rented didn't fit into the driveway. Two of the heavy wheels sheared over the lawn, leaving thick imprints in the dirt. The man at the agency couldn't believe Laurie wanted the massive jeep she described. "Unless you're going into the mountains, it serves you no purpose other than to show off." From up high in the driver's seat Laurie nodded. Showing off was exactly what she needed.

"Wow," the boy said. He opened the door and stepped off the porch. The metallic grill of the brightly coloured jeep dwarfed him. He wasn't wearing shoes.

"Would you like to go for a ride, Trevor?"

When Laurie's children were growing up, so much time and emphasis was placed on instructing them never to get into cars with strangers. Laurie supposed she had the unfair advantage of not being a stranger to the boy, and could likely have lured him into her "cool" vehicle multiple times, but she knew she only had one chance to get this right. She pushed the door open and grabbed the boy's extended arm, hauling him onto the seat beside her. She quickly backed onto the street, tearing up more grass and dirt, getting away before the new babysitter looked up from the TV long enough to notice the child was gone.

* * * *

Laurie's VCR was so much easier to operate than the sleek DVD player her daughter tried enforcing on her. She queued up the program she taped off PBS years ago. She only watched it once, but never forgot the chilling images that had been stored on a videocassette inside her cabinet since 1993.

The boy sat cross-legged, with his hands tucked beneath him. He looked like he wanted to hide. He was unhappy to be there, and Laurie thought of herself as the witch with her gingerbread house.

Nonsense. I'm not going to hurt him.

"Are you hungry? After this I'll take you home so you can have some dinner."

"Can we have McDonalds?"

"Sure. We'll go anywhere you like."

She began playing the tape.

"Can we play a game? Can we say *Bang*?"

The boy shook his head. He wouldn't watch the images on the TV, nervous. "No."

She smiled, "No? Why not?" Inside, she began to panic. The boy wasn't sophisticated enough to explain, but he intuitively grasped that what she was attempting to do was wrong. The same way the president's death righted itself, this would too, only likely with greater consequences.

You don't know that. You have to try. It would be a sin to let such a great talent go unused when it could be so helpful.

She made the decision to press on.

"Why don't you want to say *Bang*?" She paused the tape, freezing the yelling man so she could hear the boy's whispers. He sounded ashamed, as if he'd wet his pants.

"I've run out of bullets."

"Oh, that's no problem. I happen to have a box of fresh bullets right here." With exaggerated gestures, she pantomimed pulling open a wide pocket on the hip of her slacks, removing a box, flipping open the lid and offering the contents to the young boy. "Take as many as you need. Load up."

The boy seemed to be humouring her as he reached into the air box and selected bullets. He weighed them in his hand and made a face. Something was off. He put them back into the box.

"They're too big. They won't fit."

She didn't challenge him. Instead of insisting his gun was fine, that the bullets fit, she put her faith in action. There was no gun, only the boy. While his ability was real, the gun came from a world of pure imagination. So she played along.

"Do you have something else? A laser, maybe?"

The boy smiled. He pushed both hands together, forming a sci-fi zapper. Laurie imagined a gleaming, silver pistol, capable of shooting a beam of pure antimatter.

A siren passed the house. Laurie knew it was just a fire truck. Thank God. She didn't care there may be a burning building with people trapped inside. She just needed a few more moments with the boy.

Laurie noticed the computer pad her daughter gave her propped up on the couch behind them. She could feel the glare of the computer's camera. She imagined its lens stretching wide, while a whole group of people crowded on the other end, watching and listening. The CIA perhaps, furious at her meddling in the Kennedy assassination. What if foreign interests were keeping an eye on the boy, trying to determine if pointing his finger and saying "Bang!" was the end of his ability, or if he could he do other, more destructive things?

She pressed PLAY on the VCR, and the shouting man reanimated in all his furious lunacy.

A rumble came from the sky. She identified the chopping sound in the air from when she and Brad took a helicopter ride over Niagara Falls for their thirtieth anniversary. She had been so nervous, and thought it a ridiculous expense. All this time later, she was glad to have knowledge of what kind of aircraft was currently hovering over her house. This wasn't the local police looking for a missing boy. No, by the aggressive roar of the engine, this had to be people of a more serious disposition. They had probably been looking for Laurie and the boys for weeks, ever since Groucho Marx lost his clothes. They probably had a way of keeping track of any changes made.

She hadn't much time.

On the TV, a crowd watched the shouting man, thousands of them arranged into Olympic formations. Banners displaying the crooked cross dappled in the open air.

She watched the boy as he lazily dragged his hand across the screen. Static crackled, and she could see the tiny hairs on his arm stand to attention. She licked her lips and waited for him to strike with his "laser gun".

"Zap!"

The black-and-white man's uniform flew off. It seemed to soar miles into the air, like it had broken the bonds of gravity and was being flung into outer space by the strength of the spinning world. The man stopped his speech, perplexed by what had just happened. The old footage cut to the crowd wavering, like a corral of spooked cattle. When the film cut back to his face, his mouth hung open, confused as the breeze chilled his naked body, unable to determine if he were dreaming.

The foundation of the house rattled as the helicopter set down in the middle of the street, setting off car alarms, caring not who saw them. The blades continued to whirl, blasting the house with sharp air. Dirt and stones clattered against the window.

Will that be enough? Is a moment of unexplained embarrassment enough to break the terrible spell he's cast over his people?

On the TV, the man resumed his speech, pressing on as though he were not naked before his entire nation and the eyes of history. It was like some awful version of The Emperor's New Clothes, only there was no child with a voice loud enough to be heard over the adulation of the masses as they shouted *Sieg Heil!*

Outside, multiple voices shouted commands as they leapt from the helicopter. Laurie figured it must be a huge one, like the military used to deploy troops.

"There's cookies in the kitchen," she told the boy. "You'll find them on the counter. Help yourself."

While the boy scuttled off in search of treats, his laser gun back in the holster, Laurie switched the TV off, sick of looking at the black-and-white footage of her failure, sickened to think about the footage yet to come. Being naked couldn't save the president, she was foolish to think being naked could have saved the world.

Outside, the relentless wind and dust kicked up by the whirling helicopter blades slammed against the house. Before the soldiers could kick it down, Laurie opened her front door, voluntarily giving up the last moment of privacy she would ever have, prepared to be held accountable for all the things she tried to change.

DEATH AND THE VAMPIRE
James Dorr

A girl walks home alone at night. But this time Aimée was stopped by Death on the bad side of Rampart Street in the shadow of St. Louis Cemetery Number 1.

"*Bonjour*," she said, gesturing toward her assailant. "But are you really…?" The figure was tall and gaunt, wearing a hooded black robe that shaded its face and was holding a scythe, and as Aimée saw it, it was too early for Mardi Gras but also way too late for Halloween. And moreover, while not impossible but still odd even for the early hours of morning, other than them the street appeared deserted.

"I *am* Death, yes," the figure said in a deep, slightly quavering voice. Aimée wondered—was it high on something? But then Death continued, its voice gaining more confidence. "And you are a vampire."

That startled Aimée. It struck too close to home and, not only that, it seemed rather rude. "Why would you say such a thing?" she demanded.

"That you are a vampire? Remember, I am Death, and Death knows many things. That you are possibly older than you look. Maybe even as old as the ones who originally came here, according to legend. The ones some people call the 'Casket Girls.'"

Les filles à les caissettes, Aimée thought, yes. This did strike too close to home. Though Death seemed to imply they all had been vampires, not just the one, Aimée herself, who had turned her now-sisters during the long, cramped voyage from France and their stay in the Ursuline Convent just after when they first arrived here, nearly three centuries in the past. Who then, with the others, had integrated herself into the highest ranks of New Orleanian society, and indeed this night had been making her way home from Charity Hospital to the French Quarter, following a fundraising gala.

She thought for a moment of Batman and Bruce Wayne, a creature of the night himself who disguised his vocation through late night attendance at similar philanthropic affairs. Though he was a fiction while she was real—indeed was a member of the Charity Hospital Board. Where most members, to be sure, looked older than she, but which she had joined in the guise of a daughter just returned from having attended college in France, and now striving to fill the pumps of her "mother."

But that still left the problem of "Death," who seemed to know too much.

"Tell me," she asked, "if you are Death, what business would you have with me? If I were a vampire as you suggest, would I not be 'undead' already—in which case, it would seem to me, you would be better served by attending the living That is, the ones you might yet recruit to your side."

Death paused, as if puzzled. It seemed for a moment to stagger, just slightly. "Maybe," it said, "I am not here for you. How do you know a car full of teenagers might not even now be careening off South Claiborne Avenue, coming this way where it will be involved in a fiery crash? But since you *are* here, it seems to me you are somewhat troubled. Somehow unfulfilled."

"Ah, then," Aimée said, "but if I were a vampire, would not my becoming fulfilled be easy? After all, for a vampire, is not fulfilment simply a matter of finding one's supper?"

Death shook its head slowly. It opened its robe wide, spreading its arms. "If that is all you seek as a vampire, then you lack true purpose. Come, find it in my embrace."

Of course, Aimée thought. And did she not have a naturally pale complexion herself, now that she considered it, which even in dim light might have been noticed? And long, black curly hair framing her face, and wearing dark clothing this night as well? A vampire indeed! She would have to ask—had the "Goth" look already gone that out of fashion? And, as for a purpose....

At least this she understood. Death was trying—how did one put it?—to cop a feel.

She thought for a moment of one of her fellow filles, Claudette, who no doubt would enjoy the irony of this. Claudette, with her marvelous sense of humor. But she, Aimée, while she wasn't a grouch—not exactly—she wasn't overly tolerant either of things that annoyed her.

And Death was one of these.

"A moment," she said. She turned her back and, using her tongue, she moistened her teeth, then whirling she gave a little leap, bracing her hands on the tall figure's shoulders, and tore out his throat. Her mouth instantly filled, she pushed him back while twisting sideways to avoid the spurt as blood continued to gush from the wound. Sated, she checked her surroundings once more—they were still alone—then pushed Death with her foot into the gutter where, face down, he might at first just look like a passed-out drunk. And, more to the point, any trace left of her DNA would be washed away from him by the time he was finally found.

Let them think it the attack of a vicious dog, she thought, as she strode away, turning right, toward the River. It was a strange night, she thought, licking her lips, but she had learned a new thing.

While admittedly she had had better, Death didn't taste that bad.

✗

MIND ROT

Cindy O'Quinn

My mind split and gave birth to a monster…

Years went by as I lived for you. Only you. Every little thing seemed big, in what was left of my mind. Long gone the days of not sweating the small stuff. It ate its way through until all that remained was a shell. Bruised, broken and of little use in tomorrow's hell.

Like blood and rain—I saw your fears and tasted your pain.

Stuck in the bad moments of life, I forgot to enjoy the good, if there was any. Faded like newborn memories against changing seasons. Going from dark to darker as I became an expert at hide-and-go-seek. Never to be found.

I cried my tears onto Mother Earth…

She drank them up and used the salty moisture to nourish the soil. Of life. Of death. All the same while I suffered in silence, but many voiced their pain and gave name to the sickness. Practice made a perfect art of how to close my eyes.

As I counted the ways to say goodbye.

Two pieces of my mind remained. Darkness took one, and you ate the other. I woke up, and that was a good thing. It was a world with no men, and I thought that was a pretty good thing, as well, so I drove through the night…

And eventually arrived at half past giving a fuck.

✗

THE DUST OF SAGES AND FOOLS

John R. Fultz

Magtone sat cross-legged on his carpet while the world rushed by.

Forests, fields, and lakes became blurs of green and blue in the sunlight. Foothills became mountain ranges and receded again into valleys and plains. He ignored both fertile lands and barren deserts, staring always into the eastern sky. He flew toward the rising sun, and every dusk it set somewhere far behind him. At night he soared beneath stars and comets, while the moon painted his face with golden mystery.

Every few days or so he suffered the delusion that he was still wholly human, and convinced himself that he must land the carpet and rest awhile. As soon as he touched the ground his memories returned, and he recalled that he needed no sleep or food at all. Not anymore. Not since he swallowed the sorcery of Karakutas, and much of its culture, along with the power of its greatest mage. Imbibing the magic had saved him from death by stabbing, and riding the carpet had saved him from death by volcanic eruption. The great city died behind him as he sped into the unknown, seeking for signs of civilization.

Now and then he found life in the lands below, primitive villages or feudal societies establishing provincial borders. But the wilderness of the world was so vast that it dwarfed the few civilized realms he had found so far. He found the stones of ruined cities too, more than he ever would have imagined. Enough ruins to make him wonder if the world might be nearer to its end than its beginning. He recalled the words of an old poem that claimed beginnings and endings were actually the same things.

"The truth of it lies…behind the eyes," he spoke aloud the last line of the verse, as he often did when recollecting the great works. A moment of sadness stole his breath, as he realized all his favorite books and scrolls were now only so much volcanic ash, along with everything else he had ever known. Then he recalled the tales of Odaza, City of Walking Gods, the only city to compare with mighty Karakutas. Somewhere across the Sea of Ages that bastion of civilization stood, waiting for the Last Son of Karakutas to arrive.

The libraries of Odaza were legends all by themselves. The accumulated wisdom of the world and all its ages lay inscribed in those revered halls. The tales of gods roaming its streets and guarding its walls were well-believed in Karakutas, which had hosted a trading caravan from Odaza once very ten years. The wines of Odaza were the finest in history, and men gave entire fortunes for few bottles. Pirate fleets across the Living Ocean went to war over shipments of the divine liquor. Magtone himself had "acquired" several volumes of Odazan poetry, many with fanciful etchings of the terraced gardens and divine spires of the city.

Since his exile, Magtone had seen only savage cultures prone to violence, war, and the manipulation of nefarious spirits. The greater arts of sorcery and alchemy were unknown in most of the world, and now that Karakutas was gone its legend, its power, and its knowledge would die as well. Unless Magtone brought all of it to Odaza, where the magic that enabled his existence could be distilled into volumes for the great libraries.

"I must get Karakutas out of my head," he told the wind as it rushed by his ears. He burped, exhaling a small cloud of rainbows. "And my belly…"

He might expel it all now, or at least he could try. Spill the roiling sorcery that filled his body like blood, let it pelt across the blurry wilderness below. What would happen to him then? Would the carpet still fly? Would his body shrivel up like a drained wine-skin? What about his mind? If he released the sorcery that sustained him now, noble Karakutas would be truly dead, wiped from the world's memory. Even if he survived that betrayal, he couldn't live with the guilt of it. His life had gained purpose, something he had never experienced. Not until the wizard's spell made him a living embodiment of everything that made Karakutas great. It was a purpose he must fulfill.

Again and again he would come to this decision, and find himself sitting on a mossy rock, contemplating the night away until the sun rose up to call him onward. He blinked, jumped back on the carpet, and soared eastward again. Eventually he would cross the Sea of Ages and find on its far shore the gleaming spires of Odaza.

The magic roared and sparked inside his head.

Although he had often despised them, he missed the company of others like himself. Sharing wine and tales in the taverns of Karakutas he had found a sort of bitter happiness, and a grudging respect for the quality of his verse. He missed the company of women most of all, although he no longer felt lustful urges. He was a thing of magic now, but he was still mostly human. The weight of his own solitude told him that.

Magtone was lonely.

Sometimes it was this loneliness that made him descend from the clouds to seek the company of living things. The magic allowed him to speak any language, which served well when he found persons capable of conversation. That had not been very often.

When the far horizon fell away, replaced by a silver mirror that was the Sea of Ages, he stood upon the carpet and breathed the sea air deep into his lungs. Continents of clouds rolled above the endless waters, and storms raged far out over the deep. Near to the sea stood a lone mountain that was unlike other mountains. It was a city, or rather it had once been a city. Built in the shape of great mountain, it cast a dark shadow across the waves.

Magtone had never seen anything like it. Karakutas was founded in the hollow crater of an extinct volcano; but this nameless wonder was carved by millions of hands from an actual mountain of pale stone. His mind reeled at the time it must have taken to sculpt such a miracle of stonework, then reeled again pondering the catastrophe that had destroyed it. Most of the mountain-city's spires and domes had been shattered, its numerous terraces blackened as if by falling flames. The summit of the metropolis was the remnant of a mighty fortress, its outer walls all but collapsed.

Magtone muttered to himself, as he often did when inspired by strange beauty.

"A mountain of ruins by the moonlit sea…"

He found himself flying about the sad broken towers and shriveled gardens like a curious moth. The silence of the dead city was hidden beneath the constant roaring of waves on the strand, a rhythmic rumble paced like the breath of a sleeping giant. The sheer grandeur of the place was worthy of a unique verse, and Magtone couldn't resist. He had been a poet far longer than he had been a living manifestation of magical energy. If that's what he was now. No matter—he was still a poet.

The carpet came to ground inside a withered and weedy courtyard overrun with grape vines and ivy. The wild, untended vines fell to dust and blew away as the carpet settled. Magtone formed quill and paper from a few loose strands of his carpet. Lost in his own spell of twilight and imagination, he jotted down a few lines to capture the dark beauty around him.

The devastation and the grand architecture reminded him of Karakutas, not for any similarity of design, but for the sheer nostalgia of a city-dweller too long in the wild. There was not a single stone of Karakutas left intact, but the towering skeleton of this mountain-city endured here, a slowly eroding memorial to the savants that created it. How long had it stood here by the sea, and how long would it continue standing here? All things fell to dust eventually.

Magtone finished his poem. He set down his quill-and-paper at the corner of the carpet, where they melted into the weave like stains The moon rose impossibly large and silver, inflated by an aurora of ultramarine illusion. The jagged towers shone against its glow like blackened spearheads with chipped blades. Magtone walked into a public plaza full of debris which used to be the statues of kings and heroes. Granite faces large as houses lay among the rubble, their sculpted eyes long ago robbed of the jewels that once made them seem to watch over visitors to the plaza. Several sets of eroded stairs led up the mountain like roadways converging on the smashed citadel. Instead of taking all day to climb one of them, Magtone floated on the drifting carpet.

As he rose higher above the concentric thoroughfares, a dim music floated to his ears. The sea wind died for a moment, and he heard more clearly now. The sound of a piper. A series of single notes revolving about themselves to create a looping melody. Again and again the melody recycled itself, growing clearer, then less clear, and finally losing itself beneath the wind again. Magtone still heard the music, but not with his ears. It was the extranormal senses of a wizard, acquired with the sorcery he had ingested.

The piping drew him toward it like an insect to a bonfire. Rising into the more splendid quarters of the mountain-city, he saw clearly now the ghosts who inhabited it. They lurked like spiders in the wreckage that used to be their comfortable homes. When Magtone turned the lights of his eyes on their half-shadow forms, they scattered like cockroaches. Some faded to nothingness.

"Lesser spirits," he mused. "Lost souls…"

He searched the high towers for the source of the piping music, which rose louder than ever as he topped the broken walls of the citadel. There, sitting atop a charred battlement of flaking stone, was a small girl of about ten years old, her thin legs dangling over the edge. She played on a wooden flute. Her plain brown peasant frock had faded to eggshell white, and her long hair was straight and golden. She stared up at the carpet floating before the wall, and her eyes flashed like sapphires.

She stopped playing and smiled at Magtone with a weary calm, as if she saw men on flying carpets every day. In a language that no other man would have understood, she said: "Are you the Sea God, come at last to wash away the bones of Syrramia?"

"Syrramia…" Magtone repeated the name. Perhaps he had read about an ancient kingdom of that name in some antique volume, or maybe he had read that particular book inside a dream. He couldn't be sure, but the name of the mountain-city seemed familiar in an uncertain way. She did not wait for him to answer, but continued playing her flute.

The night wind ruffled his hair, and he brought the carpet lower and closer to the child.

"My name is Magtone," he said. "I'm a poet and…" He didn't want to frighten her. "And many other things…"

The child removed the flute from her lips and frowned.

"Then you're not the Sea God."

"I'm afraid not," he said. "Who are you?"

"I am the One Who Waits," she said.

"For what exactly do you wait, Young Lady?" Magtone asked.

"I already told you," she said. "The Sea God will come one day to wash this place away."

"How long have you been waiting?"

"Since the city died," the girl said. "I lost count after the first thousand years. It does not matter anyway. I must wait, and so here I am. Waiting."

"I lost my city, too," Magtone said. "And I have nothing at all to remember it by. Only memories and the magic I carry within myself. At least you have these beautiful ruins. Why do you wish to see them swept into the sea?"

"You ask many questions," said the child.

Magtone smiled. "I am a curious soul."

"And I am cursed to remain here," the girl said, "trapped in this form until the ruins of Syrramia fall into the sea. On that day I will finally be free, as my kin were freed long ago. Free to leave this world."

"What do you hope to find beyond this world?" Magtone asked.

"Peace," said the child that was not a child at all.

Magtone could not deny the wisdom of her answer. He sat the carpet down atop the fragmented wall, and went to sit beside her. "Can you tell me what happened to Syrramia? Do you know its history? The story of its downfall?"

"Why should I tell you such things?" she said, and began playing her flute again.

Magtone told her the story of Doomed Karakutas—its terrible glory and its fall from grace. The ancient lies that had lain its foundations, and the fundamental evil that destroyed it. Visions of Karakutas in its golden prime flickered between curtains of salty rain. The piper's song accompanied the images with an unnatural synchronicity.

Magtone's carpet floated over his head, keeping himself and the girl mostly dry. The enchanted fabric made tent-like sounds as the raindrops fell against it.

"There," Magtone said. "I've told you of my city. Now tell me of yours."

"This was not my city," said the child. "It was the city of my master. I was summoned here only to serve him, and I serve him still, bound by his curse until the time I have mentioned. I cannot tell you of the city's doom, but I can tell you what I knew of my master."

"He must have been a mighty sorcerer," Magtone said.

"Aelos was the High Voice of the Bronze Circle," said the girl. "A confederation of mages who rose in opposition to the Fool King of Syrramia."

"Ah, so it was civil war that destroyed the mountain-city," Magtone said. "A conflict of sorcerers and mages."

"Likely, but I cannot say. My master kept me locked in his tower, except for certain nocturnal missions he commanded me to perform. He set me loose to find his enemies, to murder his rivals, or to gather the curiosities needed for his spells. When the city died, I was locked in an iron flask, reduced to sleeping smoke and vapor. Aelos set me free of that prison, and with his dying breath cursed me to watch over the ruined city until the day it fell into the sea."

"What are you truly?"

"What do you think I am?"

"A demon? A spirit-thing? Some fearsome predator from another world, called forth by Aelos with forbidden incantations?"

The girl laughed and tossed her pipe over the wall's edge. It fell into the ruins below without a sound. "I had almost forgotten," she said. "But you have reminded me of my true nature, and the second half of my charge."

"Your charge?"

"To guard these ruins against intruders," she said. "Like you."

A blast of light from her eyes caught Magtone in the face, and he stumbled backwards. The skin of his face melted like wax, but he called upon the power within and vomited up a storm of rainbow shards. The child's body swelled to massive proportions. She stood taller than a man now, hunched and rippling with muscle, bare skin white as snow, enormous bat-wings spreading from between flexing shoulder blades. The sweet, round face was gone, and the fanged snout of a devil had replaced it. A green tongue flicked between its fangs like an angry serpent.

The rainbow shards crashed against its breast like glass against granite. Magtone leaped backwards from the wall into space, and the carpet whirled to catch his fall. The creature spread its wings and followed him into the air above the dead city.

"Come back, fleshy one!" cried the demon. "I have not eaten in a hundred years. But my appetite has returned…"

Claws snagged the edge of the carpet, and Magtone found himself caught in the devil's grip, the thunder of its wings battering his eardrums. The carpet could not move forward while the beast held onto it.

"If you're cursed to stay here," Magtone said, "to guard this graveyard of stones, then you need to understand the nature of stone."

The demon opened its maw and thrust its head across the carpet, but Magtone met it with a slap across one cheek, then the other. Rainbows erupted from his eyes and flooded into the creature's open gullet. The demon shook and made a gagging sound, then a greyish pall spread across the pallid flesh. In another second the beast and its open wings—now both comprised of dull and heavy stone—fell like a meteor into the debris of the lower city. The resulting crash-and-boom shook the remaining towers and sent a few avalanches scudding down the ragged slopes. Sea winds blew away the rising dust, and the night was clear and calm again.

Magtone came circling down on his carpet and found the demon's stone head among a pile of ancient rubble. The fall had broken off a single of its triple horns and a few of its longer fangs, but body and wings were now only pebbles and dust. Magtone lifted the demon-head and sat it next to him on the carpet, ascending again into the city's high quarters. He came once more to the garden of withered splendor, and there he mounted the stone demon-head atop the stub of a sheared pillar. He leaned his back against the slab to stare at the stars. The magic in his belly repaired his disfigured face as exhaustion fell over him. It was the first time he'd felt tired since swallowing the magic. It made him feel human again, so part of him welcomed it.

His eyes glimmered with one last spell before he allowed himself to sleep. "By the power that sustains me, let the story of Doomed Syrramia be revealed in my dreams. Sshhh! Stay quiet, demon-head, I must sleep awhile. If you disturb me, I will drop you in the sea, and your curse will never be ended."

The carpet's edge curled up to cushion Magtone's head as he closed his eyes.

"You are too curious," said the demon-head. "Such curiosity will be your undoing…"

"Silence," Magtone muttered, and the stone head said nothing else.

* * * *

In the 893rd year of its glory Syrramia welcomed home its greatest general, Oldaga the Unconquered. The general returned with an army of knights and mercenaries, bearing prisoners and wagonloads of treasures from the inland kingdoms. His name had become a terror on the lips of those who resisted the advance of the Syrramian Empire. Ten thousand slaves Oldaga brought with him from the smoldering cities of the west, and the celebration of his return lasted for months.

The Order of Wisdom ruled the city in those days, a council of accomplished sages. They also served as keepers of the empire's entire body of history and knowledge, benevolent oligarchs who used their intelligence for the glory of Syrramia. Their great-ancestors had carved the city from the holy mountain. Every succeeding generation had increased the mountain-city's legend, and in the time of Oldaga the empire's fleet had conquered a great slice of the Sea of Ages. Embassies from all over the world came to trade at the ports of Syrramia, and a traveler could find anything he wanted on its winding streets like circles within circles.

The ruling sages declared after Oldaga's return that the empire need grow no more. They knew well the reach of their power and would not dare to exceed its grasp. Distant territories would always be caught in the turmoil of rebellion, so the inner provinces must provide steady resources for the mountain-city's continuing predominance.

There would be no more wars of expansion.

The general and his knights took the news poorly. Oldaga was unsatisfied with the sages' lack of ambition, so he seized power in the city with the aid of a few clever mages. Aelos of the Bronze Circle was one of those involved in the plot. At the time, he believed himself to be saving the empire from stagnation and decay. Yet the course of Oldaga's rebellion later ran to madness and calamity. When Aelos and his Bronze Circle allies cast down the magical defenses of the Order of Wisdom, Oldaga himself put the old men to the spear. He went on to burn their libraries and execute all practicing scribes and sages-in-training.

Aelos confronted him before the blazing Hall of History. The blood of sages stained Oldaga's armor and the black beard that overflowed his chestplate.

"You need not kill the novices!" Aelos said. "And you must burn no more books!"

Oldaga waved his bloody sword and dismissed the words.

"I am king now," he said. "I will burn, kill, or fuck whatever I want."

Magtone watched the drama unfold inside his dream. He was an unseen visitor here, a floating phantom.

Aelos raised his hand to strike at the general with a bolt of magic, but Oldaga's sword was quicker. It sliced upward and took off the hand in a spurt of crimson. The glow of the uncast spell fizzled as the hand of Aelos fell to earth. Oldaga laughed, and left Aelos to squirm in his pain. A day later the usurper forged himself a crown and officially declared himself the first King of Syrramia. The general populace loved him well enough to murder those who did not feel the same, and the rest of the population quickly fell in line.

Aelos met in secret with the last members of the Bronze Circle. Half their number had died helping the Fool King take the city. Now there were only eleven mages left, and one of them with a stub where his best casting-hand used to be. A spell of numbness had taken away Aelos' pain. He would fashion a clockwork hand for himself when time allowed, but first he needed to gather the Circle while it still existed.

"What news?" asked Tremblo, wrapped in the soiled cloak of fishmonger. The humiliation of wearing a disguise in the city was a bitter thing for highborn mages.

"The Fool King has incinerated the last of the citadel libraries," reported Opolon the Swift. "We are truly too late…"

"No," Aelos said. "We can still prevail. Redeem ourselves. But we must lay low and gather our forces, heal our wounds. Let the fools think we have given up and fled the city. Then we strike at Oldaga and his mercenary mages."

In the following days the tyrant further solidified his grip on the mountain-city by having his troops destroy all schools, and any temples that could not pay him tribute. The wise and learned were hunted down and driven from their hovels, executed on the street as potential plotters and subversives. Centuries of wisdom had been lost already, and the supply of it grew less every day.

"We can wait no longer," Aelos told his conspirators. "We must strike tonight." His clockwork hand shot sparks from finger to finger in nervous anticipation.

"We are still not ready," said Pakolus the Diviner. "The stars favor a venture in another week's time."

"How many more scholars and children will die in another week?" asked Shatami, Daughter of Lightning. "How much more knowledge will be lost?"

Magtone felt the terrible weight that lay on their shoulders, and it seemed to him that this dream was as real as anything in waking life. Then he remembered that he was not only dreaming, but viewing actual history through the spell of his dreams. All of these events had actually happened more than a thousand years ago. His heart beat faster inside and outside the dream.

A tiny dragon flew into the room where Aelos met with the Circle. It landed at their feet and transformed into Zyrus, a handsome dwarf in patchwork colors. "The Fool King lies senseless at his table…drunk off his ass…"

"And his mages?" Aelos asked.

"Distracted by their unrestrained access to the King's harem."

"Disgusting," said Shatami.

"We'll never get a better opportunity," said Aelos.

The Bronze Circle stormed the gates of the High Citadel in the shapes of hulking dragons. Aelos battered down the gate by flying directly into it with the force of a living hurricane, and the other sorcerer-wyrms flew in behind him. They reigned fire across the courtyards, through the windows of towers, across the roofs of barracks and stables. The mages who rose up to confront them were confused, drunk, and caught off-guard. They died along with the soldiers loyal to Oldaga. The Fool King himself died in the jaws of Aelos, who snapped his body in half before returning to man-shape and stealing the diamond crown from his head.

In that frozen moment, with the unholy crown in the raised fists of Aelos, the bonds that had forged the Bronze Circle broke once and for all. Magtone realized this, even if Aelos did not. The victorious mage put the crown on his head and sang a spell that would bind the living city to his will. How else could he restore the glory of Syrramia if he did not rule it?

Shatami and Pakolus and Tremblo fell upon him at once, casting deadly fires and killing light across a throne room cluttered with burnt corpses. The mages fought in human form now, yet they were still as fierce and destructive as the dragons they had imitated. They fought for the crown and for the right to wear it, never once stopping to discuss another strategy. With Oldaga gone, a new game had arisen between them. A game of power that could only end in death. Whoever held the crown now would complete the spell of Aelos and rule the empire of the mountain-city forever.

A conflux of sorceries grew bright as the sun, and the walls of the High Citadel began to crack. The terrible energies of spells never meant to be unleashed by living men poured across the city like rivers of hungry lava. The earth shook and the sea roared.

Magtone's viewpoint ascended until he looked upon the crumbling city from a great distance. The battling sorcerers snuffed each other out one by one, and beauty fell to corruption as light falls to darkness. Everything alive inside the mountain-city was swept away by torrents of raging power. When it was all over, the dust of ruin clouded the sky above the mangled mountain.

The sun sank red and angry behind the western mountains. Magtone found himself in the withered garden again, but he could not tell if he still dreamed or had awakened. The stone demon-head was silent. A soft voice reached his ears, the voice of a man infinitely tired, yet heavy with hidden strength.

"...until the bones of Syrramia are swept by the Sea God into the waves."

Magtone looked past a trellis of shriveled vines. Aelos—or perhaps the ghost of Aelos—lay broken and dying at the edge of the burnt garden. A small girl stood over him, holding a wooden flute in her hands. Aelos spoke to her through bloody lips; his body was a mess of torn flesh and broken bones. The girl nodded, and went off to play her flute in the ruins.

"So this is how the glory of Syrramia extinguished itself," Magtone said.

Someone behind him laughed. He turned to see a hooded figure standing upright among the dead leaves. Its face was a smiling skull without skin or flesh. A ragged shroud hid most of its body, but its single hand was also skeletal. It held that hand cut toward Magtone, as if in welcome. Its other skeleton arm ended in a stump of white bone, where Oldaga's sword had passed through it long ago.

Magtone turned back to the dying body of Aelos, but it was gone. Only moss and shattered mortar-stones lay there now.

"Aelos?"

"Indeed," said the skeleton. Its jaw did not move, but it spoke a magical language that required neither lips nor tongue.

"Is this still a dream?" Magtone asked. He blinked at the apparition.

"It was your dream," said the skeleton. "Now it is mine."

"Evidently there was a survivor on the day Syrramia died," Magtone said.

"It depends on your definition of survival," said the skeleton. "My jumbled bones have lain here for a thousand years, waiting for someone like you to come along." The skeleton stepped closer. Magtone sat cross-legged on the ground before it. There was no sign of the carpet. It must not exist inside the dream, if that's where he was. Yet, dream or no dream, he knew the threat of Aelos' bones was real.

"Someone like me?"

"Someone with power," said the skeleton, stepping close enough to touch him. Bony fingers caressed his cheek. Magtone wanted to move, to run, to fly, but he was unable to do any of it. The half-dead thing had ensnared him with a dream trap, and it would not let go. Now it would drain his life, and with it the magic, the history, the substance of lost Karakutas. He could not let that happen. Karakutas must not be lost to the memory of the world like Syrramia had been.

The touch of the bone digits was cold as ice, and as they slid into Magtone's mouth he vomited a gout of rainbow energies. The magic flowed up Aelos' fleshless arm and lit up the dark sockets of his skull. His naked teeth chattered, and Magtone heard him laugh again, like a small boy given extra sweets. Magtone's essence spilled from his body like blood from a mortal wound. A handsome face began to form about the skull of Aelos, and his power transformed dancing energies into solid flesh, while Magtone continued retching forth digested sorcery.

"Great Syrramia rises again, like this imperishable flesh," Aelos said. "From the dust of sages and fools the first empire will be reborn. A legend returned from oblivion to carve its name across the world once more..."

Magtone ceased his magical regurgitations for a moment.

"You sound more like Oldaga than Aelos," he said.

"Shut up, False Mage," Aelos said. "I'll drink the last of your stolen power now." His living face was almost fully formed, but his skull still showed through the congealing flesh.

Magtone spoke in a piercing voice. He used the last reserves of the magic, rather than his captive mouth, to form the words: "As your shade remained to haunt these ruins, so must the shades of your brethren, betrayed and murdered by you. Let the Bronze Circle rise from these bloodied stones..."

Thunder rolled above the churning sea.

"Impossible," Aelos said. "The others did not prepare as I did. I shared none of my immortality spells. They are less than nothing now."

A mad wind blew through the withered garden, raising curtains of leaves and sand. Ten shapes like men or women standing in darkness began to move closer. Magtone went limp as the last dregs of sorcery seeped from his body like molasses pouring from an old jar. Without it he would be less than a phantom. Or perhaps he would truly die and know oblivion. But that meant the legacy and memory of Karakutas died along with him.

"Less than nothing are we?" An angry voice cracked the night. No, it was ten angry voices that spoke as one. Ten shadows flowing forward to surround Aelos. Shadowy hands grabbed Magtone's body and cast it aside like a ragdoll.

"Shatami?" Aelos said with new-made lips. "Tremblo? Zyrus?"

"We are here," said the ten voices. "And seven more."

"But I destroyed your bones...all of the city's bones...only mine survived. There are no anchors for your spirits here..."

"We are the souls of those whom you loved and betrayed," said the voices. "You are the only anchor we need."

Aelos raised his newly-fleshed fingers to touch his soft new face. His eye sockets still swam with stolen rainbows. "Syrramia must live..."

"It is already dead," said the voices. "Like us. Like you."

"No! Together we can restore its lost glory..."

"There is nothing left," said the shades. "Less than nothing."

They swarmed Aelos like a pack of wolves on a lame deer. They dug phantom claws in deep and tore his newly made flesh to ribbons. They cracked and splintered his re-forged bones. Red blood and whirling rainbow lights spewed into the air. The lights gathered and fell like rain across Magtone's sunken form, sinking into his flesh like water into hungry soil. His strength returned as the magic filled his body. He blinked and forced himself to wake up.

And the dream finally ended.

* * * *

Magtone awoke in the withered garden, where ten specters tore slices from a lump of whimpering flesh. They flickered in and out of sight against the amber moonlight. Magtone inhaled the cool sea air, glad to be breathing.

How close to oblivion he had come, before clawing himself back to life with an act of necromancy. Once again the magic of Karakutas churned and bubbled in his gut, sending ripples of pleasure through his limbs.

The ripping of flesh and cracking of bones went on for a while longer. Magtone watched the ghosts fade beneath the first rays of dawn. Not a single bone fragment or drop of blood from Aelos was left to mark his passage. It had all faded like so much forgotten verse. Or perhaps a sliver of his essence lingered here still, a spirit trapped forever in the city's ancient stones.

The morning sea glittered with reflected sunfire, and the ruins were quiet again. Above the sounds of the surf, Magtone heard a familiar piping. He looked about for the stone demon-head, but it was nowhere to be found.

Somewhere among the splendid ruins, the piper yet played.

Magtone sat on his carpet and rose into the air. The Sea of Ages glowed brilliant as a diamond plain below him. He sailed over its aquamarine depths and looked back at the grey mountain of decay that had been fair Syrramia. He sang a great and dangerous song that gathered clouds and invisible forces about him. The deep seabed rippled, and a wave of blue-green water rose from the sea. It sped toward the mountain-city, growing even taller as it rolled shoreward. When it reached the mountain of ruins, it crashed down with a chorus of thunders.

The bones of Syrramia crumbled, and it fell into the sea like a forlorn sandcastle.

In the strange calm that followed, something pale as seafoam rose from the strand on bat-like wings, only to lose itself in the swollen clouds.

"So much for curiosity," Magtone said.

After a while he turned his gaze once more to the east. The green sea was calm again. He could see no end to its dazzling beauty. How far must he travel to reach the opposite shore? He could not guess. He knew only that Odaza stood bright and magnificent somewhere across the water. Last of the world's great cities. He imagined the songs of its divine poets—not for the first time—and longed to hear godly voices praising his own verse.

And, O, there would be such wine…

The carpet carried him fast and far above the whispering sea.

✗

PUSH DAGGER
John C. Hocking

Hi, Louise. Didn't expect to see me here, did you? Why don't you sit down right there? I've got to talk to you. Sit down, Louise.

That's better. You got this real surprised expression when you turned on the light. I look a mess, don't I?

Let's talk about your husband. I've been doing a lot of thinking about him. You know, he's in the next room.

Sit down, Louise. Thank you.

Your husband, Dan, found this push dagger. Yesterday we were unloading a shipment and this crate fell off the truck and smashed open on the dock. Dan got us to shove the busted crate and the stuff that came out of it between some shelves, so if the boss came by he wouldn't see we'd screwed up. Turns out the crate wasn't for business at all but for the boss's kid. That's the dopey, goth-looking guy who the boss is always yelling at for spending so much money on books and weird crap from all over the world. And there was some pretty weird crap that came spilling out of that crate, Louise. Ugly little statues, some crystal ball-type things and a bunch of candles that smelled like dead flowers. And the push dagger, although Dan didn't show that to me until after he re-packed the crate and stuck it back together so it looked almost as good as new.

Dan had seemed kind of pissed off at me all morning. He made me move the barrels into the warehouse all by myself. He made me clean out the johns and I don't remember anybody ever doing that in the whole time I've worked there.

And he showed me the push dagger. Do you know what a push dagger is, Louise? It's a knife that fits right in your fist. The blade pokes out between your second and third fingers. It starts as a smooth cylinder, so you won't cut your fingers, then flares into a blade you can punch with. The one Dan had found in the crate was about six inches long, black, and had these weird carvings all over the blade. And it looked old. All worn and smooth like it had been handled for a long time. Dan said he was going to keep it and that the boss's kid would never know. He kept waving it around and pointing it at me, saying how it felt good in his hand.

Later, when we were closing the place down, he started talking about how he used to box and telling me about this one fight where he almost killed his opponent. He held his knuckles right under my nose so I could see the scars on them.

I was a little worried then that he'd found out about you and me. But today was different. This morning Dan came into work looking all hung over, with dark smears under his eyes and hands that shook so much he could barely sign an invoice. He was really nice to me, though. Bought me doughnuts at coffee break. Gave me half his sandwich at lunch. Put his arm around my shoulders and said, "What's mine is yours." It was kind of weird, but I felt better about it than yesterday.

Toward the end of the day he asks me if I want to go out and get a drink with him. Says he's buying. I say I'm always up for a free drink. Bobby hears this and asks if he can come and Dan says no, because he wants to talk to me about work private. Now this makes no sense but I don't worry much at the time because I've been paying Bobby twenty bucks twice a week to watch Dan during lunchtime. Bobby says that every time I've come over here to see you, Dan's just sat in the lunchroom eating his sandwich. So there's no way he can know about you and me, right?

Anyway, Dan takes me to this little hole in the wall that doesn't even bother to shovel the snow out of its parking lot. I'd never been there before but Dan said he liked the place because if he ever got too stewed it was close enough to home that he could walk. We go in and Dan starts putting away the shots like you can't believe. I try to keep up but after four I decide there isn't much point and switch to beer. At first Dan's laughing it up and slapping me on the back, but after a while he quiets down and finally he starts talking about you. I swear I got your whole life story from the second you met him until today. All the details, too. Believe it or not, even though I was nodding and keeping the major poker face, I was really laughing like hell inside. I mean, he's working into a heavy sob story about his marriage and he's spilling it to me, of all people. What a joke, huh Louise?

Finally he pays up and we leave. I have my coat open even though it's cold and I'm a bit wobbly in the knees. Outside the sun's gone down and little flakes of snow are blowing through the dark. Dan pushes me into this alley beside the bar, whispering about a shortcut to the parking lot. Soon as we're well into it I feel his hand on my shoulder and he spins me around saying something about how I'd touched his wife for the last time. He punches me hard in the chest. It seems to tear right through my body and all the air goes out of me like a busted balloon. I fall back against the wall and there's this awful pain and Dan's punching me in the face, first with one hand, then the other. He did that 'till I fell down in the slush. I think he kicked me a few times then, but I'm not sure.

It's all black for a while, then I open my eyes and see the stars up between the walls of the alley. I got no idea how long I've been there but I'm cold, colder than I've ever been. Frozen like the rock under a glacier. But there's a different kind of cold that's filling my chest, it's so cold it's like heat and it's giving me the strength to stand. I push myself up the wall, pull my wet coat closed and feel numb clear through. It's hard to walk because my legs are stiff and my coat fits funny.

Hey Louise, you know who I thought of then? You. I figured maybe Dan went home and was waiting for you to get off the late shift so he could do the same thing to you that he did to me.

So I walk all the way over here. And you know, as I was going through all that cold dark I did a lot of thinking. By the time I was outside your door I had it all figured out.

Dan was inside, but you weren't home yet, which meant that I hadn't lain in that alley too long after all. It just seemed like forever.

I walk right in. Dan jumps up and nearly falls back down again when he sees it's me. I smile, but I don't say anything. I just open my coat and show him the handle of the push dagger sticking out of the middle of my chest.

You should have seen his face.

He punched it real neat between my ribs. Right through my heart, Louise. I smiled as big as I could and pulled it out. The edge kind of stuck in the bone a little but I got it loose. Truth to tell, I was kind of sad to see it go. Dan just stood there watching and making funny sounds.

I was going to give the push dagger right back to him, but I thought of a few questions to ask first. He got it back a little at a time, and he worked really hard to answer all my questions, Louise. I put the blade in a lot of places but never into his heart, so I think when I was finally done he was done too, and probably glad it was over.

But before we were finished he told me you were acting real odd the day before yesterday. Said you were acting real high and mighty and made him kind of suspicious. Just couldn't shut up could you, Louise? So he got fed up and grabbed you and told you if you didn't do some explaining he was really going to knock you around.

That's when you told him all about us, isn't it, Louise? Except you said I made you do it and threatened to hurt you if you told anyone.

I feel better knowing these things. I don't know if I can ever really rest now, but I feel like maybe I could because I know the truth. I guess I'll see.

When I was done with Dan, I turned off the lights and sat down to wait for you. I thought a lot in the dark. After a while I got up and took the push dagger back from Dan. You see, Dan had the push dagger, but then he gave it to me. I gave it back to him, but he doesn't need it. I need it, Louise. I'm going to give it to you.

Right now.   ✗

SONG OF THE GOAT
K.A. Opperman

I have whispered in a witch's ear
All the secrets that she yearned to hear;
O'er the darkling hedge my hooves leap clear,
When the crescent moon holds reign.

I have suckled at her buxom teat,
Drinking moon-white milk till past replete;
I have felt her sighs of scarlet heat
As she strokes my night-black mane.

I have wandered through the woods at dusk,
Drinking in the autumn's deathly musk.
Many names are mine; I shed this husk
When the sabbat-fires burn bright.

I have pranced amid the shepherd's flock,
Made the chaste their silver belts unlock.
Ere the holy crowing of the cock,
Sign my book by candlelight.

ALLEN K. '91